SUITE
Temptation

ANITA
BUNKLEY

D1497060

KIMANI™
ROMANCE

To my husband, Crawford, with love.

KIMANI PRESS™

ISBN-13: 978-0-373-86080-7
ISBN-10:   0-373-86080-3

SUITE TEMPTATION

Dear Reader,

Come along on a journey with my heroine, Riana Cole, as she tangles with handsome Andre Preaux in a corporate tug-of-war. A woman on a mission, she goes after the big bonus from a major client while pursuing a man she vowed never to deal with again.

Romance in the workplace drives these two into a dangerous game; a game that is hard to resist as they travel a rocky road to lofty corporate heights, determined not to surrender to the ultimate temptation.

I enjoy hearing from readers, so please e-mail me at arbun@sbcglobal.net or send a note to P.O. Box 821248, Houston, TX 77282-1248.

Read with love!

Anita Bunkley

Prologue

June 2002, Houston, Texas

A perfect score, Riana thought, her eyes traveling over the papers that Professor Lowell had handed to her. While other students gathered their books and bags and hurried out of the lecture hall, she flipped through the multipage document, both relieved and more than a little proud of herself for having aced the Commercial Banking in Real Estate examination that she'd been preparing for over the past twelve weeks.

Participating in the Small Business Administration course at the University of Houston had been a challenging experience, and, at first, Riana had worried that at thirty-five, it might be difficult for her to recapture the discipline and mind-set of a college student in order to make the grade. But that had not been the case at all: after the first day of class, she had slipped right back into the trusty study habits that had served her well through undergraduate and graduate school, and had found the intellectual environment a stimulating change from her work as a loan officer at a San Antonio financial firm.

The number of students taking the course had been much larger than she had anticipated, and she had been pleased to find that the majority of them were mature professionals like herself who were enhancing their careers or completing requirements for their undergraduate degrees. During the twelve-week session, Riana lived with her cousin, Felicia Woods and enjoyed the girl time they were able to spend together. However, she had also made several new friends in Houston, including Andre Preaux, the fine brother who was sitting next to her, assessing the results of his own examination.

"How'd you do?" Riana asked Andre, poking him with her elbow. Tall, trim and as delicious-looking as a piece of Godiva chocolate, he had an air of masculine vitality that made him very attractive. On the first day of class, Riana had accepted Andre's invitation to join his study group, and it hadn't taken long for them to break away from the nine-member group and move their study dates to a coffee shop, then to the student lounge, and eventually to Andre's apartment, which was a short drive from the campus. In spite of her attempts to resist Andre's lingering glances, gentle touches and his focused attention on her, his charm had worked its magic, and within a week, their late-night study dates had slipped into overnight stays at his studio apartment, where Riana began spending much more time than at her cousin Felicia's house, where she was officially living during her time in Houston.

Riana's attraction to Andre had been immediate and intense, though a bit disconcerting. She had not been looking for a romantic entanglement, and certainly not with a thirty-three-year-old who was pursuing his undergraduate degree. However, at six foot two with a slim, toned physique, a voice that melted her heart and a smile that made her stomach do flips, Andre had stirred up a passion in Riana that she had not been able to contain. He was exciting, energetic, sexy and gentle—a combination that had been impossible to resist.

"What'd you get?" she asked again, praying that he had at least passed the exam: they had pulled so many all-nighters while preparing for it, even though they had taken a few breaks from the books to do *other* things.

Andre didn't answer. Slumped down in his seat, his long legs extended, his booted feet crossed at the ankles, he stared dully at the test papers crumpled in his fist. His full bottom lip was tucked under his front teeth, and the stunned expression on his handsome features was alarming. If it was any reflection of the grade he had received, Riana knew he must be crushed.

Andre was a construction worker, sporadically employed, who took classes between jobs and had only one semester left before finishing his bachelor's degree, with plans to become a civil engineer. On the surface, he appeared to be an easygoing guy who took things in stride, but beneath that calm facade Riana knew there was an intensely driven man, preoccupied with succeeding.

Without looking over at Riana, Andre handed her his test paper, a blank expression darkening his caramel-brown face. "See for yourself," he mumbled in a dispirited tone.

Riana eased the document out of Andre's hand, unfolded it, and then let out a gasp. "Andre!" She pummeled him with a fist. "Ninety-four! And I was worried you'd failed!"

Grinning in a boyishly mischievous way, Andre leaned over and touched his lips briefly to Riana's, breaking out of his fake sullen mood. "Me, fail? I don't think so. If you knew me better, you'd know that when I focus on something, or someone, I don't give up until I get what I want."

Riana slapped him playfully on the arm and shoved his test paper back at him. "Oh? And what exactly does that mean?" she teased right back, relieved that their study sessions had paid off, in spite of so many interruptions.

"I got you, didn't I?" Andre replied, his brown eyes bright with a sheen of satisfaction.

Riana shook her head and forced a half smile, knowing what she had to say, and knowing that her words might hurt. "Yes, I guess you did…for a while. You know, hanging out with you has been great fun, Andre, but I'm returning to San Antonio tomorrow. I've accomplished what I came to Houston for, so I have to get back to work."

"I know, I know," Andre mumbled rather grumpily. He ran a hand over his close-cut hair and then shifted back in his seat, eyes focused on the ceiling, obviously frustrated with the situation. "Couldn't you stick around for a few more days?"

"Impossible."

"Oh, so I guess Sweetwater Finance can't function a day longer without you, can it?" His words had a hard edge, conveying his irritation.

Riana chewed her lip. Why did Andre have to make their parting harder than it had to be? She wasn't going to lie: she was eager to return to work and assume her new position as vice president of commercial loans at the company where she'd worked for seven years. Her career was finally taking off and she had a busy life back home waiting for her. After laboring in every department of the financial firm she was about to enter the select ranks of upper management, where she would earn the kind of money she deserved. Nothing was going to sidetrack that. While many women her age were longing for a serious romantic relationship, a husband, a house in the suburbs and a few perfect children, that was not what preoccupied Riana. Not now, at least.

"Whether or not Sweetwater Finance can get along without me is not the point," she told Andre, shaking her head.

"Well, what is?" he tossed back, looking at her in a way that let Riana know he expected an answer he could live with after she was gone.

"We both knew my stay in Houston was only a temporary thing. We agreed to a no-strings-attached relationship, remember?" Impulsively, Riana reached out and massaged Andre's neck, wishing their situation was easier to fix. "I'm not happy about leaving you, either, but this is the way it has to be."

Andre covered Riana's hand with his, gripping tightly, as if holding on to her now would help him hold on to her forever. "We could do a long-distance thing, you know? San Antonio is only a couple of hours away. Every other weekend. I could take vacation time. We could…"

"No, Andre. That's not what I want," Riana cut him off. She didn't want to scramble around and try to patch together a relationship that, she kept telling herself, had run its course. She didn't want to sit around and wait for his phone calls, think about him all the time, live for his next visit, exist on the edge of potential disappointment. The stress of such an arrangement would be too unnerving, and a clean break was the only way she could ever handle leaving. He had to accept her decision. "It's time we went our separate ways," she calmly told Andre.

"Why you gotta sound so final? We can still stay in touch." He jerked away now, turning angry.

"Because tonight has to be our last night together," Riana answered, wanting to bring closure to this crazy, wonderful, out-of-the-blue affair and end it wrapped in his arms. Andre was not like any man with whom she had ever been involved. He had turned her emotions inside out and turned a fleeting attraction into a dangerously seductive whirlwind romance, pulling her into a steamy liaison that had evolved with heart-stopping speed. As impulsive as the affair had been, Riana had no regrets, and the only way she could get on that plane the next day and say goodbye was to convince herself that their paths had simply crossed unexpectedly. That leaving now was the best thing to do. That at least she would have sweet memories to hold on to, to remind her of this blissful time.

Andre slid closer and traced an index finger along Riana's cheek, somber dark eyes fastened on hers. "I really don't want you to go."

"I have to."

"I'll call you every day," he insisted, not hiding his anguish over the imminence of their parting.

"Don't. Trust me, Andre. It's best if we don't try to make more of our time together than it was. When I get home, I'm going to be swamped at work, consumed with learning my new job, and too busy to handle a long-distance relationship. Let's leave it as it is, okay?"

"Riana. It might take time and patience, but we could work it out. We can visit back and forth, talk on the phone, try to keep this together. I love you, you know that, don't you?"

A wave of uneasiness rose inside Riana. *Love? Oh, I wish you wouldn't say that,* she worried, unable to deny that she had feelings for Andre. But love him? No, she didn't dare consider that: he had made it clear that he planned to stay in Houston once he finished school. She was building her career at Sweet-water Finance and had no plans to leave San Antonio anytime soon. Why struggle to fit Andre into her life? Why force a re-lationship to stay alive when it might be best to let it go? Their lives had intersected at the wrong time and there was nothing to do but accept it.

With a sigh, Riana laced her fingers through Andre's and gave his hand a firm squeeze. "I'm not happy about this either, but we've gotta do what we've gotta do. However, I have to say, I will miss the hell outta your blueberry pancakes and whipped butter cream," she managed with a light laugh, desperate to ease the tension that still held them firmly in their classroom seats.

Andre nodded, a twinge of a smile tugging at his lips. "Ready to go?" he finally asked, words low and husky. "I sure don't want to spend one more minute of my last night with you sitting in this room."

"Yeah," she told him, pulling her purse strap over her shoulder. "Let's get out of here."

The best feature of Andre's cramped studio apartment was the oversized Jacuzzi tub in the bathroom, which he had filled with strawberry-scented water. He climbed in first, settled down among the frothy bubbles, and then extended a hand to help Riana in. Muted candlelight bathed the room with a golden glow, highlighting Riana's perfect figure while teasing it with flickering shadows. Andre's gaze swept from her long, bronze legs, to the curve of her hips, to her heart-shaped face framed in light-brown hair, worn parted on the side, swinging against her cheek.

Andre kept his eyes on Riana as she slipped down in front of him and settled on her knees, the fluffy bubbles reaching only to her waist. Dipping one hand into the water, he scooped up a handful of the sweet-smelling foam and lathered it over her shoulders, her neck, her firm round breasts, pausing to rotate his thumbs over her dark, pointed nipples. Riana moaned and edged closer, bringing her own sexy scent to him.

Andre inhaled sharply, and then ducked his head and feathered his tongue over her shoulder, licking away the strawberry-scented bubbles clinging to her skin, while his hands made their way around to her back to bring her flush against his chest.

The feel of her body pressed to his, so wet and slick and smelling so good made Andre grow hard in an instant. He

covered her lips with his in a bold, demanding kiss while he
worked one hand down her spine, onto her thighs, and into the
tangle of curly hair between her legs. Her gasp of pleasure
broke off their kiss, forcing Andre to lean back and gaze at her
for a short, sweet moment, entranced by her golden-brown
eyes. She smiled at him. He crushed his mouth to her neck and
held his breath in his lungs, clinging to her for one last time,
fearing what the next day would bring.

When Riana shifted and parted her legs, Andre rose on his
knees and cradled her hips with both hands, his fingers locked
as he pulled her to him. Inch by inch she moved closer, slick
with soap, radiating her own sugary heat.

With a gentle lift, he easily slipped inside her, moaning
aloud, and not caring that tears had sprung unexpectedly into
his eyes. A swirl of emotions inundated him, cascading through
his body: sadness, regret, longing and fear.

She's leaving tomorrow and I have to let her go, he told
himself. *Maybe I can't hold on to her forever, but I can make
love to her tonight in a way that she will never forget, sending
her off with the knowledge that I've given her all I have.*

Determined to savor this final night in her arms, he knew
he'd have to use a great deal of restraint to make sure that he
satisfied Riana completely before he lost all control. With their
bodies joined, Andre felt the burn of his need for Riana trace
through his veins. She rocked with him, gripping his shoulders,
arching her back, her legs around his waist, holding nothing
back. It excited him to feel the raw sensuousness of her passion,
to know that she was in total surrender as their soul-searing
rhythm churned the sparkling bubbles. For as long as he could
hold her, he tasted and teased and explored her bronze body,
moving deeper and deeper into their own erotic world until they
climaxed together and collapsed.

Later, lying in bed with Riana's damp hair pressed into his

chest, Andre cradled her tenderly. He felt strangely agitated, yet content. A shiver of sorrow descended as he mentally surrendered to Riana's decision. He loved her. He craved her. But he'd have to learn to live without her.

She was right. There was no way they could make plans for a future. What did he have to offer a successful, smart woman like Riana? He was still a struggling student while she had her master's degree, a secure career and would soon be a VP with a major financial institution. He was a construction worker with rough hands, a paycheck that barely covered his living expenses, and a wardrobe that consisted of jeans, work boots and a few dress shirts, while she wore chic designer clothes and thought nothing of dropping a few hundred dollars for dinner in a fine restaurant.

Her life was on a fast track to success, while his was tentative, unstable and shrouded in past mistakes. It hurt so much to admit that she was right, they didn't belong together, and it would be selfish of him to pressure her about it. She deserved more than he could offer, and until he accomplished what he planned to do, he didn't deserve her love.

Chapter 1

San Antonio, Texas, four years later

After the producer's assistant attached a small black microphone to the lapel of Riana's burgundy suit, he gave her a thumbs-up and disappeared into the dark shadows surrounding the brightly lit set. Riana stared at the television camera that was positioned directly in front of the sofa where she was sitting and took a deep breath, eager to get the interview started. She crossed her hands and placed them in her lap, making sure that her silver watch, her Tiffany charm bracelet and the diamond-and-ruby ring on her right hand were angled toward the camera.

Her mind clicked through the short list of talking points that she wanted to address, hoping that Sheri Sherman, the host of *Community Business Focus,* would not hog the interview, as she was known to do. Sheri was a gregarious, energetic television personality who conducted extensive research on the major players in the local business community and loved to pass along her knowledge in a chatty, informal style. It was well known that her guests had to seize control of the interview from the beginning. However, an appearance on Sheri's half-hour show could be more valuable than a sixty-second prime-time commercial, and every businessperson in San Antonio coveted an invitation to sit down and talk with her.

"Let's do it," Sheri called out to the floor director as she swept onto the set and sat down in the fake Louis xv armchair next to the sofa. She was dressed in a bold red pantsuit with black satin lapels. The ruby and silver beads around her neck were oversized, dramatic and genuine; as were the rings she was wearing on each finger. With a flip of her long thin braids, she turned to Riana and blessed her with a wide grin. "You ready, girlfriend?"

"Absolutely," Riana replied, licking her lips and praying that she didn't have lipstick on her teeth. *Too late now,* she told herself as the director counted down from five and then leveled a pointed finger in Sheri's direction.

"Hello, everyone," Sheri began. "Welcome to *Community Business Focus,* where you get to meet the up-and-coming business leaders of our city. My guest today is Riana Cole, CEO of Executive Suites, Inc., an executive search firm based here in San Antonio." Sheri shifted slightly and turned her attention to Riana, flashing another TV-perfect smile. "I'm so happy to have you here with me today, Riana."

"My pleasure," Riana replied in her most professional tone.

"How about a little background. You're a native of San Antonio, aren't you?"

"Correct. Born and raised right here, though I did leave to attend the University of Texas at Austin, and after getting my undergraduate and my master's degree in Economics there, I came back home. I love this city and wouldn't think of living anywhere else."

"I know what you mean. You still have family here?"

"Only a sister. My parents retired and moved to San Marcos in the Hill Country a few years ago, but they come back to the city quite often. It's hard to leave San Antonio completely."

"So true, so true. But San Marcos is just up the road. I know it means a lot to have family nearby." She widened her grin and slid her tongue over her shiny white teeth, as if making sure *she* didn't have lipstick on them. "Now, I understand that your company, Executive Suites, Inc., was responsible for getting Jerry Holmes, our new Director of Visitors and Tourism, to come to San Antonio last year. Our city has always been considered a great draw for tourists, but he is doing a fabulous job of marketing San Antonio to the world. So many international events are coming our way now. We're lucky to have him here."

"That's right," Riana agreed. "My company was tapped by the city to provide turnkey recruitment services for that search. It took some doing, but we were able to convince Mr. Holmes to leave Denver and come to our fair city. We also work with major corporations who are seeking highly qualified personnel."

Sheri nodded. "So, you're a headhunter?" Laughter followed. "Isn't that another word for what you do?"

"That's exactly what we do," Riana stated with a smile, launching into her first talking point. "When a hard-to-fill position opens up within an organization, a public entity or a corporation, and the job calls for a specially trained person, human resource managers turn to me. I have a worldwide database of candidates and the ability to find the right person for the job in record time. Executive Suites, Inc., can save CEOs and human resource managers a great deal of time and expense."

"How did you get started?" Sheri asked.

"Four years ago, I was stunned when my boss at the financial firm where I had been working for quite some time suddenly informed me that the VP position he had promised was not going to come through. In fact, they let me go."

"Uh-oh," Sheri interjected sympathetically. "I know that hits home with a lot of my viewers. I've even found myself holding the dreaded pink slip more than once. You know the media industry is a tough business…."

"I'm sure it is," Riana stated, cutting off her host, eager to get her story told. "So, after I left the finance industry, I drew unemployment and looked for work. But every time I reached the interview stage for a position I really wanted, I was told that I was overqualified. I looked for six months. It was a discouraging, exhausting process, and it finally wore me down. I just gave up."

"I know what you're saying," Sheri added with a short laugh. "Looking for work is *work!* Stressful, too."

"Exactly," Riana agreed. "So, I decided to start my own executive recruitment firm to match professionals, who are too often considered *overqualified* for the jobs they want, with the right employer. After doing my research, I applied for and was granted an SBA loan and then I purchased a franchise from Executive Suites, Inc.—a national recruitment firm with offices in ten major cities. I hired an assistant and prayed I would be successful. Three months later the business took off when I snagged two corporate accounts. It's been booming ever since."

"Wonderful! And so inspiring. And I must say you look successful, my sister. That suit is too sharp!"

"Thanks. Appearances do count, you know? If you dress the part and act like you've arrived, you're halfway there," Riana added with a confident tilt of her head.

"So true. Good advice. You took what could have been a de-

feat and made it work for you! Exactly what our viewers need
to hear. So, I understand your company is now one of the top-
grossing recruitment firms in the state."

"Yes, it's an exciting time for me."

"How many recruiters do you have on staff?" Sheri
wanted to know.

"Ten, and I have plans to expand into other markets very soon."

"Can you tell us where?"

"I hope Houston first, then Waco, Amarillo, perhaps."

While the camera continued to roll, Sheri leaned toward
Riana, tapping her gold pen on the notepad on her lap. "What
about your personal life, Riana? Anything you'd like to share
with my viewers? Are you married, divorced, single? A working mom? My audience is always interested in hearing about
the personal lives of busy career women like yourself."

Riana gave her host a timid smile and lifted both hands,
palms up. "I'm afraid I don't have much to say on that subject.
I'm single, not in a serious relationship and not really looking
for one. Running my company takes all of my time and energy.
I don't see myself pursuing any romantic interests anytime
soon."

"Well, good luck. I'm sure you'll be successful." Sheri
turned from Riana to address the camera. "Now, folks, I have
to take a quick commercial break. Make that money, you know?
But when we come back, Riana is going to give you tips on
how to draft an effective résumé and tell you what you need to
know before you go out on that next job interview."

An hour later Riana was behind the wheel of her champagne-
colored Lexus and headed back to her office, a seven-room suite
on the twenty-third floor of the Crockett Building in the heart of
downtown San Antonio. From her windows high above the city,
she could see the famous Alamo, the bustling River Walk and the

outline of Mission Concepcion, one of the oldest Spanish missions still around. Traffic was extremely heavy, as it always was during the summer months, when tourists crowded the downtown area in search of a glimpse of Texas history and a fun time in the fiesta-happy city.

When Riana pulled into her private parking spot in the garage adjoining her building, she remained in her car, taking a moment to reflect on her interview. She was relieved that her appearance on Sheri's show was over and felt satisfied with the way it had gone. Riana got plenty of airtime in order to get her story out. Things were definitely on a roll!

Looking forward to the rest of her day, Riana got out of her car, took the elevator up to the twenty-third floor and pushed through the double glass doors of Executive Suites, Inc.

"Saw you on TV this morning," said Tanisha, Riana's efficient office manager, a dedicated sister who had been with Riana since the office first opened. A petite, fair-skinned young woman with a gentle voice and a steel trap for a mind, she took her job seriously, earning total respect from the staff. With Tanisha in charge, Riana never had to worry about any of her employees slacking off or taking advantage of the fact that Riana was often out and about, networking to bring in more leads. "Good job," Tanisha continued. "The phones have been ringing like crazy."

"Really?" Riana commented, accepting the stack of pink message slips that Donna, the receptionist, handed to her. Riana glanced through them, amazed at how quickly she was getting results from her appearance on Sheri's show. Now, she better understood why those in business in San Antonio worked so hard to keep Sheri happy.

"The school district, two banks, your sister, Britt, and someone from the Allen Group called," Donna prompted, referring to the pink slips in Riana's hand. "Very important to call George

Allen back *today*. His assistant said that he wants information about your services, and that he has a rush job. The man wants to talk to you ASAP."

"Right," Riana agreed, recognizing the name. George Allen was president of the Allen Group, well-known as a major builder of exclusive gated communities, skyscrapers, industrial complexes and huge shopping malls. His name and photo turned up regularly in newspapers and magazines whenever he broke ground on one of his trendsetting projects or donated a chunk of cash to a charitable organization. He was one of the ten wealthiest men in Texas, and his activities were tracked by national publications.

Riana stuffed the messages into the side pocket of her attaché case and headed down the hallway toward her office. Pausing at her door, she turned around and called back to Donna, "I'm gonna give Britt a quick callback first, and then please get George Allen on the phone right away."

"And I want to hear what he has to say," Tanisha interjected, crossing her fingers at Riana before disappearing back inside her office.

Seated at her desk, Riana punched the speed dial to her sister's house, knowing it was best to call Britt back first, before her kids returned home from swimming lessons, the library, a Scout meeting or wherever they'd been shipped off to for the morning. Britt was a stay-at-home mom with five children under the age of twelve who lived in the suburbs with her husband, John, a mild-mannered veterinarian. Even though school was out for the summer, Britt didn't let her children sleep late and watch television all day. She made sure they followed as rigorous a routine of activities during the summer months as they did when school was in session.

"Hi, Britt," Riana greeted, distressed to hear her youngest niece, Wendy, wailing in the background. "What's up?"

"Do you really want to know?" Britt said on the edge of a sigh.

No, not really, Riana thought as she listened to Britt's run-down of her hectic morning. Typical suburban-mom stuff. Nothing Riana could relate to, but she held her tongue and let Britt vent for a few minutes, her monologue interrupted by attempts to shush Wendy. It was difficult not to hurry Britt off the phone, but Riana knew her sister needed the release of talking about her troubles with someone. Today, it was Riana.

"Anyway, the real reason I called…" Britt finally got to the point.

"Yeah, right," Riana prompted, eager to get off the phone and call George Allen back. "I only have a few minutes. An important call to make." Tapping her pen impatiently on her blotter, she waited.

"I know. You're always so busy. Anyway, I saw your interview with Sheri Sherman this morning," Britt started, voice dropping a few octaves.

"Oh? Good. What'd you think?" Riana asked, pleased that Britt, who took little interest in Riana's business, had been watching.

"I'm worried about you," Britt tossed out, her tone a bit accusatory. "Don't you realize how dangerous it was for you to say what you did?"

"What are you talking about?" Riana asked, sitting up straighter, puzzled. *Dangerous? What was bothering Britt, who overreacted to everything?*

"I'm talking about your comment. About not having time for a personal life," Britt clarified. "You just told the world that you're not interested in men. It sounded so strange, almost as if you were, you know…gay or something. Why did you have to do that?"

"Oh, my God! Britt. How can you say that? You know that's not what I meant."

"That's how it came off."

"I simply said that I don't have any interest in pursuing a serious romantic relationship," Riana defended herself. "It's the truth. So what?"

"Well, you'll never get married if you keep broadcasting the fact that you're too involved in your work to give a man the time of day. I don't understand you, I really don't."

Stiffening her spine, Riana kept all emotion from her voice as she told her sister, "I'm not concerned about what people think. If I never get married, that's fine with me, Britt. I'm perfectly content with my life as it is and I have no desire to complicate it by bringing a man into the picture."

Britt's remarks stung Riana. After hanging up the phone, she sat quietly, unable to believe what Britt had said. *Me, gay? Not hardly,* Riana thought, shaking her head, her mind suddenly turning to memories of the time she had spent with Andre Preaux. Even though it had been four years since she had felt Andre's lips on hers and held his body close, it seemed as if she had made love to him only yesterday. Why wouldn't those memories fade?

Chapter 2

Andre paused to catch his breath when he came to the end of his circuit on the jogging trail that wound its way through Hermann Park. Holding on to the back of a park bench, he began a series of stretching exercises while studying the rain clouds that were beginning to darken the jagged Houston skyline. The hot, humid day was coming to an end, and he was glad he had made it to the park in time to get in a good run before the evening rain took over.

Running cleared Andre's head and gave him time to review what he had accomplished at the office. It had been a satisfying day at A. Preaux and Associates, his newly established urban planning and architectural firm located on the top floor of Prairie Towers, a six-story art-deco structure he had rescued from the wrecking ball.

He had prepared a bid proposal for a warehouse renovation project, completed the preliminary sketches for a city-sponsored health center, and prepared his presentation for a gathering of area business owners to discuss his vision for a strip shopping center. Of the projects he was currently working on, the city contract excited him the most. The government design would add another valuable reference to Andre's short list of satisfied clients and add to his renovation fund for Prairie Towers.

Years ago, when the business center of Houston had suddenly shifted westward, companies had vacated office buildings like Prairie Towers for steel-and-glass towers that shimmered in the sunlight. Andre had watched the property deteriorate during punishingly hot summers and through tropical storms that had ravaged it inside and out, while praying that no one would snatch it up before he accumulated sufficient money to buy it. Last year he had managed to purchase the deserted building for a fraction of its value, using every cent of his savings and going into debt, with little left over for the major renovations it would require. Though Prairie Towers was in a fairly dilapidated state, its address still drew respect, and that was what mattered to anyone purchasing real estate in Houston.

Andre had great plans for the 1950s structure, deciding to do most of the work himself, but for now, the building remained vacant except for the top floor, which Andre had divided in half with one side used for his loft-style living quarters and the other half converted into his office space—with two desks, a computer, his drafting table and a bookcase—sufficient furnishings for himself and Lester Tremaine, his part-time assistant, and the only associate at A. Preaux and Associates.

Now, Andre scanned the buildup of cars lining Fannin Drive, ready to head home and add the last coat of sealer to the hardwood floors he had just refinished in his living area. Once he'd completed that work, his loft apartment would be fully renovated and he could turn his focus on the unfinished walls of his office.

"Traffic's gonna be hell," Andre muttered to himself as he

mopped his face with a small white towel and finished his stretching routine. The darkening rain clouds served as a warning that the weather was surely going to make his rush-hour drive time even more sluggish.

Just as he was about to head to the opposite side of the park where he had left his newly washed Pathfinder, the first drops of rain hit the ground, and within seconds, a full-blown downpour erupted. *Twelve dollars wasted,* he thought.

Seeking cover, Andre jogged over to a nearby pavilion where a lone man was watching the rain.

As he approached, Andre recalled that the man had been under the pavilion when he had first arrived at the park, and had stayed there while Andre raced past him repeatedly during his six-mile run. The stranger didn't look like a homeless person, and didn't appear dangerous or threatening, so Andre relaxed, thinking that he might be an office worker who had come out to the park to simply get some fresh air.

Ducking under the shelter, Andre nodded to the stranger. "I knew it was coming," he casually remarked to the man, who was dressed in neat khaki slacks and a white open-collar shirt. His fair complexion was ruddy, as if he'd been out in the sun too long without a hat, and his dark-blond hair, cut short and spiky, resembled a military buzz. Reflective black circles of glass shielded eyes that Andre sensed were sweeping over him.

"Typical July in Houston," the man replied, coming over to stand beside Andre.

"Right," Andre replied, easing back a bit while rethinking his earlier conclusion. His mind whirled back to a recent news report about a well-dressed mugger who had been spotted hanging out in city parks, waiting for unsuspecting victims to beat and rob. It seemed that no one could be trusted nowadays, but Andre hated to automatically assume that every stranger he met was potentially dangerous.

"Are you Andre Preaux?" the man suddenly asked in a strong, official manner, as if he had been waiting for Andre all along.

The question shocked Andre, who stepped away several feet and leveled a curious eye on the red-faced man, whom he now could see was lanky and slightly stooped. His shielded eyes told Andre nothing, staring back at him as if they were simply two black dots pasted on a face for show. "Why? Who are you?" Andre wanted to know, certain he had never seen this person before.

The man reached into his pants pocket and pulled out a slim black wallet, which he flipped open with one heavily freckled hand. "Charles Frazer, FBI. Are you Andre Preaux?"

Too startled, and too cautious, to speak, Andre moved his head up and down.

"Good," the man said, turning away from Andre to walk over to one of the metal picnic tables in the center of the pavilion. Once he was seated, he motioned Andre over. "Sit down, please. I want to talk to you."

"About what?" Andre asked, slowly making his way toward the table as he tried to grasp the inference of the FBI agent's presence in the park. The man knew him. Had called him by name. What could he possibly want?

"It's about your brother, Jamal Preaux," Frazer clarified, removing his glasses to reveal pale-blue expressionless eyes.

"Oh." The word erupted from Andre's mouth, flying out like a tiny dart. He digested the agent's comment, fearful about what was coming next. After having pushed Jamal out of his mind and out of his life for so long, Andre had begun to believe that no one knew about his estranged sibling, but apparently, the FBI did, and the realization was disturbing. "My half brother, you mean," Andre corrected, cautiously taking a seat across from Charles Frazer.

"Okay, fine. Your half brother," Frazer conceded with a

slight smirk. Barely moving his lips, he went on. "When was the last time you saw him?"

That was a question that Andre didn't want to answer, and one that he had hoped no one would ever ask. He could feel his pulse begin to race as he considered whether to cooperate with this man before he knew what was really going on. After all, he was not obligated to answer any official's questions without a lawyer present, and how did he know that this man was really an agent with the FBI? "Why do you want to know?" Andre ventured, stalling, groping for any reason to avoid this conversation.

"Have you seen or heard from Jamal Preaux recently?" Frazer pressed, toying with his sunglasses, his blue stare cutting into Andre's brown eyes.

Slowly, Andre forced himself to calm down, deciding to answer as truthfully as possible because to do otherwise would only make him appear as if he had something to hide, which he didn't. "No. I haven't seen Jamal recently."

"What about his wife, Kay Lamonde Preaux? Heard from her?"

Again, Andre replied, "No," his voice unexpectedly dropping to a whisper.

"You were in Jamaica last September, weren't you?" Frazer pulled a small notebook from the pocket of his limp white shirt, thumbed to a page and studied it, as if verifying his facts. "September 2005? Did you see your brother then?"

Knowing it would be stupid to deny that he had traveled to Jamaica because it was so easy to check travel and passport records, Andre had no choice but to confirm the agent's statement. "Yes," he confessed. "I went to Jamaica in September. I saw my brother then."

"What was the purpose of your visit?"

"Vacation."

"Where did you see Jamal?"

"He came to see me at my hotel in Kingston."

"Are you two close?" Frazer asked.

Andre hunched his shoulders, beginning to feel cornered. "No, not really." Biting his lip, he paused, and then added, "We've had our differences over the years. I'd like him to come back to the States, bring his family and settle down here."

"You ever talk about that with him?" Frazer asked.

"Yeah, sure. But I guess he loves the island life too much to give it up."

"What does your brother do for a living?" Frazer plodded along, his tone growing more efficient with each word, his manner more insistent.

"I don't really know," Andre answered in a constricted voice, praying that he sounded convincing. "Odd jobs. He told me he repairs houses, does fix-up stuff. His wife, Kay, is an artist. Sells her paintings in a local market."

"I see," Frazer said as he made a few notations on a page in his notebook before flipping it closed and taking out one of his business cards, which he slid across the picnic table to Andre. "You still live at Prairie Towers?"

With a jerk of his head, Andre confirmed the man's question, a coil of apprehension forming in his gut. This man knew where he lived. Knew he had a half brother living in the Caribbean. He'd intercepted Andre in the park. How long had the FBI been watching *him?* "Yeah, that's where I live and where I work. My office is in the same building."

"You own the building, right?"

"Yes, I do," Andre snapped, not liking the way this interrogation was going.

"Where'd you get the money to buy a piece of property like that?"

"Where anybody gets money to buy something they want. I earned it. I saved it. Borrowed some from the bank." Now,

Andre was really getting pissed. What right did this man have to ask such questions, which he certainly didn't have to answer? "What difference does it make how I financed my property?"

"Just wanted to know. For the record," Frazer calmly clarified.

"Well, is there anything else you want to know?" Andre tossed out, raising his chin in a defiant jut, ready to be finished with this vague interrogation.

"Not right now, but stick around. I may want to talk to you again."

"Why?" Andre demanded, now suspicious. "Let's dispense with this cat-and-mouse bull. What's this about? Do I need to get a lawyer?"

Agent Frazer's features turned even more solemn and his eyes lowered into hooded blue slits, the first sign of emotion that Andre had seen. "Do you think you need one?"

"No, not at all," Andre boldly countered, determined not to waver.

"Then, you have nothing to worry about, okay?"

"Sure, sure," Andre replied as he picked up the card and studied it. "But can't you tell me what's going on? Is Jamal in trouble?"

"Well, let's just say that he's a person of interest in a complicated situation. He seems to have disappeared. Along with his family. We'd like to find him and his wife, ask them a few questions, that's all."

The self-assured expression on Frazer's face told Andre that he wasn't going to get more than that. "I'll let you know if I hear from him," Andre promised.

"Thanks," Frazer replied before adding, "Looks like the rain has slacked off. I'd better make a run for it." He slid his sunglasses back over his eyes and pushed up from the table, preparing to leave.

Andre didn't move.

Frazer stepped out from beneath the shelter and looked up

at the clearing sky, one hand in his pants pocket, his back still to Andre, and then he twisted his upper torso and turned around. "Don't leave town without letting me know," he called out over his shoulder, before hurrying across the wet grass to the parking lot where he got into a black compact car.

"I'm sure I won't," Andre said to himself, feeling as if he'd been kicked in the stomach. *I should have known this day was coming,* he thought, gripped with the same awful sense of dread that he'd felt the last time he saw Jamal.

Chapter 3

After holding for a full five minutes, Riana finally got George Allen on the line, and it was hard for her to contain her excitement when he finally told her what he wanted.

Swiveling around in her chair, she positioned her back to her office door and faced the sun-splashed windows that overlooked downtown San Antonio. A ripple of anticipation came over her as she took in the details of the most important assignment she had ever been offered. Adding George Allen's company, the Allen Group, to her client list would be a major coup, and she didn't care if he asked her to locate a multilingual nuclear scientist who could also sing the blues and write country songs, she was going to accept this assignment. No way could she underestimate the importance of snagging this account.

"So," she finally said when Allen finished, "you're constructing a minimum-security prison outside of San Antonio to be named Tierra Trace—specifically for adult women and female juveniles, right? Is this a federal project?"

"Exactly, my company was awarded the contract to design and build Tierra Trace, which will be closely monitored and controlled by government regulations. It's an unusual approach, in that the complex will house inmates who have been selected to enter advanced professional training and college-level classes in order to reenter society and be productive. Minimum security, white-collar crime. It's not going to be a place for people to simply sleep, eat and watch TV to pass the time."

"Interesting," Riana commented.

"The location and design of the various units within the complex will be crucial to the success of this project."

"What's the size of the complex?" Riana asked.

"It'll be modest in size, divided into three distinct areas with separate buildings for adult women and juvenile girls. It will also have a small unit for pregnant women or those with newborns who need to keep their babies with them for a while. Lots of green space and utility areas all around. Each of these distinct groups has vastly different requirements and I am convinced that housing inmates with similar personal situations and similar needs will impact the success of this plan. This is the first of its kind in the country, and if it's successful, others will follow."

"It's a most unique approach," Riana said.

"Yes, it is," Allen stated with pride. "It must be functional, have clean lines and incorporate all the high-tech security equipment and state-of-the-art sanitation requirements available, along with instructional and recreational areas."

"How can Executive Suites help?"

"I want you to recruit a leader for my design team. I need a space-planning architect to help pull my vision together," Allen said, and then added, "I've been thinking about using someone new to the industry, an unknown who can bring a fresh perspective."

"You want me to recruit a novice architect who's just launching a career? Why not go after the best, most experienced person for the job?" Riana wanted to know.

"When I saw you on *Community Business Focus* this morning, I was very impressed with your story. I thought, 'Why not hire an up-and-coming search firm to use on this project? And while I'm at it, why not go after a hungry architect who really needs the work?' This is not one of my bigger projects by any means, but it's a very important one, and whoever comes on board will get a heck of a lot of exposure. I want you to find me an unknown with talent. I'm sure you can locate a professional who understands what I need and who can deliver."

"Thanks for that vote of confidence. What's your time frame?" Riana asked, swiveling back around to grab her pen and take notes.

"I'll be out of the office next week, but when I return, I'd like to meet with you and go over a short list of candidates. Think you can get some names together by then?"

"No problem," Riana replied, her mind already whizzing ahead to the recruitment resources she planned to use.

"The design team won't actually meet for at least ninety days at the outside, but I want to get the candidate—man or woman—on board right away. Sound like an assignment your firm can handle?"

Riana took a deep breath, crossed her fingers and told George Allen, "Yes. Executive Suites will find the perfect match between your company and your project. You will not be disappointed."

"Good. Now, I'm going to have Pat, my human resources manager, call you with the job description. She'll give you all the details and work with you to finalize the contract, now that you've accepted the job. She'll draft your contract, go over it with you, and when it's all set, I'll talk with you again."

Immediately after hanging up, Riana turned to her computer and got to work. With the next day being the Fourth of July, the office would be closed, so she wanted to get a head start on this assignment. She pulled up the database of clients currently enrolled with Executive Suites and quickly highlighted the names of three architects whose credentials were impressive. However, she knew she could not stop there. On a task like this one, she would have to utilize all of her recruitment sources and screen a wide range of potentials. She could tell that Allen was a demanding man who expected the best from people he worked with, and she was going to deliver exactly what he wanted.

After creating a folder to hold the information she found on the first three candidates, she turned to her database that contained the names of the presidents of professional agencies and organizations within the building and architecture industries who had helped her with her recruitment needs in the past. After carefully preparing an e-mail blast that detailed her requirements, Riana sent the announcement to everyone on the contact list, hoping that someone would give her a lead.

So far, she had never failed a client, and it was this sense of confidence—her assurance that the ideal candidate was out there somewhere—that drove her to push so hard and to set her personal needs aside in order to make her company grow.

So what if her sister, Britt, referred to Riana as a workaholic clotheshorse who would probably wind up a lonely spinster? Riana had no intention of slowing down, or of focusing on her social life instead of her company. Britt was just jealous, and she certainly had no trouble accepting the clothes that Riana offered her when she cleaned out her closet at the end of each season.

Riana's mother, Karleen, who had worked part-time during

the summer months at the neighborhood ice-cream shop when her daughters were young, also accused Riana of taking her work much too seriously. Karleen wanted more grandchildren to spoil, a second son-in-law to pamper and another big wedding to plan. In her opinion, Riana was using her work to avoid commitment, afraid that a man would want to come in and take over her business under the guise of relieving her of the stress that comes with owning a demanding franchise.

Even Riana's father, Sam, now retired from his government job as a city health inspector, concurred. He worried that Riana might be sacrificing too much for the sake of making money. Getting rich was not that important, he often told her. A fancy car, expensive clothes and nice jewelry meant nothing if you didn't have someone with whom to share and enjoy such perks. Money wouldn't bring his daughter happiness, he would say, urging her to take a hard look at her priorities.

Riana disagreed with all of them. She was proud of what she'd accomplished, and she thrived on the financial freedom that she had earned. She was content to immerse herself in the world of negotiations, contracts and deal-making to the exclusion of an endless and often frantic round of galas and benefits and shallow happy hours and boring stand-up cocktail parties just to search for Mr. Right. She gave generously to the charities that mattered by writing checks at the end of the year, and had long ago given up worrying about finding a mate. If it happened, fine, but she sure wasn't going to lie awake at night worrying about when, or if, someone to love—who could fit into her world—would come along.

Now, clicking through her e-mails, Riana saw that two of her professional colleagues had already replied to her request for leads for potential candidates to fill George Allen's search. The first message, from the president of the American Association of Urban Planners contained the résumés of two of their members who were seeking projects: Sandra Morehouse of Oklahoma City and Robert Fountain from Dallas. Riana closely scrutinized their credentials, made a few notes about Sandra, who had five years of experience and a short list of clients, and then Robert, whose work was starkly simple and not very attractive.

Impressed, but not quite satisfied, Riana moved on to the second message, from the membership chair of the National Association of Builders and Architects. The contact, with whom Riana had worked on two other assignments, was offering up only one name, and when Riana read the e-mail, she froze. Andre Preaux, of A. Preaux and Associates in Houston, winner of the prestigious 2003 Space City Improvement Award for his design of a low-rise complex for marginalized senior citizens in Houston. Heart thumping in her chest, she began to read aloud from the screen.

"'Andre Preaux, a newcomer to the industrial architectural and design scene, brings twelve years of experience in the construction business and a recent degree in architecture from the University of Houston to his innovative designs. In his award-winning project, Arbor Oaks, he grasped the big-picture demands of the problem of limited housing for elderly seniors on fixed incomes and was able to effectively tie the project to the goals and the needs of an underserved group of citizens. He cut through tangled red tape and finished the complex in record time while honoring city ordinances and following housing guidelines to achieve a final project that surpassed the original plans. His use of innovative design concepts for the handicapped and those with limited mobility, his incorporation of environmentally friendly materials, and his involvement of the local residents allowed him to prove that there can be equitable access to affordable housing for all members of the Houston community.'"

It can't be the same man, Riana kept telling herself, frowning at the photo of a professionally attired caramel-colored man in a business suit and tie. His hair was longer, his smile seemed brighter, and he looked more mature than the thirty-seven years she knew him to be. He also looked confident and polished, as if he possessed secrets to his rapid rise that he did not plan to reveal. She had never seen Andre wearing anything other than scruffy jeans or slacks and a shirt, never a suit. This man was dressed with ultimate care, sending a message of impressive style. Even the address of his firm was impressive: Prairie Towers, in the high-rent, Main Street, museum-district area. Apparently, he was doing quite well, and he was just as disturbingly handsome as she remembered. Even more so, Riana had to admit, wondering for the thousandth time if they could have made it as a couple.

Frantically, she scrolled through his résumé, eager to read everything she could about his background, his work, his education and his future plans. She was stunned. How could this be the same man who had worn faded jeans and work boots to class, who had swept her into a whirlwind romance before she'd realized what was happening? Was this the same man whose heart she knew she had shattered four years ago when she had left him behind to pursue her career?

Slumping back in her chair, Riana stared at the monitor, not seeing anything, unable to stop the flood of memories she'd been holding back for years easing into her mind. As she sat there, sensations she had struggled to forget swept through her. The feel of his fingers on her skin as he held her chin and kissed her good-night. The clean soapy smell of his skin after they'd bathed together in his bubbly Jacuzzi tub. The scent of their soul-touching bodies after a long night of making love. The taste of his lips, plump, full and warm over hers.

An ache of longing flashed through Riana, tearing into her heart and holding her still. Sitting there, she felt a lump of regret begin to swell, reigniting the misery she'd suffered through during those miserable days after her return home. It hadn't taken long for Riana to admit that she had miscalculated everything back then: her job security at Sweetwater, the depth of Andre's feelings for her and her ability to get over him.

Andre had called her once, had e-mailed her twice, but she'd never responded, unable to go back on her decision to put her career first and sidestep the temptation of entering into a long-distance relationship. She had simply eased her way out of his life as smoothly as he had entered hers, fully aware that she had left him feeling confused and disappointed about her actions. However, she'd had little choice at the time, and after weeks of crying herself to sleep at night or lying awake second-guessing her decision to walk away from Andre, she had finally managed to let go of him and put her energy into building her company.

Now, Riana moved her index finger over the delete button on her keyboard, prepared to erase Andre Preaux from her computer screen as well as her life. But she couldn't press the key. As much as she wanted to push his résumé aside, it was impossible. Dammit! Andre had all of the credentials that George Allen was looking for and there was no way she could exclude him from her short list. In fact he might be the ideal candidate.

Riana clipped one more yellow rose from the chest-high bush in the center of her rose garden, placed it in a basket and decided that the six full blooms she had picked were more than enough for a nice bouquet. She headed into the potting shed at the far end of her compact, well-landscaped yard and put her tools away.

When she had left her office at six o'clock that evening, she hadn't planned on working in her garden, but when she walked through the door she was too keyed up over having seen

Andre's photo on the Internet to simply flop in her easy chair and watch the evening news on TV as usual. She had to stay busy, keep her mind off him. So she'd put on her jeans, a T-shirt and her leather gardening gloves and headed into her rose garden to shift her thoughts from the ghostly past.

Riana pulled off her gloves, hung them on a hook in the shed and wiped perspiration from her forehead with the back of one hand. The early-July evening was sultry, humid and still pushing ninety degrees even though it was nearing dusk: a typical day in the Alamo city. However, Riana had no complaints. She was used to the steamy summer days that never seemed to cool and knew that grumbling about the heat did no good; it would end in its own time, and that could be as late as mid-October, or even Thanksgiving Day some years.

As she made her way back toward the house, she surveyed her colorful flower garden with pride: it was one of the reasons she had purchased this house on Puerto Valdez Avenue. The Craftsman-style bungalow had cost twice as much as she had planned to pay when she decided to become a homeowner, but it was worth the investment. Her house was close to downtown, on a quiet tree-lined street, and just the right size for a single person.

For Riana, living on Puerto Valdez Avenue was like residing on a tropical island of calm and peace. She thrived on the privacy of the mid-town neighborhood, where every street ended in a wide cul-de-sac, and the only vehicles cruising past belonged to a resident or someone who had business being in the area. The chirps of birds and the rustle of tropical foliage drifted over smooth green lawns that fronted the tidy homes, which were set back from the street and divided by hedges of blooming oleanders along the driveways.

Inside, Riana went into her recently updated kitchen and looked into the fridge: orange juice, bottled water, a diet drink, a pint of cottage cheese and a carton of eggs. She shouldn't have been surprised. There were two things Riana did not do: cook or clean house. A housecleaning service descended on her home once a week to keep it spotless, and she drank juice for breakfast, had lunch delivered to her office from a nearby health-food store and usually picked up a salad or pasta for dinner from Central Market on her way home. Today, she had been so preoccupied with memories of her time with Andre she had forgotten all about food.

After taking out the can of diet drink, she shut the refrigerator door and poured it into a glass, sipping it while she arranged the yellow roses in a white glass vase, impressed with the size of the blossoms.

Finished with her arrangement, she placed it on the coffee table in her muted beige-and-cream living room, and, grabbing her diet drink, went into her home office for a quick e-mail check. However, instead of logging into her mailbox, she punched in Andre's Web site address and held her breath as she gazed at his photo and read his résumé over and over, unable to tear her eyes away from his face or get her mind off the only man she had ever loved.

What am I doing? she silently fretted, sensing his presence wrap around her, her heartbeat steadily increasing. *Why am I acting as if I care? As if he means a thing to me?* However, she knew the answer. She loved Andre, and the realization was not one she could ever escape.

Since moving back to San Antonio, she had acquired an interesting circle of friends and had dated often enough to suit her needs. However, too often, when she did meet a man who interested her, the relationship quickly fizzled when he realized that his role in her life would be solidly paired with her devotion to Executive Suites, Inc.

Riana was well aware that her strong work ethic turned

some men off, but in Riana's opinion, everything was as it should be. She was living the good life—in a home that she owned, driving the car that she loved, dressing in stylish, well-made clothes and investing in her future. This was all she'd ever wanted to do and she had no plans of changing anything in order to please an insecure man or her overprotective family.

I was right to leave Andre, she told herself. *If I hadn't, I never would have accomplished the goals I set for myself, and I never would have created the company I love so much.*

Becoming a successful businesswoman had been Riana's dream since she was young, going back to the days when she had taken the city bus across town to the private school that she and Britt had attended. Cruising through the crowded business section, she had gazed out the windows, fascinated by the women in tailored business suits, carrying expensive looking attaché cases who hurried across intersections and along the streets, going in and out of the multiwindowed buildings. She had always wondered what they did behind those heavy doors of brass and tinted glass, in those rooms looming high above the city.

During her senior year of high school, Riana accepted a part-time job at a national life-insurance agency whose offices filled seven floors of a building in the heart of the business center. Thrilled to finally be a part of the fascinating world she had longed to explore, she quickly imitated the dress, the stride and the in-office mannerisms of the women with whom she associated. Her salary was low, her job was tedious, but she went to work every afternoon with a smile on her face and an intense desire to do her best. That approach, coupled with a positive attitude, soon caught the attention of Madeline Betts, the vice president of the insurance company.

Madeline took Riana under her wing and coached her on the ins and outs of the insurance business. Told her how to get what she wanted from the corporate managers—all males—who dominated the company and presented great challenges for women with drive and purpose.

Learn to be tough, but fair, Madeline had told Riana. Be persistent, but not overly aggressive when negotiating. Never take anything or anyone for granted. Don't compromise, if doing so would leave you with regrets. And most important of all— never burn bridges, or let anyone burn them for you. We're all too interconnected to take such a chance.

Riana had thrived under Madeline's tutelage, and when she applied for admission to graduate school at the University of Texas, Madeline Betts wrote the glowing recommendation that Riana believed had won her a full scholarship to the master's program in the College of Economics. With her advanced degree, she had been quickly snapped up by Sweetwater Finance where the most important thing she learned was how *not* to run a company. Getting fired had definitely been a blessing in disguise.

Now, as she studied Andre's Web site photo, she wondered if finding him again would turn out to be a blessing or a curse.

Chapter 4

It was difficult for Riana to gauge George Allen's reaction to the candidates she had presented for his consideration and she was beginning to get nervous. Ten days had passed since he'd first contacted her and it was time for him to let her know whom she ought to pursue. With a great deal of care, he read over each résumé, made a few notes in the margins and then set it aside before going on to the next.

At last, he removed his glasses and placed them on the conference table, prepared to reveal his decision.

"They all look good, Riana," he finally said, drumming two fingers on the hard, polished wood. "Tomas Segovia has great credentials, but everything he's done looks the same. Nothing innovative there," Allen replied, thumbing his chin as he leaned back in his big leather chair. "Sandra Morehouse's last job was extremely well executed, but it wasn't well received by the county officials." Allen tucked his bottom lip beneath his teeth as he considered another résumé. "Now, this young man takes a fresh, bold approach to his designs. Exactly what I've been thinking about for Tierra Trace." He focused on Riana when he said, "I think what Andre Preaux did with the Arbor Oaks design was most impressive. He just might be able to deliver what I want."

Allen's comment threw Riana momentarily off guard, though she knew it shouldn't have upset her at all. He was right: Andre's striking design, which had addressed important environmental, residential and economic factors had made it a winner, making Arbor Oaks stand out from the plethora of average projects that the other architects and planners had completed. However, all of Andre's talent didn't erase the fact that it was going to be very difficult for her to approach him, and she didn't dare reveal her concerns to George Allen.

"His firm is very small. In fact, he may be a one-man shop. And other than the senior citizens' facility, he hasn't done much to prove his talent," Riana quickly tossed back, a worry frown creeping over her brow.

George Allen nodded his understanding, but countered her concern with a statement that made Riana's stomach tighten. "I still think he's the one. What draws me most to Preaux is that he took risks with unusual materials and he got the job done in record time."

I once took a risk on him, too, and got involved in record time! But I let him down hard and I doubt he's forgotten, Riana silently recalled, wishing she could remain impartial.

"Reminds me of myself when I started out," Allen continued. "All I needed was the right break. Someone to connect with my vision. I see no reason why I shouldn't at least give him first shot." He arched a brow at Riana, who smiled demurely and inclined her head. "Set up an interview. I want to know more about Andre Preaux. If he doesn't work out, we'll move on to someone else."

"That's a good approach," she agreed. "Let's hope Preaux is interested in meeting with me. From the look of his Web site, I gather he's a pretty busy man. I haven't spoken to any of the candidates yet, but I'll contact him first, have a friendly chat and explore his future plans. Then I'll know how to move ahead."

Allen turned his perceptive gaze on Riana, shaking her out of her miserable dilemma. "If he works out, this project may go down on the books as my riskiest one ever. My first time using Executive Suites as my search firm, and now I'm actually thinking of hiring a novice architect to help design my complex. Some people might think I'm crazy, but this is what keeps me excited and engaged in doing business: the discovery and promotion of new talent. Riana, here's what I want you to do. Schedule a personal interview with Andre Preaux as soon as possible, don't just talk to him on the phone. Go to see him. I'd like you to spend time at his office, see where he works. Check out his surroundings. If possible, feel out colleagues about his work ethics, his management style, his temperament. And for this project, I'll have to have a criminal background check on him, too. You know what I'll need."

"Yes, I do," Riana replied, girding herself for this difficult recruitment task. If she had to go to Houston and face Andre, she'd go, and she'd recruit him for the job and earn a nice fee from George Allen, too. And while she was at it she might as well make the trip do double duty and take care of some business while there. "I'd been planning on going to Houston anyway," she told Allen, sounding as casual as she could manage. "I want to check out the Executive Suites franchise there. It's not doing well, the owner wants to sell, and I'm considering buying it."

"Good idea. I heard you talking about your expansion plans when you were on *Community Business Focus*. Houston's a good market for recruitment. As I've always said, the only way to be successful in business is to grow, grow, grow. Staying small never leads to anything but remaining exactly where you are."

"I agree," Riana replied, her mind already spinning with ideas about how to approach Andre. She'd have to plan her tactics carefully, remain totally about business with no treks down memory lane, no conversation about regrets, no emotion. She would plunge into the task fully prepared to get the job done in record time and then, she hoped, she'd never see or speak to Andre Preaux again.

"I'll get back to you as soon as I've interviewed Preaux and give you an update," she told Allen, ready to get started.

"I trust your company to do its job," Allen agreed with a nod. "And I look forward to your take on how you think Preaux will fit in with my plans."

Riana swallowed, her mouth nearly too dry to speak, her stomach sinking fast. "I know you want the best for the Tierra Trace project, and that's what you'll have."

"Tell you what, if Preaux turns out to be the right person for the job, and you can get him in place within a very short time frame, the Allen Group will pay Executive Suites a fifty-percent increase in our contracted fee."

Stunned, Riana blinked. "Fifty percent? How generous," she commented, knowing what Allen meant. If she did *not* come through within his time frame, he would have no problem taking his business elsewhere. This was a test. He had backed her into a corner and she could not let him down. The Allen Group account was hers. All she had to do was remain detached during the recruitment process and not allow herself to get personally involved with her former lover.

Felicia turned to her computer, punched up her e-mail and began reading through the latest security updates, trying to figure out which ones directly applied to her area of the airport when her phone rang. She answered without taking her eyes off the screen.

"President's Lounge. Felicia Woods speaking."

"Hey, Felicia, it's Riana."

Now, she shifted her attention away from the pages of dense text that were beginning to blur anyway and swiveled back in her chair. "Riana. Well, I needed this break. Good to hear from you, cuz. How's it going?"

"*Very* well. Can't complain at all. Things are definitely moving in the right direction."

"That means business must be booming," Felicia responded, nodding as she listened to Riana's quick update on the activity in her office. "You sure sound chipper," Felicia commented, a touch of envy in her voice. "Wish I could say I felt the way you sound."

"Pretty hectic?" Riana commented.

"Girl, this place is a madhouse. The members aren't so bad. I do get a crazy one now and then, but mostly it's just this place. Long hours, no respect, touchy folks who always have something to say. But what am I gonna do? Can't quit. I have too many years invested in this job to up and walk away." A pause. "Anyway, what's up in San Antonio?"

"I just signed with a very important client and I have an assignment that's going to bring me to Houston."

"Fabulous. It'll be great to have you around. And you'll finally get to meet Malcom, too."

"You two are still dating? I can't believe it."

"Yep, and we're getting along fine."

"This must be a record for you, Felicia. Guess you got him hooked, girl. How long has it been now?"

"Eight months. The reason I think this one has lasted so long, and why we get along so well, is because he's never around," Felicia laughed. "Dating a pilot is fantastic. He's away long enough for me to really miss him, so every time we get together, it's like the first time. Strange, but it works for us."

"Can't wait to meet him," Riana replied. "However, I'm gonna be so caught up in work I doubt I'll be hanging out with you guys very much."

"Oh, I'll make sure we get you out to have some fun. Been thinking about throwing a party as soon as I finish fixing up my place. It's a mess right now, so you might not want to bunk with me this time around."

"Oh, no problem. Don't worry. I made reservations at the Extended Stay America near downtown. Something like a mini apartment. Executive Suites has a long-term contract with them. I might have to be around for a while."

"Sounds good. Tell me all," Felicia said, listening while Riana filled her in on her assignment.

"Andre Preaux? *Your* Andre?" Felicia exclaimed, jaw dropping in surprise. Scratching her forehead, she thought back to the time when Riana had been totally smitten with Andre, but too stubborn to admit it. "You've got to be kidding! Who woulda thought?"

"Exactly. But I *have* to get him to accept the position. Big bonus for my firm if I do."

"Girl, he might not even talk to you, let alone let you recruit him! You dumped the guy, broke his heart and never looked back. Things could get ugly."

"Oh, I don't think so," Riana replied. "This is a huge opportunity for him. The Allen Group carries weight."

"Maybe so, but Andre Preaux is probably carrying one hell of a grudge."

Chapter 5

Lester Tremaine answered the phone at the beginning of the second ring as he always did, convinced that answering too quickly made him seem too anxious, and if he waited until after the third ring he risked missing the call. His method worked, and many of Andre's clients complimented him on his prompt response to their telephone calls, as well as his polite greeting. A graduate student in engineering at Rice University, Lester assisted Andre in his research by sorting through the requirements of potential projects, organizing files, handling the mail and generally staying on top of the city and county regulations that affected licensing and building permits.

"A. Preaux and Associates," Lester stated with the crisp assurance of a man in charge. "How may I help you?"

"Hello. This is Miss Cole, calling from Executive Suites, Incorporated, in San Antonio. Is Mr. Preaux available?"

Remaining silent, Lester ran the name of the caller and the

company through his mind, certain he had never heard of either, and he didn't recognize the voice. He had a gift for being able to recall every voice he had heard, whether in person, over the phone, on the radio or TV. This was someone new. "And this is in reference to…?" Lester prompted, doing his job. Andre trusted him to screen all calls and weed out sales people, telemarketers and those seeking information that was readily available on the A. Preaux and Associates Web site. No way was he going to bother Andre with things that he could take care of himself.

"I'd like to discuss a possible project in the San Antonio area with him."

"Well, yes, of course. However, I'm sorry, he's not in right now, but I'll be happy to give him your message. Where can he reach you?" Lester inquired as he wrote down the information he knew Andre would need.

After clicking off, Lester studied the message with interest. *Executive Suites?* he mused, twirling his pen. *A big hotel project, perhaps? An office building?* He hoped so. Andre needed something right away because the contract with the city health-center complex had been awarded just yesterday to a large, well-known firm, leaving Andre very disappointed. All they had going now was a remodel of a small boutique that had suffered a minor fire and the strip shopping center for Richard Vail, an independent builder in town. After those projects, Andre's calendar was open.

Lester was a talented twenty-six-year-old who was openly gay, meticulously thorough and dedicated to his work at A. Preaux and Associates. His slight build, creamy buff-colored skin and tightly curled copper-brown hair made him appear much younger than he was, and he still got carded whenever he ordered a drink.

During the two years that Lester had worked for Andre, he

had come to think of his boss more as a colleague and good friend than simply his employer. They took on each project together, working as a team to bring it in on time and in a way that ensured a positive reception. Lester had been up front with Andre when he was first interviewed, telling him that he was gay and in a stable relationship with a partner. Andre had not flinched or looked at him as if he were an oddity or made any comment other than, "I'd be happy to have you work for me, if the hours fit your class schedule." And after that, he and Andre never again mentioned the difference in their sexual orientations.

In fact, there were times when Lester felt as if Andre envied him for having found someone to love, and he often wished that Andre would go out on more dates. However, Lester stayed out of Andre's personal life and went about his business, which revolved around his work, his classes and his live-in partner, Todd.

When Lester's cell phone rang, it jolted him out of his hopeful musing and brought him back to the reality of the moment. He pulled his tiny phone from his shirt pocket, squinted at the caller ID, grinned, and then flipped open the cover immediately, eager to talk to Todd.

"You're downstairs already? Are you calling from your car?" he asked in a rush of words, wondering how Todd, who managed a cellular phone kiosk in the Galleria, had maneuvered through noon-hour traffic so quickly. "Okay, I'm on my way out now," Lester chirped, juggling the phone with one hand as he shut down his computer and grabbed his keys to the building with the other. Before leaving for his standing Wednesday lunch date with Todd, Lester made sure he placed the phone message from Executive Suites on Andre's desk.

Andre placed the white bag containing his Southwest chicken wrap sandwich and diet soda in the center of his desk, preparing for a quick lunch before heading off to a meeting with a county commissioner who was unveiling plans for a new recreational facility in his district. He was anxious for the opportunity to bid on another well-funded government contract that would keep his name out front.

Just as he was about to take a sip of his drink, he noticed the message slip that Lester had propped against his telephone and picked it up. The note was neatly printed in Lester's block-style script. Miss Kohl of Executive Suites, Inc? Who was that? Andre wondered, studying the area code. West Texas. New Braunfels? Kerrville? San Antonio, perhaps? He'd never heard of the company and didn't recall ever having done business with a Miss Kohl. Hopefully, the call was worth returning.

"'Interested in talking to you about a project,'" Andre read aloud as he set the piece of paper on top of a stack of folders and dove into his sandwich, thankful for the peace and quiet.

As much as Andre liked having Lester around and depended on his reliable assistance, today it felt good to have the office to himself. Lester was a valuable asset to the company, and Andre hoped to bring him on board full-time after he received his degree.

During the time Lester had been employed, Andre had gotten to know and like the young man. Surprising them both, they had become good friends, even though their lifestyles were worlds apart. They enjoyed discussing current books and movies and, of course, the latest trends in building.

Lester was a good listener, an extremely creative person who was bubbling with ideas, and he was easy to have around. In a two-man office, that was important, and Andre knew he could trust Lester to say or do what was in the best interest of the firm without worrying about him making huge mistakes.

However, at times like this, when Andre wasn't swamped

with work and things were slow, he had to focus on maintaining a positive attitude. His bank account was holding well for now, but his phones were much too silent, and, except for the space he'd carved out for himself on the top floor of his building, Prairie Towers remained in the same state it had been in when he bought it.

Andre shifted in his chair and surveyed the stripped walls of his office, the rough cement floor, and the open ceilings where pipes and wires showed through. His living suite was in good shape, but his office was begging for a redo. Andre knew he could turn Prairie Towers back into a showplace of an office building that would entice forward-thinking companies and small businesses to clamor for space. It was going to cost a chunk of cash and take a healthy line of credit to pull everything together, but he would do it, he had no doubt. He had hoped the city contract would come through, but since it hadn't, he could stay busy enough with other projects and keep financial pressures from building.

Andre lifted a stack of folders containing pending projects off his file cabinet, planning to go through them one more time. He found a great deal of satisfaction in his work, and nothing was more exciting than juggling two or three projects at the same time while researching prospective bids on others. Working under pressure kept him energized and positive, but when things slowed down his mind tended to fill with a jumble of worries about failure and loss, bringing him face-to-face with his past. Why couldn't he shake that faded old shadow of the man he used to be?

Andre's father, Rex Preaux, had been a Louisiana roughneck oil-field worker who migrated from one end of the Gulf Coast to the other, taking dirty offshore jobs wherever he could get them. He divorced Andre's mother, Lorene, and disappeared when Andre was four years old, leaving behind a son with a huge hole in his heart. That was the first time that Andre experienced a true sense of loss, and the pain never fully left him, not even when he eventually reunited with his father.

As he grew up, Andre blamed his mother for running his father off, refusing to believe her story, which he finally managed to persuade her to tell him—that Rex Preaux had left her for another woman. Andre's disappointment fueled a deep rage against his mother until Rex finally returned to Baton Rouge three years later with his new wife, proving that Lorene had been right, because Rex also brought along his second son—a skinny three-year-old named Jamal.

Rex and his new family settled down in a house only four blocks from his first family, and Andre was happy to have his dad back. However, his happiness quickly vanished when he overhead Rex telling Lorene that he would never again set foot in her home or have anything to do with his first-born child. This declaration crushed Andre, and he again blamed his mother for failing to bring his father back into his life.

As they grew up, Jamal and Andre attended the same school, played basketball in the same neighborhood streets, and actually became very close. Too close, according to Lorene, who watched Andre imitate Jamal, whom she called a wild, impulsive child who was leading her son astray.

Like water draining into a sewer, Andre was quickly sucked into Jamal's fast life, thrilled to be earning chunks of cash while hustling drugs with his baby brother. Jamal rose to the position of leader of their gang, and life was good, Andre thought, until the local police arrested him for selling drugs to an undercover cop: marijuana and cocaine.

Andre had been seventeen years old at the time of his arrest, young enough to be tried as a juvenile. The only good thing about the crushing blow was that his record would not become a permanent blight on his past. However, by the time the judge sentenced him to two years in Jena Juvenile Justice Center, the facility was full, he had turned eighteen, so it was off to federal prison to live among the hard-core adults who literally scared Andre straight.

During his incarceration, Andre experienced a deep sense of failure at having disappointed his mother, as well as himself. Choking back his sorrow, Andre turned his back on his rebellious brother and his emotionally distant father, and reached out for his mother's forgiveness.

Lorene responded, arriving at the prison once a week with words of encouragement to fuel the flicker of hope that Andre struggled to keep burning. He didn't want to turn into a mean, surly brute of a man, like those he faced in the prison walkways every day, and he never wanted to be locked in a cage again.

Lorene's weekly visits were the only pleasant periods during Andre's incarceration, but even they didn't last long—six months into his sentence, she died unexpectedly of pneumonia, leaving Andre devastated with grief and furious that he couldn't attend her funeral to say goodbye.

After serving his time, he left Baton Rouge, moved to Houston, and started working jobs on construction sites, leaving his family back in Louisiana and his stint in prison to fade from his memory. He was twenty-two years old when he decided to take the steps to make something of himself, and the first thing he did was get his GED. Next, he enrolled in college and earned a bachelor's degree in civil engineering, finally becoming an architect in his midthirties, in charge of his life at last.

Andre knew what he wanted now: a major project that was well funded and highly visible, one that would ensure the future of A. Preaux and Associates. He couldn't think of failing. He'd come too far to lose everything he'd worked so hard to accomplish.

After finishing lunch, Andre glanced through the mail that

Lester had opened and neatly arranged it in a folder in order of importance. He set most of it aside, but did zero in on a pale-blue envelope, which he opened right away, glad to see a check for sixteen thousand dollars from the boutique owner whose shop he had recently redesigned. Next, he picked up the message from Miss Kohl and punched in the number, curious to see what she wanted.

"Andre Preaux returning a call to Miss Kohl," he told the woman who answered. A soft Spanish ballad filled the line while he waited, making him smile. Something about the tune was gently pleasant and made a statement about the company. *Innovative branding,* he thought, knowing he would remember this company because of the song.

"Hello." A woman's voice interrupted the music. "This is Riana Cole."

"Riana?" Andre repeated, gripping the phone as he leaned over his desk. A black hole opened in his stomach. "Riana Cole? *C-O-L-E?* Is that how you spell it?"

"Yes, Andre. It's me. Your former classmate in Commercial Banking in Real Estate."

And former lover, too, he thought, swept back four years by the sound of her voice. The stream of longing that hit him, caught him by surprise. He had thought he was over her, and would never feel this way again, but here it was—that sensual mix of joy and desire that had captured his heart back then.

"I'm…I'm surprised," he began, unsure of what else to say. "I never would have dreamed I was calling *you.*" He eased lower in his chair and sucked in a long breath, anxious to regain his composure, wondering just what she wanted.

Surely, she must think I hate her for walking away, for not giving our relationship a fighting chance, he thought. *But it was her decision to end it, and all I did was honor her wishes, as difficult as it was.*

"You work for Executive Suites?" he commented, finding his voice. "I thought you were a VP at Sweetwater Finance," he pushed ahead, not wanting to get caught up in thinking about their past.

"I don't *work* for Executive Suites, I own it. The VP position at Sweetwater didn't work out, so I created my own company and hired myself," Riana replied in a surprisingly light tone, going on to tell him about her executive search firm.

The sound of her voice stirred up old emotions, making it difficult for Andre to concentrate on what Riana was saying. As he listened, her face emerged slowly into his mind. The way her fine brown hair swayed across her cheek. Those soulful eyes that had made him go weak whenever he'd looked into them. Her slender hands on his back, trailing fingers down his spine. The easy way she had fit with him. A lump of regret clogged his throat, holding back the words that he knew would mean nothing to her, even if he managed to say them.

"Good for you," Andre told her when she finished filling him in on the past four years. The fact that she hadn't mentioned marriage or children or even a serious personal relationship didn't surprise Andre. Riana had accomplished exactly what she'd set out to do: become a successful businesswoman. Clearly, she had not let anything or anyone compromise her dream.

"…so I'm recruiting a leader for Allen's design team on a minimum-security prison for women and juveniles," Riana was saying.

Suddenly, Riana's words jerked Andre back to the conversation. "What's that again?" he asked, head tilted to the side. "You said you want to interview me for a possible job with the Allen Group?" Now, he pushed aside the emotional effects of his telephone reunion with Riana, eager to talk business.

"Yes, George Allen has contracted with my executive search firm to screen and recommend an architect/planner to lead the design team on a moderate-sized prison compound," Riana told Andre.

"Really? Why me?" he wanted to know, aware that Allen could get anyone he wanted. What architect or space planner wouldn't jump at the chance to work with the well-respected builder?

"Apparently, Allen wants a fresh approach and he liked what you did with the senior citizen project for which you won the Space City Improvement Award."

"Really?" Andre commented, still unable to believe he was talking to Riana.

"Yes. You've done very well for yourself, Andre. You have your own firm, and I see you're located near the museum district."

"Right. Prairie Towers. I own the building," he replied with pride.

"Very nice. You're certainly moving in the right direction. Congratulations. I'm happy for you."

"Thanks," Andre managed, "but I'm only just beginning. I've got great plans for my company."

"I'm sure you do. And George Allen wants to be a part of your plan. He's considering several candidates, but you're at the top of his list. And that's why I'm calling, Andre. This is strictly business. Allen would like me to interview you and report back to him. That's it. So, as far as I'm concerned this is only another job. One that I'd like to complete with as few complications as possible," Riana finished in a tone so cool it made Andre flinch.

I guess the sweet, passionate woman I fell in love with has vanished, Andre surmised, deciding to play the game her way. The position she had outlined was exactly the kind of project he had been praying would come his way, but could he trust Riana to be fair and impartial when it came to recommending him? Or would she simply go through the motions to satisfy her client, and not truly promote him as a serious candidate?

Would she build up his hopes, only to draw back and leave him hanging, as she had done once before?

Proceed with caution, Andre told himself as he listened to Riana lay out her plan.

"It all sounds very interesting," he admitted to Riana. "However, I need a lot more information before I could even consider such a project," he stated, not wanting her to think that he was sitting around waiting for something to fall his way. "Besides, I'm swamped with proposals right now. There're quite a few projects that I'm considering."

"I understand. Just say yes to an interview, okay? Allen wants me to have a face-to-face with you, and if you agree to meet with me, I'll be happy to drive into Houston tomorrow."

It pleased Andre to hear an edge of desperation in Riana's voice. He smiled to himself. She might be trying to play it cool, but she needed him and he had the upper hand.

As much as he would like to snag a job with the Allen Group, he wasn't going to make Riana's task an easy one. She hadn't made things easy for him when she simply vanished out of his life, so why should he worry about her feelings now?

"Hold on, let me check my calendar," Andre told her as he put one hand over the mouthpiece of the phone and stared at his near-empty monthly planner, where only an appointment with his dentist and a meeting with a local builder had been penciled in. "I'll have to squeeze you in. Tomorrow won't do. Gee, the timing is so bad on this, but I do want to hear more about the position. Okay, what about Friday?" he finally offered.

"Fine," Riana replied in a less than enthusiastic manner. "It would have to be late. I have an afternoon appointment that will probably run until at least three o'clock."

"I'll be here."

"Fine. Where do you want to meet?" Riana asked. "Your office? I'd love to see it. I know it's gorgeous."

Her words made Andre tense. "I…I think," he stumbled, not eager for Riana to see his building in its current state, or for her to take the unpredictable service elevator to his crudely pulled-together office. "It might be better if we meet someplace else. I'm having my office repainted right now, and things are a bit cluttered."

"We could meet at my hotel," Riana offered. "I'll be staying at the Extended Stay America downtown. There's a conference room in the business center. I could arrange to…"

"No," Andre interrupted. "Since you'll be tied up in a meeting until late afternoon, why don't we meet for dinner?"

"Dinner? Uh, Andre, this is not going to be a social meeting. Let's keep things simple, okay?"

"Well, drinks, then," he pressed. "I could meet you at the Downtown Aquarium. Bagby at Memorial. Not far from your hotel and it's the hottest new spot in downtown now. I haven't been there yet, but I've heard the Dive Lounge is a quiet place where folks can actually carry on a conversation."

The line remained free of conversation for a few seconds.

"That would be fine," Riana finally agreed. "I'll meet you there around five-thirty."

Andre got up from his desk, went to the window and looked down six floors to the busy street, where he saw Lester getting out of Todd's maroon Mustang, a vintage model that the guy had beautifully restored.

How much should I tell Lester? Andre wondered, knowing the first thing Lester would ask about was the telephone call from Miss Cole, whose name he had misspelled. *Not everything. Only what he needs to know for now,* Andre decided just as the elevator doors opened.

"Where'd you and Todd go for lunch this time?" Andre turned to ask, leaning against the wall by the window. He knew that every Wednesday Lester and Todd tried out a new restaurant and then provided their friends with sample menus, detailed descriptions of the interiors and reviews of the waitstaff and the food.

"Cantonese today. The Jade Monkey, over on Kirby. Not a very appetizing name, but the food was to die for." Lester held his stomach and groaned. "If you go, don't go alone. No one person could possibly eat an entire entrée. I think I'm gonna burst."

Andre gave Lester a skeptical look. "I know you'll work it off, don't worry."

Lester removed his sunglasses, carefully folded them closed and then put them in the top drawer of his desk. "Speaking of work," he began. "Did you get the message I left for you from the lady in San Antonio?"

"Executive Suites. Yes, I did, and I called her back."

"So…?"

In a teasing fashion, Andre rocked back on his heels, crossed his arms on his chest and raised his chin, pausing before he answered. "The Allen Group is interested in hiring me for a design project."

"Get outta here! You're gonna work for *the* George Allen?"

Andre grinned and nodded. "Hopefully."

"Fantastic!" Lester's creamy tan face lit up, his thin lips widened into a smile, forcing his eyes into dark half moons. "When will you know for sure? What's the project? How much are they going to pay? Do you have to provide…?"

Holding up one hand in a signal to slow down, Andre interrupted Lester's string of questions, and then told him all he knew, omitting the fact that he and the recruiter had been in a serious relationship four years ago. At least it had been serious for Andre.

"So, I probably won't know anything for a few weeks, but I did agree to meet with Miss Cole on Friday. At the Dive Lounge. I need to get more details."

"Hum. The Dive Lounge? Pretty fancy place." Lester placed his fist on his chin, watching Andre closely. "This recruiter is going all out."

"I chose the location. Thought it might be easy for her to find since she's staying at ESA downtown. And by the way, Riana Cole's name is spelled *C-O-L-E,* for future reference."

Lester grimaced, and then lifted a palm toward Andre. "Sorry. Guess I should have asked how to spell it since I didn't know who she was. It didn't throw you, did it?"

If you only knew, Andre thought, but told Lester, "Nope. Not at all."

"Good," Lester replied, turning away from Andre to answer the ringing phone. "Oh, I know you'll impress her. Don't even worry about it. That job is yours."

Andre turned back to the window and watched the cars whizzing along the street, thinking about Riana, realizing how much she had accomplished. She had done exactly what she'd set out to do, while he was still waiting for a big break. Could this job with the Allen Group be his ticket to the kind of professional success he yearned for? If so, he had to do everything possible to make sure Riana recommended him to lead the project.

However, as soon as that thought slipped into Andre's mind, another worry surfaced: Charles Frazer and his damned questions. Who would want to hire a man under FBI surveillance? Could his youthful mistakes cost him the opportunity of a lifetime? Suddenly, life seemed more complicated than ever.

Chapter 6

The drive from San Antonio to Houston provided Riana with plenty of time to think about seeing Andre again, as well as her upcoming afternoon meeting with Rodney Roberts, the owner of the Houston franchise of Executive Suites, Inc.

After a careful review of the numbers and a lengthy session with her accountant, she was anxious to branch out and expand her business. Her bank had preapproved the purchase of the franchise at a price she felt was fair, pointing out that an attractive purchase point for Riana was the location of the office, which was locked into a long-term lease in a prime real-estate area—one she could never afford at today's prices. All she had to do now was to seal the deal with Roberts, who should be easy to work with since he was anxious to sell.

The Houston branch had been understaffed and poorly managed for years and Riana sensed that it was going to take a hands-on, focused effort on her part to turn things around—

and that would require her personal attention, as well as an extended stay in Houston. As daunting as it seemed, she was eager for the challenge, and with Tanisha managing the San Antonio office she could split her time between her two franchises until she recruited the right person to run the Houston office.

But now, Andre Preaux was complicating things. She had never dreamed she would ever see him again, let alone have to recruit him for a client.

"Oh well, Houston's a big city," she said, taking the exit off Interstate 10 to merge onto the Loop. "This place is big enough for both of us. Once I finish this assignment for George Allen and he hands over my hefty bonus, I'll never have to speak to or see Andre Preaux again."

After checking into her hotel room, which was a two-room mini-suite with a small kitchenette that had a refrigerator and a microwave oven, Riana went out to explore her floor, and was happy to find a sunny laundry room at the end of the corridor, a godsend for long-term guests like herself. She'd packed enough clothing and toiletries for a five-day stay, but hoped she wouldn't have to be in Houston that long.

Returning to her room, she unzipped her garment bag, took out the contents and laid them on the bed, thankful that her navy-blue suit had emerged unwrinkled. Planning to go directly from her meeting with Roberts to see Andre, she'd had to choose just the right outfit to carry her through both meetings, making sure she made the right impression. Now, she had to hurry and get dressed.

However, Riana took a moment to assess the skirt to her suit—short and hip-hugging, yet stylishly appropriate. The fitted jacket accented just the right curves, projecting a feminine, but businesslike image while the gold buttons at the front and on the cuffs added a touch of classy sparkle. The dark-blue peep-toe pumps she planned to wear were both sexy and comfortable, expressing her trendy, but sensible approach to fashion. Her white slouch leather bag trimmed in bright golden studs completed the look that she had gone to great lengths to put together for...

For whom? she asked herself, confronting her inner thoughts about seeing her ex again. *Am I dressing for a meeting with Rodney Roberts or for Andre Preaux?* Either way, she decided, giving up a sigh, everything had to be perfect.

Talking with Andre had shaken her more than she could have imagined. His voice still swam in her mind. Recalling his deep rich tone made her shiver. When she sat down with Andre, he'd see for himself that she had made the right decision by focusing on her career instead of entering into a long-distance relationship that probably would have fizzled. Now, she had it all: the thriving business, the house in town, the luxury sedan, the financial security she longed for. How could he fault her for following her dream, once he saw what a successful businesswoman she'd become?

Riana stripped off her jeans and her red T-shirt while heading into the bathroom, feeling confident that Executive Suites, Inc., of Houston would soon be hers, but wishing she didn't feel so nervous about seeing Andre again.

Riana's meeting with Rodney Roberts went much more smoothly than she had expected. The owner of the Houston franchise was eager to get out from under the pressure of his rapidly failing enterprise and was gracious enough to make arrangements for Riana to work out of one of his vacant offices while she was in town, and for as long as it took to finalize their deal.

"I really appreciate you allowing me to work here. I have so much going on in the office in San Antonio that I must stay on top of, and being here will provide me a chance to observe your staff in action, too," she told Roberts as they finished a tour of the six-room suite.

It had not taken long for Riana to zero in on a major problem with Roberts's operation. His laid-back, hands-off management style had led to a too-relaxed atmosphere, with staff coming and going as they pleased and generally doing very little work. With headphones in their ears, half of the staff had not even looked up to acknowledge their boss's presence when he was showing her around. Food and drink containers sat on most of the desks. The walls were painted a dingy lavender-gray and unappealing dark-blue commercial carpet covered the floors. The suite was devoid of any sense of personality or community, leading Riana to conclude that morale must be as low as the recruitment stats on the last quarterly report that she had reviewed.

What these people need is someone to help them get motivated to succeed, including a system of reward, Riana thought. She firmly believed that most people wanted to do a good job and would come through under the right circumstances. Clearly, Rodney Roberts was not cut out to own an Executive Suites franchise.

"I'm happy to help any way I can during the transition," Roberts replied, leading Riana into the conference room. He sat down across from her and tented his fingers under his chin, "I want to do everything I can to make this deal happen. Here are my annual summaries for the past three years that you asked for. Not so great, as you'll see, but I'd like to know what you can make of them. I thought I was doing everything by the book, but nothing seemed to work. Don't know what the problem was."

"Thanks," Riana said, accepting the stack of papers. "This will help me a lot."

"I truly didn't realize what I was getting into when I bought this franchise," Roberts went on. "I was a successful used car salesman in this region when I retired and bought this franchise, thinking I could do this kind of selling just as easily. But selling trucks and selling a CEO on a candidate are two entirely different processes. I'll take vehicles over people any day."

"Executive recruitment *is* an art," Riana agreed. "You have to truly want to get to know what makes a person tick, and then, understand how to tap into that person's heart to make it work for you. I love it. That's why I want to expand into the Houston market. Let's make this deal, okay?"

"That's what I hope will happen."

"Good," Riana replied enthusiastically, praying her meeting with Andre would go this well. Roberts was straightforward about what he wanted and had no trouble getting right down to business, while Andre just might muddle the situation with his need to play her off. She wasn't about to let her emotional reaction to seeing him again complicate things, and once the Roberts deal was sealed, she planned to focus completely on getting Andre on board with George Allen, concluding the negotiations as soon as possible.

"I have another meeting to rush off to," Riana told Roberts. "I'll review your summaries over the weekend, and perhaps we could meet on Monday morning? What time do you get in?"

"Eight o'clock. Let's meet at eight-thirty. The earlier the better, if that's all right with you?"

"Fine. I'll be here," Riana replied with a smile as she shook his hand.

With her first round with Roberts completed, Riana was ready to move on.

It was five-twenty when Riana turned her car into the main entrance of the Downtown Aquarium, a six-acre entertainment and dining complex on the edge of downtown Houston. A huge Ferris wheel rose from the center of the adjoining park, which was well-known for its 500,000-gallon aquatic wonderland, an upscale restaurant that provided an underwater dining experience and a variety of amusements and gift shops.

Riana cruised the huge parking lot, looking for a space and finally found one at the far rear of the lot, where a chain-link fence separated the parking area from the lushly landscaped tropical grounds. She was early, as she had planned to be, and hoped she'd be able to grab a table, watch for Andre and observe him before he spotted her.

Once she arrived at the lounge, the hostess escorted her to a quiet booth at the side, where a glowing tank of exotic fish had been built into the wall. The lounge was much more intimate than she had thought it would be and it reminded her of a small jazz café that she and Andre had frequented when they were together. *Why did she have to think about that?*

After settling down in the booth, she pulled out her notepad and reviewed the notes she had taken during her conversation with George Allen, determined to keep the discussion with Andre focused on the benefits of working for the Allen Group and the perks he would receive during his transition from Houston to San Antonio. Feeling satisfied with her approach and ready to meet with Andre, she set her notepad aside and looked up.

"Damn," she whispered, both shocked and impressed with what she saw. Andre was standing at the entrance of the softly lit lounge talking to the hostess. For a split second, Riana panicked, wondering if she'd made a huge mistake by taking on this assignment. He looked too damn good to be true.

We should have met in the hotel business center, she thought, suddenly feeling vulnerable and more than a little guilty. When she had dumped him, she'd never looked back, moving on with her life without thinking about his feelings. She couldn't say she was proud about what she had done, but she had convinced herself that leaving him was her only option at the time.

Tugging at her suit jacket, Riana squared her shoulders and braced herself for his greeting, wondering why she was so damn nervous. What did she have to worry about? He was coming to see her because she could help him with his career. He needed her. She certainly didn't need him. Or did she?

Chapter 7

Riana watched as Andre made his way toward her, relieved to see a smile on his face. All of a sudden, she felt cautiously optimistic that their reunion might come off smoothly. However, the sight of him was still unnerving. She took him in from head to foot, her lips parted, feeling the long-dormant spark that had first drawn them together reignite with a snap and sweep through her like a brushfire out of control. A tremor passed from her heart into her legs and disappeared into the floor beneath her feet, leaving her feeling suspended. As much as she hated to admit it, not only was the attraction still there, it was heart-stopping and impossible to ignore.

"Riana," Andre breathed her name, looking down at her with the kind of intensity that commanded attention. "It's good to see you again."

She couldn't move, didn't speak and simply looked up at him, startled by how much, yet how little, he had changed in the four years since she had walked out of his life. His powerful build, toned by years of construction work and fine-tuned by his passion for running, was nearly visible through his clothes. His sturdy, slightly square jaw and the intensely focused gleam in his brown eyes, made him look wiser and more observant than before, even somewhat daunting. She noticed that his dark-brown hair was now cut short, but he still wore it with a razor part on the right side, accenting the clean crisp image he projected. He was dressed in dark slacks, a pale-blue dress shirt and was wearing an interesting tie sprinkled with geometric squares in a blaze of blues and yellows. Instinctively, her eyes swept to his left hand: no ring. *That's interesting,* she thought, hating herself even for checking that out.

"Andre," Riana finally replied, rising to extend her hand, a smile teasing her lips.

Andre met her handshake, and then covered their clasp with his free hand, as if conveying his genuine pleasure at seeing her again.

"Sit down, please," she said, deliberately pulling her hand away while using a tone that was welcoming, but cool. She hoped he got her message. All she wanted to do was talk about the job offer in a calm, professional manner, and not divert into personal matters or confessions of regret, remorse or any kind of trip down memory lane. When they finished their meeting, they would go their separate ways.

However, as soon as Riana was seated across from Andre, she felt the years of separation melt away. She could hardly keep from smiling when she saw him splay his fingers at his waist, as he always did when he first sat down. When he held his head at that adorable angle that made him appear both curious and studious while checking out his surroundings, she knew he was using his architect's eye to assess the structure.

And when he nodded his approval of the place and winked at her, her heart did a tiny involuntary flip. "I like it," he said.

Oh, yes, this was the same Andre who had stolen her heart and made it impossible for her to forget him.

As they prepared to place drink orders with the waitress who suddenly appeared and broke the tension, Riana was reminded of the many times they had sat like this on fun-filled dates while checking out a new restaurant or a smoky jazz club, blissfully living in the moment. At that time, she had been hell-bent on simply having a good time, fully aware that the day would come when she would have to leave Houston and forget about Andre. If only she had known how hard that was going to be.

Before Riana could respond to the waitress's inquiry, Andre quickly spoke up. "A Cosmopolitan on shaved ice for the lady," he said, one eyebrow raised at Riana, a grin of satisfaction creasing his sculpted cheeks.

Riana leaned back in the booth, unable to keep from returning his smile, both disturbed and pleased by this intimate gesture. Clearly, he wanted to let her know that a part of her remained with him, that what they had shared was not forgotten. "You remembered," she murmured in a voice that came out as a near-whisper.

"How could I forget?" His remark was low, strong and void of hesitation. "I haven't forgotten anything about you. Or *us*," he added more forcefully, leaning slightly forward.

Determined not to waver, Riana inclined her head, acknowledging his right to remember, and in as clear a voice as she could manage, she told the waitress, "And a vodka martini for him, two olives." In the silence that followed, Riana realized that her words had come out easily, as if they had never been apart.

Andre laughed, nodded and tilted his head toward the waitress. "I guess that's it."

With the ice broken, but the atmosphere still hotly charged, Riana eased back in her seat and focused on Andre. "You've accomplished so much since the last time I saw you."

With a shrug, Andre nodded. "I had to play catch-up, remember?"

"Don't say that," Riana replied, her remark tight with emotion. "We weren't in a race."

"At times I felt like we were."

"No, we were simply in two different places professionally—and personally—when our paths crossed. I think we both knew that from day one."

"Maybe so, but now the playing field has leveled."

With a finger to her chin, Riana studied Andre. "Yes, things are very different. For both of us."

"Are you happy, Riana?" Andre wanted to know.

She nodded, pushing aside a stray lock of hair. "Yes, I am. Things couldn't be better. My company is doing fabulously well. I bought the cutest house in San Antonio. I…"

"But what about *you?* Personally?" Andre pressed, and then boldly added, "I see you're not wearing a ring."

Riana glanced down at her left hand and then made a fist. "No, I'm not. And there's no one waiting back in San Antonio, eager to put one on my finger."

"No?" Andre's eyes widened dramatically. "I'm surprised… or, maybe not," he decided. "Clearly, you've put your career ahead of your love life. As you've always done."

"Andre, please don't go there. I don't want to discuss our past. We had a wonderful time together, but it's been over for a long time. We've both moved on. However, since you mention it, I see that you're ringless, too."

"Damn straight." He rubbed his ring finger with his thumb, his words disturbingly obvious.

"Haven't found the right woman?" Riana quipped, immediately regretting her remark. Why had she asked that? Why allow herself to get sucked into a discussion about Andre's love life? He must think she was someone who cared about who he spent his time with.

"Oh, I found the right woman four years ago," he tossed back. "And I learned a great lesson from her."

"What?" she weakly managed, unable to keep from asking.

"To put myself first."

Riana made no comment, but simply leveled a knowing gaze on him.

With a lick of his bottom lip, Andre continued. "You see, I've been too busy finishing my degree, purchasing my own building, and launching my architectural firm to get bogged down in a relationship," Andre went on. "Becoming a successful architect is all I'm into now. Nothing else matters."

Riana's chest fell as she expelled a low breath, surprised that she had been holding air in her lungs so long. His words stung like nails driven into her heart, but she knew she probably deserved that slap, yet couldn't let it show. "You've made your point, Andre. I hope you get whatever you want. You deserve all the success in the world."

"I'm working at it," he replied with satisfaction. "Every day."

The waitress arrived with their drinks, interrupting their brittle banter and giving Riana an opportunity to compose herself. Their exchange had left her shaken and confused. Did he hate her? Or did he still love her? Had she been right to walk away? Or had she blown the best thing ever to happen to her? Either way, it was clear that he was not going to make it easy for her to forget what she had done.

Deciding to move quickly toward her mission, Riana launched into the background on the Allen Group and its recent projects in the San Antonio area. Between sips of her drink, she gave Andre a detailed description of what George Allen wanted, working hard to keep her presentation focused on the Tierra Trace project.

"Sounds perfect," Andre finally responded with enthusiasm, as if they had not sparred verbally earlier. "It's not every day that a newcomer like myself gets a shot at working with a builder like George Allen. What an opportunity."

"I knew you'd be eager for this," Riana replied, relieved that Andre was responding in a positive manner. He had paid close attention to every word she had spoken and seemed impressed with the benefits of signing on with the Allen Group. He understood what would be expected of him and had assured her that he was up to the challenge of such a project. Things *were* coming together, but she would have to get closer to Andre before she could safely recommend him.

"In order to complete my part of the process, I do need to spend some time with you at your office," Riana began. "Kind of hang out with you, meet your staff, observe you in action. That kind of stuff, okay?"

Andre grimaced and lifted one shoulder, sending a negative reaction. "Why?" he wanted to know.

"You do want me to draft a positive recommendation, don't you?" she ventured.

"Sure, but there's no reason to come by my office."

"Oh? Why not?" Riana replied, struck by the sudden change in Andre's tone. He sounded wary, as if he'd lost some of his earlier enthusiasm. "I don't want to intrude, but Allen wants my take on your style of operation. How you interact with clients and staff. Management style. I think that's fair, don't you?"

"Sure it's fair, but my office isn't big. I only have one employee. A part-time student who's in and out. I'm pretty much a one-man operation."

"I understand. No problem. I'd still like to chat with…"

"Lester. Lester Tremaine," Andre finished.

"Right." She scribbled his name in her notepad. "He's the nice young man I spoke to when I called your office. Maybe I could meet Lester tomorrow?"

"Tomorrow's Saturday," Andre bluntly reminded her.

A sheepish smile came over her face when she realized how quickly she was trying to move the process along. "Right. Next week, then? Monday or Tuesday, perhaps?" she pressed ahead, thinking, *This is not going to be as easy or as fast as I expected.*

"I'll call you on Monday, after I check with Lester and see what his class schedule is going to be like. Might as well come when we're both there."

Riana nodded, and then pulled a sheaf of papers from her black attaché case. "I'd like you to fill out a few forms right now, so I can begin your background check tomorrow."

"Background check?" Andre repeated. "What does that require?"

"Oh, standard stuff. Criminal, security, credit. Drugs. The usual." She chuckled knowingly under her breath. "Don't be alarmed. Sounds a lot more serious than it is. If we're lucky, I'll be able to wrap this whole thing up in a few days and get the package off to Allen by the middle of next week. Once he's reviewed it, he'll move to the next stage: a personal interview."

Twirling his martini glass between two fingers, Andre remained thoughtful for a moment. "I don't know," he murmured with hesitation, watching Riana closely. "You know, on second thought, you'd better give me a few days to think all of this over. You see, I'm in the middle of drafting several important bids right now. I don't want to waste your time. Maybe I shouldn't make any decisions about taking the job with Allen until I wrap up some loose ends."

"What are you talking about? I thought you just told me that you really wanted to go for this position?" Riana snapped, setting the papers aside while a sense of deflation hit her like a slap in the face. How dare he lead her on and let her believe he was eager for the job, and then pull back like this? *Shows how much he knows about doing business in the big leagues,* she thought.

"I do. But I need to clear up a few things."

"What things? What's going on, Andre? Getting cold feet about taking this on?"

"Not at all," he snapped. "I didn't say that. But I do deserve time to review Allen's proposal to be sure I make the right decision."

"All right. But don't put me off. If you really don't plan to follow through with this I have other candidates who would jump on this offer and I have other things I could do with my time."

"I understand, and I'll have an answer for you next week, early."

"Okay," Riana stated, forcing annoyance out of her voice as she dug into her briefcase again to find a card. "Here's my number at the hotel. I'm in room 408. Call me if anything changes, otherwise I'll expect to hear from you on Monday?"

"Right. And thanks," Andre replied, as he reached for the folder that the waitress was about to place in the center of the table.

"I'll get that," Riana rushed to say. She took the leather folder from him before he could protest, slipped a twenty-dollar bill from her wallet, and placed it inside before handing the case to the girl. "Keep the change," Riana blithely told the waitress.

Silence hung between them while Riana gathered her things. Standing, she looked down at Andre, her eyes as cool as her tone. "Don't blow this, Andre. Allen has several other prospects. If you want this job, you'd better grab it."

"You'll get my answer soon," Andre promised, rising and extending his hand.

"Good." The handshake she gave him was short, firm and

very businesslike, one she hoped conveyed her disappointment in the outcome of the meeting. She had planned to start the background checks the next day, work through the weekend, and wrap up the interviews at his office on Monday. Obviously, he planned to drag the process out much longer than she had expected. Without another word, Riana turned on her heel and walked away.

Is he stalling on purpose? she worried as she walked toward the exit. She could feel his eyes on her back and hoped he was noticing the way her skirt cupped her butt and how toned and shapely her legs were. *Give him something else to think about until Monday. If he's trying to make me squirm and beg him to do this, he's taking the wrong approach. I need this contract as much as he does, and he'd better get his act together because I'm not leaving Houston until I get what I came for.*

Riveted at the table, Andre watched Riana walk away, unable to keep his eyes from traveling over her back, across her full rounded hips and down to those luscious bronze legs that he had once felt wrapped around his waist. He ached to hold her, kiss her, tell her how much he had missed her. With a dry swallow, he pushed back the bite of desire that gnawed at him, desperate to keep his emotions in check.

She was more beautiful than he remembered, and just as plucky and stubbornly independent as before. He hoped he hadn't blown his opportunity to work for the Allen Group by putting Riana off for a few days, but things were a bit complicated now. Once he settled the issue with the FBI, he'd submit himself to her background checks, but until then, he had to keep Riana in the dark, and feeling positive about him, too. He couldn't let her leave like this.

"Riana!" Andre called, hurrying out the front door and

across the parking lot, which was now shaded in purple twilight. "Wait up!"

Riana whirled around, car keys in her hand, glaring at him. "Why? I thought we were finished. You said we'd talk early next week."

The edge of irritation in her voice frightened Andre, but he refused to let it get to him. Taking long strides, he closed the space between them, took her keys from her, and put a firm hand on her arm. "Yes, I did, but I don't want to wait any longer for this," he told her, guiding her beneath a fringe of fragrant oleanders.

"Andre! What are you doing?" Riana sputtered, clenching her teeth as she tried to jerk away.

"I'm going to kiss you," he whispered, pulling her to him without giving her a chance to protest. He draped one arm around her shoulder, captured her golden-brown eyes with his, and then bent down and nibbled her bottom lip. Tentatively, testing her, tempting her to react. When she didn't jerk back, he crushed his lips to hers in a demanding—nearly punishing—kiss that forced the breath from his body. He could feel her quivering, relaxing and then stiffening in his embrace, but still he did not let her go.

Riana pummeled his back with her fists and strained against his chest, as if she were very angry. However, he could tell that she wasn't seriously trying to get away, only registering her complaint.

Deciding to test her even further, Andre tightened his grip and deepened the kiss, sliding his tongue over hers, plunging the depths of her familiar, fiery lips.

Suddenly, Riana opened her mouth more fully. Andre slipped one hand beneath her suit jacket and caressed the bare skin of her back. As soon as he touched her, she thrust her hips forward and gasped, lessening her struggle, silently admitting defeat as she swept her hands to the back of his neck and brought them even closer.

The instant they were joined, Andre felt the years slide away as her touch reignited the fire that he had never been able to extinguish. He had never stopped loving Riana, even while cursing her for breaking his heart. His need for her was permanently branded into his soul, whether he liked it or not.

"Oh, Andre. Don't. Please," she uttered when they broke away. Placing her hands on either side of his face she paused to study his features.

He watched her, knowing what she wanted to say, and knowing why she couldn't say it. All of a sudden, he was overcome by the realization that Riana *did* want him. She *had* missed him. And she hadn't pushed him away. He pressed his cheek to hers, bringing them so close that her thighs were rubbing his growing erection. Andre knew he was headed into a real danger zone.

Suppressing the groan of desire that burned in his throat, he forced himself to step away, and with a swift turn, he maneuvered her back against the side of her car. He leaned over her, his mouth only inches away. The thought that they might be able to recapture what they had once shared coursed through Andre in sweet waves of hope.

Taking deep breaths, he let his eyes roam her face in the leafy shadows that played across her features. "You're all I want, Riana. All I've ever wanted," he confessed, as if defeated.

A whistle of air eased from between Riana's lips. Ducking under Andre's arm, she stepped out of his embrace, crossed her hands at her waist, and hugged herself as she looked at him, her body rigid and tense. "I can't do this, Andre." Her voice cracked with the admission. "I can't. This is a huge mistake."

"What is?" he asked softly, his chest rising and falling as he struggled to gather his composure.

"Falling back into a relationship with you," Riana said, taking care to speak each word clearly, slowly, as if doing so would give her answer more weight.

"Why?" Andre wanted to know. "Finally, the timing is right, isn't it? I'm establishing myself professionally. Your business is solid, and if I'm lucky, I might one day work with the state's most respected builder. What could be better?"

"I didn't contact you so we could pick up where we left off. I have a job to do and I need to concentrate on what I came here for—to recruit you, not make love to you."

Now, Andre stiffened as he assessed Riana, a smirk tugging at his lips. "Isn't that the same line you used on me four years ago when you walked away from what we had? Business first, love can wait?"

"That's not true. And you know this is different. I don't deny that I care for you, but don't push me, Andre. Don't compromise this assignment. It could be very important for us both."

Andre laughed under his breath and made a fist with one hand. "Once again, Riana, you're right. This Allen Group job could be the break I've been waiting for, and I certainly wouldn't want to do anything to compromise it." With a curt chuckle, he dangled her car keys with one finger. "Here. You'd better get going. It's late."

With a jerk, Riana snatched the keys, opened her car door and looked back at Andre. "I just don't want to complicate the situation, okay?"

"I wouldn't dream of complicating your life, Riana," Andre coolly replied.

With a final glance, Riana got into her car and drove off.

Andre remained beneath the blooming oleander as he watched Riana leave, more determined than ever to break through that tough-girl shell of hers and prove to her that they weren't finished yet.

Chapter 8

*A*s much as I want and need this job, I can't move too quickly, Andre decided as he exited the parking lot and started home. His love for Riana throbbed in his heart, but his strange encounter with the FBI agent still pounded in his head. The conversation he'd had last week with Charles Frazer kept resurfacing to play over and over in his mind, and until he was certain that his juvenile arrest could never pop up and hurt him, he wasn't about to start filling out papers for Riana or submitting to any background checks.

If only I hadn't gone to Jamaica to try to talk some sense into Jamal. I should have known he wouldn't listen. If he wants to live life on the edge, let him. I don't know anything, I didn't see anything, Andre kept telling himself as he pulled into a parking space at the side of his building.

He sat in his car for a long time, debating his next move,

though he knew there was only one thing to do. Go to see Frazer, find out what the agent had on him, and tell the man everything he knew.

At ten fifty-five the next morning, Andre walked into the Federal Building in downtown Houston and told the guard that he had an appointment with Agent Charles Frazer.

"Frazer don't work on Saturdays," the guard calmly countered.

"I spoke to him on the phone this morning. He said to meet him here."

"Hold on," the guard told Andre, turning to pick up his phone and punch in some numbers. After a few seconds, he nodded at Andre and passed him through the metal detectors. "Seventh floor. End of the hall."

A short elevator ride took him to the seventh floor, where he was greeted by the straight-faced Frazer and escorted to a cubbyhole of an office at the end of the corridor.

"Glad you called, Mr. Preaux. Come on in. Want coffee? Water?" Frazer offered as he folded his lanky frame into a chair behind his gunmetal-gray government desk.

"No, nothing, thanks," Andre replied, eager to get this meeting over and done with. He kept his jaw clenched and his back poker-stiff while Frazer flipped open a folder and pulled out a photograph, which he shoved across his desk toward Andre.

"Can you identify anyone in this picture?" Frazer asked.

Andre picked it up, nodded his head in the affirmative and then told Frazer, "That's Jamal, my half brother on the left. I don't recognize the other two men standing with him." Andre kept his eyes glued to the photograph, relieved that he could tell Frazer the truth. He had never seen the other two men, who were dark-skinned, mean-looking and dressed in jeans and black T-shirts with black head-wraps.

Frazer leaned forward and tapped the photograph, placing his finger on the man in the center of the trio. "That's Eddie Brooks. Jamaican undercover police. You're holding the last photo ever taken of him. Alive, that is."

Andre tensed, but decided not to comment until he'd heard everything the agent had to say. He set the photo aside, and then picked up another one that Frazer passed to him. It was a struggle, but Andre managed to remain composed as he stared at Eddie Brooks again, now dressed in a blood-splattered policeman's uniform and lying in a ditch.

"That's how the authorities found Eddie in September. Stuffed in a drainage ditch in Spanish Town. Fifteen bullet holes in his body. Jamaican police have been working this case for months, and it wasn't until they found this photo of Eddie with Jamal that they connected him to your brother."

Disturbed, but determined to remain in control of his emotions, Andre faced Frazer with an inquisitive expression and asked, "Who's the third guy in the photo?"

"Rugo Barril. A known drug dealer who was on Jamaica's most-wanted list."

"Where is he? Where'd the police get this photo?" Andre asked.

"Rugo is dead. Killed in a house fire in Spanish Town. This photo was found in the ruins, and it may be a vital link to solving Eddie's murder."

"And what's all this got to do with me?"

"Eddie Brooks disappeared during the time that you were in Jamaica visiting your brother. JCF—the Jamaican Constabulary Force—recovered his body from the drainage ditch shortly after. Apparently, Eddie was involved in an undercover operation investigating a drug gang that Jamal is thought to be connected to. Our records show that Jamal is wanted on drug charges in Miami and Georgia. From the looks of this photo your brother is in pretty deep with the Jamaicans. The U.S. Marshals' Service has two deputies stationed in Jamaica. We sent a guy looking for Jamal, but he's had no luck." Frazer leaned away from Andre and tilted back in his chair. "You know anything that might give us a lead on finding him?"

Old fears set off alarm bells inside Andre's head as he searched for a plausible, yet non-incriminating, way to answer. Jamal's danger-filled world was finally colliding with his and there was nothing he could do to stop it. He didn't know anything specific about Eddie Brooks's murder, but he did know that something had gone down at that house in Spanish Town and he had heard gunfire while he was there. He'd fled the scene before he learned too much, and then he'd fled the country just as quickly.

Bravely, Andre faced Frazer, hoping he looked calmer than he felt. "I lied to you when I told you that I met Jamal at my hotel in Kingston."

"I see," was all Frazer said. He slumped back in his chair, preparing to listen to whatever Andre was going to say. "Go on."

"I met up with him at a house in Spanish Town."

"Most likely the same one that burned down."

"Probably so," Andre agreed. "I went there to talk to Jamal, persuade him to come home, bring his family back to the States. I told him I'd help him start over here, if he'd get out of Jamaica and clean up his life."

"Clean up his life? So you knew what Jamal was into?"

"Yeah, I knew. Drugs. Marijuana, mostly. He ran with a posse of thugs who were known drug dealers. I remember the house was small, dark. A gray house at the end of a narrow road. A dicey neighborhood, that's for sure. I heard gunshots more than once while I was there, but I guess that goes on all the time."

"That may be true, but members of the JCF don't get killed every day." Lips pressed together, Frazer waited for his words to sink in. "If you know anything at all about Jamal's connection to Eddie Brooks's death, you'd better tell me now."

Knowing his facade of innocence was quickly slipping, Andre inclined his head in agreement and slowly began to tell Charles Frazer what he knew.

"As I already told you, I've known for some time that Jamal was in trouble. He was always a street hustler. Started out in the streets of Baton Rouge when he was twelve years old. Back then, he ruled the neighborhood trade and I even worked with him at one time. Stupid, I know, but I was young and thought I was a tough guy."

"Ever been arrested?" Frazer asked Andre.

"I could say no. But I guess you already know the real answer," Andre quipped, not naive enough to think that Frazer hadn't already thoroughly investigated his background.

"Yeah, as a matter of fact, I do," Frazer admitted. He reached for another piece of paper in his folder and focused on it. "You were sentenced to two years at Jena Juvenile Justice Center, but wound up going to the federal penitentiary in Louisiana instead. For possession of marijuana and cocaine. You did your time and walked."

Andre frowned. "Then you must also know that my record should have been expunged long ago. I was tried and convicted as a juvenile," he defended. "My lawyer assured me that I would never have to reveal my arrest to anyone. It would be as if it had never happened."

"That's the way it should have gone down, but since you did your time in a federal prison, those records aren't so easy to erase."

"Longest, most miserable two years of my life. Enough to

scare me straight. After I completed my sentence, I moved to Houston. Been clean ever since."

"Okay. Tell me about Jamaica. What made you decide to try to convince Jamal to leave?"

"Kay called me."

"Jamal's wife?"

Andre nodded. "Their marriage was falling apart, but she wanted to hold it together for the sake of their son. She asked me to talk some sense into Jamal. Get him to give up the street life, the hustling, the dangerous stuff."

"How well do you know Kay?"

"Not that well. She's Jamaican. Jamal met her when he went down there six years ago. They got married right away, she got pregnant and my nephew was born shortly after. Lonny. He's five now. I flew in a few times to see him, maybe two or three times, I don't know. Guess I wanted to make sure Kay knew that I was there for her. That she was family."

"So, she felt close enough to you to ask for help when she realized what Jamal was into?"

"Yeah. She seemed desperate. She left Jamal last September. Begged me to convince him that he ought to get out of Jamaica, come home to the States. She sounded afraid."

"Of whom? Jamal? Other people? Was he abusive?"

"No, it wasn't like that…" Andre paused to gather his thoughts, wanting to respond correctly. "He's a possessive, controlling type, and the men around him know that he doesn't let go of anything easily. He refused to give Kay and Lonny their passports. Said they weren't going anywhere. I got the impression that Kay was worried because she'd seen too much…knew things, you know? The men who hung with Jamal were real tough characters."

"Sure. And that's exactly why I'd like to talk to her."

"Jamaican police can't get to her?"

"Naw. She, Jamal and the kid, they've all disappeared. And not surprisingly, nobody's talking."

"Why involve me? There's nothing I can do."

"Yes, there is," Frazer countered sternly. "You can tell me everything, and I mean everything you saw and heard while you were in Jamaica."

For the next hour, Andre took Frazer through his trip step by step, leaving out nothing. It wasn't until he got to his last day on the island that his voice began to break. "That's when I went out to Spanish Town to see Jamal. Kay was there, waiting when I arrived. Anyway, I started talking to Jamal about leaving Jamaica. He refused. I asked him to let Kay and Lonny come back to Houston with me. While we were talking, three men arrived. Right away, Jamal started yelling at them, turned real ugly. He went into a back bedroom with them and I got the feeling that it was time for me to leave. I wasn't wrong. When I heard gunfire coming from the back room, I grabbed Kay, pushed her into my car and we split," Andre finished.

"Where'd you go?"

"I beat it back to Kingston. Kay insisted that I drop her off at a café in town. Said she'd be fine. A friend of hers owned the café and was letting her and Lonny stay there."

"What was the name of this café?"

"Oh, I don't know. I wasn't paying much attention. A hole-in-the-wall kind of place. All I remember is that it had a red door. I took off back to my hotel after I dropped her, packed my bags and went to the airport. I got on the next plane to Miami. That's all I know."

"You never contacted the authorities?"

"For what? I didn't see anything. I didn't have anything to report. When I got home, I just wanted to forget the whole mess."

"Could you identify the men who showed up at Jamal's that night?"

"Probably not," Andre replied. "They were wearing head-wraps and dark glasses, and to tell you the truth, I tried not to look in their faces."

"You willing to help us find out who killed Eddie Brooks?" Frazer pressed.

"If I can," Andre slowly agreed, dreading the implication of his decision, but what else could he say?

"Good." Frazer rounded his shoulders and crossed his hands on the table, as if preparing for a serious discussion. "You're probably the only person Kay Preaux will trust. This is what we'd like you to do."

Feeling vaguely disturbed and uneasy about what he was getting into, Andre scooted to the edge of his chair to listen, wondering why he didn't feel relieved to have finally unbur-dened himself of the secret he'd carried for so long.

Chapter 9

After a long session of reviewing reports, Riana needed to escape her hotel suite and get some fresh air, so she called Felicia from her car and quickly accepted her cousin's invitation to drop by for a glass of wine and a long-overdue catch-up gabfest.

Felicia answered the door with a paintbrush in her hand and a floral print scarf tied around her head. A swipe of apple-green paint was smeared across her nutmeg-brown cheek and her denim coveralls were dotted with matching spots of green.

"Girl, come on in," Felicia invited, greeting Riana with a one-armed hug while holding her wet paintbrush high and offering one side of her face for a quick hello kiss. Stepping back, she removed her protective plastic goggles and left them dangling around her neck as she beckoned Riana inside. "Follow me and excuse the mess," she called out leading Riana toward the back of the house, down a corridor carpeted in plastic.

Outgoing, vivacious and bursting with creative energy, Felicia was an admitted HGTV junkie and amateur interior decorator—the job she would prefer to do full-time instead of dealing with fussy travelers in the airport's Presidents' Lounge.

"Well, what do you think?" she asked Riana, sweeping her arm in an arc around her newly painted kitchen. "Like the color?"

Riana gave the walls a quick inspection and then smiled. "Yeah, I do. But weren't the walls in here already green?"

"Celery green. This is crisp apple-green. Martha Stewart. Don't you love it?"

Shaking her head in amazement, Riana laughed. "Right. Crisp apple-green is definitely much better than celery. Wonder why I didn't realize *that!*"

Felicia waved a gloved hand at Riana and rolled her eyes. "Don't get smart, now. I haven't seen you in ages and you come in here dissin' my decor?" With a chuckle, she removed her work gloves and went to the refrigerator, which was covered in protective plastic, too, and pulled back the drape. "As soon as I'm finished redecorating, I'm throwing a big party. Really big. Gotta come, so you can meet Malcom."

"Malcom. Tell me more about him," Riana said to her cousin, who changed men as often as she changed hairstyles. Today she had her long black hair pulled back in a ponytail, but tomorrow it might be a mass of tightly wound straw curls dancing around her face.

"Umm," Felicia hummed, head to the side. "Malcom is a pilot for United. Thank God, not Continental, or we'd talk shop all the time. It's bad enough that we both work for airlines and hang out with the same folks. He's easy on the eyes, never been married and doesn't seem to be carryin' a lot of extra baggage, if you know what I mean. He just might be a keeper."

"For you that used to mean two months," Riana teased. "Sounds like Malcom's gonna be around for a while."

"We'll see," Felicia hedged, smiling. "Anyway, you gotta stick around for my party. I've decided it'll be next Saturday."

"What's the theme this time?" Riana inquired, knowing her cousin always had a theme for her much-anticipated get-togethers. When Felicia was in college at Prairie View, she started her tradition of boy/girl, theme-based parties that never failed to impress. Black Cats and Kittens for Halloween, Soulful Santa and his Helpers at Christmas, Red Hats and Pink Hearts for Valentines Day. People flew in from out of state, drove in from across town, or walked over from their dorms to Felicia's off-campus apartment to be a part of the action. Frenzied, pulsing and well-publicized, her bashes often lasted into the wee hours of the morning.

"I'm thinking Gems and Jeans," Felicia tossed over her shoulder. "Tight jeans and lots of bling-bling. Oughta be live, don't you think?"

"Might be," Riana agreed, settling on a barstool. "I'll be here, even if I have to drive in from San Antonio."

"Good, now all I have to do is finish this room. Just need to put on the cabinet hardware and hang those Ted Ellis prints I finally had framed. Then, install my new faucets. Brushed nickel. Really sharp. They're gonna set the whole place off."

"You know, you're becoming a real tool-belt diva. I'm impressed with what you've done here," Riana commented, giving her cousin's work a thumbs-up of approval. "This kitchen is the bomb. As is your entire house, I might add. When you get finished here, I may have to hire you to renovate and decorate my new office space."

"What new office?" Felicia asked as she poured wine into two glasses. "You moving out of the Crockett Building? I thought you loved your space."

"I do, and I'm not talking about my San Antonio office.

I'm in the middle of negotiations for the Executive Suites franchise here in Houston. If it comes through, I'll be dividing my time between San Antonio and Houston, running back and forth."

"Fantastic. It would be great having you in town more often."

"Right," Riana agreed. "I like it here, and you know what I miss so much when I leave Houston?"

"What?"

"Sunday brunch at PJ's," Riana said, running her tongue over her lips, and then making a smacking sound as she laughed. "Smothered chicken and peach cobbler. All that good food and good music, too. Nothing like that back home." She shook her head. "Why don't we go tomorrow?"

"Can't. I gotta work. I got suckered into filling in for the night manager at the Presidents' Club, tonight and tomorrow night. Maybe another time?" Felicia offered.

"Sure, I'll be around for a while."

"Well, as I said," Felicia started, "my throw-down Jeans 'n' Gems party is next Saturday. Want me to fix you up with someone, so you won't be all alone? There's this real cute flight attendant I know…"

"Absolutely not," Riana interrupted, rather sharply. "I mean it, okay? No blind dates, please."

"All right, all right, Miss I-Don't-Need-A-Man." Felicia rolled her eyes and mocked a dramatic grimace. "Feel free to come alone." Then Felicia stopped and pointed a paint-smeared finger at Riana. "Unless you want to bring Andre."

With a squint of one eye, Riana eased her wineglass down, taking her time as she got her words together. "Andre? Why would I want to do that?"

"Girl, you've definitely got a situation on your hands. How can you expect to get close to Andre Preaux again and keep it all business? What's up with that? How'd the reunion go, anyway?"

"All right, I guess. I have an assignment, and I'm going to complete it."

"It's not that simple and you know it," Felicia countered. "Dish, girl. Give me the 411. I want an in-depth update on what happened when Andre saw you. I rarely see him around town, but then I don't run in his circles, you know?"

"All I know is that he's still single, an architect who's becoming fairly well-known. He's won a few awards for his urban-planning projects. He owns his own building in the museum district...."

"Get outta here? Pretty pricey real estate over there. What's his place like?"

"Haven't seen it. Being painted or something, so we met at the Downtown Aquarium. The Dive Lounge?"

"Right. Been there. Love it. So, you guys had like a date?"

"No! Not a date," Riana snapped. "Strictly business."

"So, even though he's still single, is there a woman in the picture?" Felicia probed, squirming on her barstool, anxious for the details.

"A woman? I have no idea."

"You didn't ask?"

"Why should I?"

"Because you know that man was the love of your life and if you had had any sense, you'd have kept him around." Felicia set her glass down on the gold-specked granite counter with a sharp crack. "You know that's the truth, isn't it?" Felicia finished, in a case-closed kind of tone.

"Well, if you must know, I don't think Andre is involved with anyone else."

"Why do you say that?"

"Because he kissed me in the parking lot last night."

"You guys kissed?"

"Unfortunately, yes. He caught me in a weak moment, but

I put him straight right away. I do *not* have time for a romance, I do *not* want to get back with him. It's over and I don't plan to start up again with him."

"That's a lie and you know it, Riana. This assignment is too weird. You coming to Houston to recruit Andre? It's fate. I swear, I can feel it. You two are not through with each other. Not yet."

With a gulp, Riana drained her drink and then waved the empty glass in Felicia's face. "Oh, yes we are. I'm about as finished with him as I am with this wine."

Giving Riana one of her honey-who-do-you-think-you're-foolin' looks, Felicia took Riana's glass out of her hand and promptly refilled it. "Now, you know you're talkin' crazy. And you two *kissed?* Well, you'd better bring Andre to my party, you hear? There's a whole lot left between you two, so before you do or say somethin' really stupid, you'd better get it together, girlfriend."

Suppressing her urge to lash back in denial, Riana huffed an unintelligible response and shook her head, knowing Felicia spoke the truth.

After arriving back at her hotel, Riana changed into some comfy shorts and a long shirt and settled down to review the annual reports that Rodney had given her. But as she paged through the papers, her thoughts kept drifting back to Felicia's remark: *There's a whole lot left between you two.* The words had hit Riana hard, forcing her to make a decision.

If Andre loves me, he won't turn down the Allen deal, she decided. *I have to get close to him again, not push him away. I must convince him that we belong together, and once he thinks we're back on track, everything will fall into place.*

Chapter 10

With a zip, Andre closed the outside pocket of his carry-on bag and reached for his car keys, one eye on the clock. Five-ten. His flight to Miami, connecting to Kingston, left at seven thirty-five and the airport was always crowded on Saturday nights. Andre knew he'd have to push hard if he planned to make it through the tangled security lines and board the plane on time.

A final check—passport, ID, cash, his iPod and a paperback copy of Walter Mosley's latest book. He had everything he needed, except a sense of assurance that he ought to be making this trip.

When Charles Frazer had asked him to fly down to Jamaica and talk his sister-in-law into cooperating with the authorities, Andre had been very reluctant to agree to the assignment.

Let the authorities handle it, he had told the agent, not about to get retangled in Jamal's messy world. But Frazer had insisted. Kay would talk to Andre, she trusted him, and if she could provide information to help them find Jamal or solve Eddie Brooks's murder, the agency would do all they could to protect her and help her leave the island if that was what she wanted to do.

Still, Andre had resisted getting involved until he realized that it might be useful to have a man like Frazer indebted to him. He thought about his juvenile criminal record, how it was dogging him like a shadow, how he worried that it could rise up and cause unnecessary trouble one day. Charles Frazer might be the solution to his problem, so Andre had changed his attitude from skepticism to one of full cooperation. Why not? He had more to gain than to lose.

Usually, Andre's past life as a petty criminal remained a vague memory of a misguided street thug who hadn't cared about anything but keeping a wad of cash in his pocket while following his kid brother around. There had been times when that period in his life seemed to be no more than a very bad dream, but now it felt like an old wound about to reopen and he knew it would hurt like hell. If helping Frazer might make it go away for good, Andre was willing to take the chance.

Eager to get going, Andre gave his loft apartment a final glance and was heading to the door just as his office phone rang. He started to ignore it, but thinking it might be Frazer with some last-minute directive, he hurried around the wall divider that separated his loft living space from his office and grabbed the phone.

"Hello."

"Hi, Andre. This is Riana."

"Oh. Yeah. Hi," he replied, surprised to hear her voice. After the way she had sped off the night before, he had not thought they would talk again until next week. "What's up?" he asked, trying to sound nonchalant, though ecstatic to hear her voice. He could still feel her body pressed against him, the way her soft curves had fit into his contours. Just thinking about her made him flush with desire, and he wished he could reach out and touch her right then. But he couldn't. He had to leave. He was under a time crunch and he couldn't miss his flight.

"I—I just wanted to see if you might be interested in going to Sunday brunch at PJ's with me tomorrow," Riana asked.

Andre let the line hum empty for a few seconds, his stomach caving in. He knew it had taken a great deal of courage for her to call him, and he could tell from her voice that she expected him to react positively to her unexpected invitation. *Oh, God,* he silently groaned. *Riana is actually coming around, and I can't even meet her halfway.*

"Maybe talk a little more about the job?" Riana advanced her mission, clearing her throat with a tight, short cough.

A beat. He could detect the nervous timbre in her voice and envision the expression on her face: those beautiful lips of hers slightly parted, a hint of a furrow across her smooth brown brow, a perfectly polished fingernail touched to her cheek. As much as he wanted to grab this opening, accept her invitation, and move their relationship to the next level, he couldn't. He had to keep his promise to Frazer and play this situation cool. "I wish I could," he told Riana. "But I'm going to be busy tomorrow. All day. Got a lot of work to do, so I plan to stick around here and focus on a few things I need to finish."

"Oh, sure. I understand. Just thought I'd check," Riana managed, her voice trailing off in disappointment.

A stab of regret hit Andre. He wished he didn't have to lie to her, wished he could hang out with her all day and spend a lazy Sunday afternoon doing nothing except what they wanted to do, as they had done when they were together. But he had a fast trip to take, a brother to locate, a frightened sister-in-law who needed his help, and he couldn't tell Riana anything about it. Frazer's orders. Keep quiet.

"Appreciate the invite, Riana, but maybe another time," he finished, keeping strength in his voice. "Uh, look. I've gotta go right now. We'll talk soon, promise. I'll call you after I talk to Lester and I'll set up a time for us to meet. Okay?"

"Right. Call me Monday, if you can. Even if it's late, so I can plan my time for the rest of the week."

"Will do," Andre told her, and then he eased the handset back into its stand and let out a low, long breath. "How the hell did I get into this?" he muttered, not looking forward to the long flight to Kingston.

"Forget you," Riana shot back crossly as she slammed down the phone. "He's going to work all day tomorrow? On Sunday?" He had never been so dedicated before. When they were together, Sundays had been their special days, when they strolled through museums, ate ice cream in the park or snuggled in a dark theater to watch a foreign movie and munch popcorn.

Now, she doubted he was telling her the truth. Andre probably just wanted to put her off because of the way she'd acted the day before. Well, two could play that game. She would go to the buffet at PJ's alone and enjoy herself, too. And the next time he started talking that mess about how he felt about her, she would remember how he had turned her down. Oh, no, she wasn't going to make things easy for him now. In fact, she was going to do everything in her power to make him sorry he refused the only olive branch she intended to extend.

Frustrated and a bit humiliated to have been so flatly dismissed, she shoved the papers she'd been reviewing aside, snapped on the television and yanked open the door to the hotel minibar.

The red leather bag on the counter caught Felicia's eye immediately, and she knew at once that Mrs. Wilson, who was a regular visitor at the Presidents' Club, had left it behind in her hurry to get to her gate. Snatching the purse, Felicia raced to the door, flung it open and scanned the crowd, relieved to spot the woman far down the terminal. "Damn. She sure walks fast," Felicia commented, plunging into the throng of travelers who were making their way through the busy airport.

Walking quickly, Felicia managed to catch up with Mrs. Wilson, and tugged the sleeve of her blouse. "You left this in the club!" she shouted over a loudspeaker that was announcing the departure of flight #333 to Miami.

"Oh, my God. Thanks!" the woman gushed, clearly grateful for Felicia's delivery. "I didn't even miss it."

"No problem. Just glad I got to you before you boarded," Felicia replied, giving the woman a short wave of her fingers. "Have a great trip!" she called out while watching the passengers begin to board.

"Hmm," she murmured when she saw a man who looked familiar hand his ticket to the attendant and pass onto the Jetway. "That looks like Andre. In fact, I'm sure it's him. Going to Miami?"

Curious, Felicia made her way over to the computer terminal at the check-in counter and asked the attendant if she could review the passenger list. A quick scan confirmed her suspicion: It was Andre Preaux all right, and according to the manifest, he was on his way to Kingston, Jamaica. "Interesting," Felicia murmured under her breath, wondering if Riana knew that the guy she professed so hard not to care about was off on a tropical jaunt.

Chapter 11

The buffet line at PJ's snaked halfway around the open dining room, but Riana didn't mind, knowing the food would be worth the wait. She sipped her second mimosa and focused on the music that the jazz quartet was playing, feeling mellow and self-satisfied for deciding to get out of her hotel suite and join the other Sunday diners who were waiting their turn at the lavish buffet—an excursion into the heart of a delicious soul-food banquet.

The large round tables that filled the main dining room at PJ's contributed to its friendly, homey atmosphere, and after piling her plate with smothered chicken, spicy ribs, creamy macaroni and cheese and tender greens she found a seat at a table with several other solo diners and settled in to savor the food that she had missed so much.

After a delicious meal, which ended with a slice of pecan pie and a taste of PJ's famous peach cobbler, she knew it was

time to go. Feeling deliciously guilty for indulging so blatantly, Riana left the restaurant in high spirits, determined not
to let Andre's absence get her down.

The July day was hot and clear, with a searing sun that
blazed round and bold overhead. During her drive back to the
hotel Riana thought about how she wanted to spend the rest of
her day. She could stroll the Galleria in cool, blessed air-
conditioning, or go for a swim in the hotel pool, or maybe drive
down to Galveston to take in the beach, though she didn't
really want to go alone.

Impulsively, Riana reached into her purse and removed the
computer printout of Andre's Web site that she had made before
leaving San Antonio. "A. Preaux and Associates. Prairie Towers. 11780 South Main Street," she read from the paper, glancing quickly at the Mapquest directions on the page. "Wonder
what he's doing now?" she said, thinking that it might be a good
idea to pay Andre an impromptu visit and see if she could
convince him to take a break from all that work he had said he
had to do. As annoyed as Riana had been with him the night
before, she knew she'd have to put her emotions aside if she
wanted to get Andre to accept George Allen's job. Time was
of the essence. If she could spend some time relaxing with
Andre today, it might help move things along.

Turning left, Riana swung off the Loop and headed south
on the feeder road until she came to Main Street. After checking
the numbers on the street signs, she turned right and drove
several blocks.

This is not exactly the museum-district end of Main, she
thought, scrutinizing the dated strip centers and shabby office
buildings lining each side of the street. When she came to a stop
at a red light, she double-checked the Mapquest address, looked
over to her left and saw Prairie Towers.

Riana's mouth dropped open and she had to blink several

times when she realized that the aging, abandoned-looking structure, was indeed, Andre's building. The sight was not a pretty one. After making a U-turn at the light, she came to a stop in the empty parking lot and sat there, taking in the structure, which had boarded-up windows on the lower floors, a stained stone facade, a cracked asphalt driveway, and a faded sign over the heavy wooden door that read Prairie Towers. Back in the day, it had probably been a showcase of modern architecture, but now it was simply a distressed, neglected property in need of great repair.

I see why he didn't want to meet with me here, she thought, looking around and not feeling particularly safe. Hers was the only car in the parking lot, making her think that Andre must not be there. Broken bottles, a moldy old mattress and several rusty grocery carts bulging with plastic trash bags—clear signs that the homeless had most likely taken up residence in the field—filled the overgrown lot next door. When a pack of mean-looking stray dogs appeared from behind the building and meandered across the street, Riana shook her head in dismay.

Quickly, she pulled out her cell phone. With a press of the number four, she speed-dialed Felicia, hoping her cousin was not still asleep after having worked the night shift at the airport.

"Good. You're up," Riana started right in as soon as Felicia answered.

"Barely," Felicia mumbled. "God, I was tired when I got home. The night shift is hell. Remind me never to volunteer to work it again."

"I hear you," Riana sympathized, and then jumped directly into her reason for calling. "Guess where I am?"

"No idea. My head is still cloudy. Where?" Felicia asked.

"Sitting outside Andre's office in the *museum district,*" she said in a very sarcastic manner.

"Oh, yeah? What's it like. Gorgeous, I'll bet?"

"Not hardly," Riana shot back, going on to describe the aging, dated structure in front of her. "Girl, I'm shocked. Andre did say that he was having his office painted, but he never told me he was working in a place that looks as if it ought to be condemned. This building needs serious renovation. I can't believe he deliberately tried to mislead me about this. Why would he do that?"

"Who knows? But he *is* an architect, so he must see potential in the location and the building or he never would have bought it."

"Maybe so, but he didn't have to lead me to believe that he owned some nice building in the museum district when it's really a dump at the far edge of downtown, almost under the Loop."

"Hey, he's a man. They have their pride, you know, so don't spend too much time trying to figure him out. And by the way, your boy Andre seems to be full of surprises," Felicia coyly mentioned. "Did you know that he's in Jamaica right now?"

"Jamaica? What are you talking about?" Riana's reaction was swift, almost defensive.

"Well, all I can say is that I saw him board Continental Flight #333 to Miami last night, with connections to Kingston. I checked the passenger list. It was Andre all right. Off to the big island for some fun and sun!"

Felicia's words made Riana's stomach tighten, forcing her to take a deep breath before she could respond. "You gotta be kidding. Why would he do that? He's supposed to call me next week to set up an appointment to meet him here. In this dump! Damn, what's going on?"

"Well," Felicia said with a cluck of her tongue, "I guess he'll be calling you long distance from Jamaica."

What is Andre trying to do? Riana worried after clicking off.

I thought I knew him well enough to feel comfortable recommending him for this job, but now I don't know. How can I trust him to tell me the truth when he's being so mysterious and devious?

Chapter 12

Andre tossed his straw shopping bag onto the bed and locked his hotel-room door, taking care to engage both the dead bolt and the chain latch, suddenly feeling very vulnerable. He had spent the morning roaming the crowded streets of Kingston, pretending to be a tourist out on a shopping trip as he picked up a few items of clothing and began his search for the café where he had left Kay and his young nephew, Lonny, ten months ago.

Andre had been wrong to think that he would be able to go directly back to the nondescript eatery in the heart of the city, and after spending hours winding his way on foot through the dense downtown area, he had not found the small, red-doored café that he remembered.

Now, Andre walked over to his window and pulled back the drapes to peer out over the city.

Where are you, Kay? Jamal? Andre silently questioned,

struck by the beauty of the gray-green mountains which rose before him, shrouded in mist. A bright-blue sky wrapped the horizon, merging with an equally blue expanse of sea, masking the violence and bloodshed that lay beneath the surface of the serene, tropical facade.

Upon his arrival Saturday night, he had asked the hotel desk clerk for a map of the area, explaining that he wanted to do some independent exploring. Immediately, the wiry gray-haired man had warned Andre to stay away from certain areas because unfortunately, crime was abundant in the western and southern parts of the city and most of downtown Kingston was not safe, especially after dark.

This was not news to Andre, who had heard that few tourists—particularly Americans—left their fancy hotel resorts in Ocho Rios or Negril to visit Kingston, a tough, widespread city that was rife with gang-controlled neighborhoods known to erupt into violence at any time. However, this was where he had to start if he wanted to accomplish his mission.

Andre studied the view to the west. From his location in the southeastern part of the island, nestled at the foot of the craggy Blue Mountains, he could see crime-ridden Spanish Town in the distance, defined by the Spanish Town Road, which snaked its way into the violent district that even many Kingstonians avoided.

With a shudder, Andre inclined his head toward the sprawling metropolis, knowing that his search might very well require that he infiltrate the rotting slums and dark nooks and alleyways of the mountainside town, plunging into the dangerous mix.

Turning from the window, Andre shook out the contents of his shopping bag. A red, white and green striped knit cap that fit snugly on his head. A faded orange T-shirt with the muted shape of a marijuana leaf stamped across the front. Dark wrap-around sunglasses. Brown cotton pants with frayed cuffs. Sneakers that had seen better days.

As he began to change clothes, he mentally plotted his approach. His plan was to devote today and tomorrow to his search, and if he wasn't successful in finding Kay or Jamal, at least he hoped to gather leads to follow up on later, when he could return and take his time looking for them. With Riana waiting for him to call and set up a meeting early in the week, he couldn't afford to spend day after day wandering the streets of Kingston or Spanish Town and chance blowing his most important design opportunity—and destroying Riana's trust.

God, he missed her so much. If only he had come to Jamaica for a vacation with Riana and not to infiltrate Jamal's dangerous world. That's what he and Riana needed—time alone, away from work, isolation from the world as they focused on their relationship. Andre felt certain that if he could ever whisk Riana off for an intimate weekend, they would quickly rekindle the love he knew she still had for him.

Later, he told himself, jerking his thoughts back to the moment.

Once Andre had dressed in his new street clothes, he checked out his image in the mirror and nodded. A stubble of beard bristled on his cheeks, giving him the rough, unkempt look that he hoped would help him blend in with the locals and allow him to move around without being pegged as an American tourist. If he was lucky, he'd get close to the people and find someone who might know where Kay or Jamal had gone.

Andre picked up his wallet from the bed, removed all of his American money, and replaced it with Jamaican dollars. Next, he pulled out the only photo he had of Kay, which had been taken shortly after she and Jamal married. She was standing in front of a garden, wearing a white cotton dress and a white gardenia pinned in her reddish-brown hair, which she wore loose and long in a tangle of waves. Curvy and soft, she had rich mahogany skin and the kind of shape that made men—and women—give her a second glance: voluptuous but not overtly sexy.

In the photo, Kay faced the camera with a glint of humor in her wide-set eyes, making Andre wonder just what she had been thinking about when the picture was snapped. Though he didn't know Kay as well as he wished, he did know that she wanted to raise her son in a safe environment and he was going to do whatever he could to help her.

I'll be fine, Andre told himself with a final glance in the mirror, ready to head out.

Traveling by local bus, Andre made his way up and down the streets of Kingston until he finally saw the red painted door of a café in a ragged section of the city where dogs and barefoot children wandered the dust-covered street. The sign above the door read Sun Grille, and the lettering looked as if it had been recently repainted.

Andre jumped from the bus and crossed the street, entering a café that smelled of jerk and coconut and honey-sweet mangos. When the rich scents hit him, he realized that he was hungry, having forgotten all about breakfast in his hurry to get to the market.

He nodded to the extremely large woman sitting beside an ancient cash register just inside the door and eased toward the rear of the dim room, where reggae music erupted from a juke-box and rickety square tables were crowded side by side.

He ventured a glance around. No one had paid any attention to him at all, and he let his shoulders sag down in relief as he picked up a greasy plastic-covered menu and studied it.

Right away, a young girl with a blue bandana tied around her hair approached and asked him what he'd like to eat. Not wanting his lack of an accent to give him away and reveal him as an American, Andre turned the menu toward the waitress and simply tapped on the fish sandwich with fritters, and then muttered quickly, "A beer."

"And whot kinda beer you be wantin'?" the waitress asked impatiently.

Andre shrugged, indicating that he'd leave it up to her. With a lift of her hands, she walked away and disappeared into the kitchen, which was clearly visible from where Andre sat.

While waiting for his food Andre listened to the reggae music and watched a group of old men at the next table play a vicious game of dominoes. They laughed and hooted and slapped down their tiles, clearly enjoying the game.

"Here you go, mon."

Andre reached for the frosty bottle of beer while nodding his thanks. When he looked up, he froze. Kay was standing behind the girl, looking at him with such an intense frown on her face that it made Andre jerk back in surprise. Her long reddish-brown hair was pulled back from her face and tied up in a loose ponytail with a bright-red scarf. She looked tired, older than thirty, as he knew she'd be by now, and the glint of humor that he remembered in her eyes was no longer there.

"I hoped you'd be here," Andre managed, as soon as the waitress walked away, feeling a jolt of relief that it had taken less than a day to find her.

"But what in hell are *you* doing here, Andre?" Kay hissed the words and stepped closer to the table, as if using her body to shield him from the rest of the customers.

"Looking for you," he answered, now tilting back to focus on her face. "I flew in last night. Been searching all morning for this place. Are you okay? And Lonny? How's he doing?"

"Why? Why are you asking? After all these months. Why now?" Kay's words tumbled out in a desperate string, linked together as one long question.

"I think you know the answers," Andre countered, recalling

Agent Frazer's theory that Kay might know something about the murder of the undercover cop. "Where's Jamal? I want to talk to him."

With a shake of her head, Kay backed away a few steps. "You shouldn't have come here, Andre. You must leave. Now."

"Not until I talk to Jamal. Tell me where he is."

Kay parted her lips and sucked in a long breath. Andre could see the fear in her eyes, but he also recognized a glimmer of reprieve. She wanted to talk to him, that much he knew, because if she had wanted to dodge him, she could have easily stayed in the kitchen. But she had approached him. Why? And how could he get her to speak with him alone?

"I'm staying at the Crown Kingston Hotel. Room 705," Andre rushed to say just as the waitress appeared with his food.

Kay bit her bottom lip and stepped aside to let the girl place his sandwich on the table, and then, with a blink of her wide-set eyes, she turned around and walked away.

Andre spent the remainder of his day sitting in his hotel room, reading his paperback book and praying that the phone would ring. He had found Kay, all right, but he hadn't made any headway at all on what he'd come to Jamaica to do. As the hours slipped past he feared she was not going to contact him, forcing him to go up to Spanish Town and start asking questions, something he truly didn't want to do.

At last, the phone rang. Andre snatched it up. "No, I don't want a copy of the evening paper," he snapped at the desk clerk, immediately regretting his tone. "I'm sorry. I was distracted. Are there any messages for me?" he ventured in a much more pleasant manner, knowing that a shift change or a general lack of urgency might have allowed a message to get lost.

"No, sir. No messages for you."

"Thanks," Andre murmured, just as he heard a soft tapping sound on his door. Thinking that the clerk had sent up the newspaper anyway, he jerked open the door.

Kay was standing there, looking forlorn, no expression on her face. Her hair was loose now, framing her face in an explosion of unruly curls, and she was wearing a plain yellow cotton dress that hung from her shoulders to her ankles, hiding her lovely figure. She glanced from side to side and then stepped into the room before Andre could invite her in. Once the door was shut, she leaned against it, assessing him with wide, fear-filled eyes.

"Andre, I can't stay long. I might have been followed, and I don't want you caught up in this."

"In what?" Andre asked, taking Kay by the hand to lead her to a chair. He sat on the edge of the bed across from her. "Tell me what's going on."

"I'm sure Jamal is dead," Kay said, her words flat with dread.

"Why do you say that?"

"A boat exploded in Port Kaiser three days ago. I know the boat. Jamal and his 'friends' have been on it many times and I'm sure he was on board when it blew up. The news reports said that drugs packed in plastic bags were found floating in the water, and that three men died. Don't ask me for more details because I can't give you any, but one of the men responsible for the explosion came to see me. He said Jamal is now at the bottom of the sea."

"A drug war?" Andre prompted.

"It goes on all the time," Kay answered with a quick tilt of her head and a look that told him all he needed to know.

The news jolted Andre, like a solid hit to the stomach, even though he should have been prepared for something like this, considering Jamal's risky lifestyle. "If it's true, I'm sorry. I really am, but we both know Jamal made a lot of bad choices and took too many chances. He was my half brother, I tried to help him once, but he didn't really want to change."

"I know," Kay admitted. "He only listened to himself."

Andre hunched forward, eager to get what he came to Jamaica for. "I couldn't help Jamal, but I may be able to help you, Kay. Do you know anything about the murder of a JCF man named Eddie Brooks?"

"No, I've never heard anything about that," Kay said. "But Jamal probably knew something, though I doubt he was involved in the man's death. I admit, I knew what Jamal was into. I didn't like it, but I couldn't keep him away from the street life that he loved. He ran drugs, yes, but I know he didn't like guns. Never kept one in the house, and he told me more than once that he would never shoot a man, and I believed him."

"When Brooks was working undercover in Jamal's drug posse, he turned up dead, shot many times and dumped in a ditch. Do you know who might have done such a thing?"

"Who? No. But I could make a good guess. So many mean, coldhearted men toting guns moved in and out of Jamal's life. I have no proof, so how can I tell anyone what I suspect? My life and my son's life would be in great danger."

"Did the authorities question you about the explosion? About Jamal's connection to the drug wars?"

"No. I think some money must have changed hands high up for the JCF to leave me alone. I'm okay, as long as I keep my mouth shut. I go to work in the café's kitchen and live in two rooms upstairs. I sell my paintings in the local market and I'm certainly not hiding. But I have enough sense not to talk to anyone who can cause me trouble."

"You should go to the police and tell them what you know," Andre urged.

"Oh, I don't think so. Why do that?"

"You've seen things, heard things. You can identify people who may need to be questioned."

"Impossible. I will not talk to the police," Kay shot back. The fright in her voice convinced Andre that his sister-in-law was terrified of what the men in the local drug posses would do to her if she started talking. He understood her fear. He'd seen the roving gangs of hard-looking men who swaggered through the streets of Kingston, itching for any excuse to prove how tough they were. "Would you be willing to talk to my FBI connection in Houston?"

With a tilt of her head, Kay considered his question, and then said, "In Houston?"

"Yes, on the phone."

"Maybe. I don't know."

"I wish you would. His name is Charles Frazer." Andre grabbed a notepad off the dresser and scribbled a number on it. "Here. Call him, talk to him, he wants to help you, if you'll help him."

Kay took the paper and folded it into a tiny square, which she tucked into the palm of her hand and then sat waiting, for what, Andre didn't know.

"Face it," Andre continued, hoping she'd consider giving Frazer a call. "If Jamal is dead, Kay, you and Lonny could come back to Houston with me. My flight leaves tomorrow at three. I'll pay for your tickets. You can get out of here and put all of this behind you. We'll work out a way for you to stay."

A ripple of concern eased over Kay's face, making her appear more frightened than when she arrived. She stood and went to the window, keeping her back to Andre, who could see that evening had descended on the city and a blanket of bright lights glowed outside.

"I wish I could go with you," Kay told Andre, now turning to face him. "But I don't have a passport. Jamal took it from me long ago, and I don't know where it is."

"Apply for another one."

"I could, but it would do no good. My name is on a no-fly list. I can't enter your country. Someone wants to make sure I stay put."

"We'll see about that," Andre vowed, making up his mind to help Kay and his nephew get out of Jamaica. After all, clearing her name might mean clearing his, and he intended to do both.

Chapter 13

Riana arrived at the Houston office of Executive Suites, Inc., at eight o'clock sharp on Monday morning, feeling confident that she and Rodney Roberts would be able to wrap up their deal in record time so she could concentrate on Andre—as soon as he called to set up their meeting.

Stifling a yawn, she entered the elevator hoping she'd be able to shake the lethargy that gripped her, brought on by lack of sleep. All night long, her mind had spun with possibilities about why Andre had gone to Jamaica after telling her he was going to stick around his office and work all day Sunday. None of her attempts to come up with a rational answer made any sense. If Andre had had a business meeting or a conference to attend in Jamaica, why hadn't he simply told her about it? And if he was off to the island for pleasure, or to meet a woman, perhaps, why go now? Why would he do such a thing during the middle of negotiations for a design job that might greatly enhance his business? No. He was up to something, playing games with her, and she was not going to let him get away with making her look like a fool.

Riana checked her cell phone to be sure it was on, and then switched it to vibrate. No way was she going to miss Andre's call. She had a lot of questions to ask, and he'd better have some answers.

As she entered the Executive Suites office, what struck her immediately was the absence of noise. In fact, it was downright quiet. Back home at her office in San Antonio, on a Monday morning telephones buzzed constantly, people's voices hummed as they busily interviewed candidates in person and on the phones, and the click-click of computer keyboards added to the rush of activity.

Pausing in the reception area, Riana cocked her head to one side and listened, distressed by the obvious signs of lack of productivity. *No wonder this office is underproducing,* she thought. *No one is doing any work!*

"Hello, Terri," Riana greeted, taking care to use the receptionist's name, before nodding hello to Iris, the office manager, whose cubicle faced the receptionist. Iris was an overweight, lethargic-looking woman seated at her desk eating a sausage-muffin sandwich and holding a huge cup of coffee. "How're you today, Iris?" Riana added cheerfully, pointedly staring at the oversized fast-food cup. One of her sacred rules was no food or drink at workstations—other than a bottle of water or a small coffee cup. Obviously, Rodney Roberts didn't care.

"I'm here," Iris replied with a grimace and then a groan. She rolled her eyes and rotated her neck from side to side, swinging her long dark-blond hair off her neck. Her face, a pale oval set with two clear-blue eyes, was devoid of makeup, which might have greatly enhanced her appearance. "Mondays are always a killer," Iris mumbled before taking another bite of her muffin. "But I'm here," she added between chews.

"Good to see you again," Riana went on, determined to ignore Iris's complaining nature. "Is Mr. Roberts in yet?"

Iris's blue eyes widened in surprise. "Oh, no. On a Monday?" She chuckled and glanced at her clock. "Probably won't see him for another hour, at least."

Forcing back her reaction to this announcement, Riana faked a smile. "Oh, well, I'll just wait for him in my office. I have plenty of work. Let me know as soon as he arrives, okay?"

"Sure," Iris replied, reaching for the phone, which was ringing for the first time since Riana had arrived.

Riana made her way down the hall, surveying each employee's cubicle as she went, and once inside her office, she had to stand still for several minutes to gather her composure, resisting the urge to go back out there and yank every bag of fast food off each staff member's desk and give them the kind of lecture they desperately deserved. As far as she could tell, all of them were spending the morning either reading the newspaper, eating breakfast or lazily surfing the Internet. What a waste of time, money and talent, she calculated, dreading the possibility that she would most likely have to fire everyone and hire an entirely new staff.

Putting that thought aside, she opened her briefcase and pulled out the annual reports that Rodney Roberts had given her on Friday. She set them on the corner of her desk, a cheap particleboard structure that had seen better days, preparing for her meeting with Roberts. She prayed that the situation might not be as bad as it appeared on paper.

Next, Riana removed her laptop from its case, set it on the desk and signed onto the Internet to check her e-mail. When a very low signal message popped up, she frowned and tried again. After another failed attempt, she stepped across the hall and stuck her head into the cubicle where a young lady, whose nameplate read Sara Thomas, was engrossed in applying a coat of clear polish to her beautifully manicured fingernails. Sara was the only African-American on staff, and also the only one not eating at her desk. However, in Riana's opinion, doing nails was not much better.

"Uh, I'm having trouble logging on to the Internet," Riana told Sara, who glanced up briefly, and then resumed her task. "Anything wrong with your signal?" Riana asked.

Sara frowned, clearly puzzled. "Nope. I got online a few minutes ago. Took a while, but it always does. Better check your phone line. Might be the connection."

"Oh," Riana uttered, realizing what must be the matter. "You mean your office isn't wireless? You don't have DSL?"

"Are you kidding? We don't have high-speed anything. Takes forever to get connected."

"What?" Riana shot back. "Surely you're kidding."

"Not hardly. Rodney's way too cheap to spring for anything that might make life easier around here."

"I see what you mean," Riana replied, easing back into her office. "This place is gonna need a complete overhaul," she said under her breath, eager to sit down with Roberts and see just how much it was going to cost to bring this franchise up to her standards.

At nine-thirty there was still no sign of Rodney Roberts. Riana ground her teeth in annoyance. She had not turned her franchise into the highest performing unit in the state by arriving late at the office, making people wait for her, or acting as if time were not the most valuable thing in life. After all, what was there, except time? And how you used it determined how happy, content, or miserable you were going to be.

At nine forty-five Rodney Roberts stuck his head into Riana's office and flashed a sheepish smile.

Riana swallowed her irritation, curious about what he had

to say. "Gee, what happened? I thought you said we'd meet at eight-thirty."

"Well, I had hoped to get an early start, but I got sidetracked. Just couldn't get out of the house. My oldest son…"

"You knew I'd be in early to meet with you. Why didn't you call?" Riana cut him off, watching Roberts carefully as he eased down into a seat across from her desk.

"Didn't think I'd be this late," he mumbled, lifting a corner of his mouth in a smirk of unconcern. "So, where do we stand?" he began, shaking off his apologetic mood.

Deciding not to belabor the point, Riana knew she was not in the mood to haggle with the man and wanted to finish with this business as quickly as possible so she'd be free to go over to Andre's office as soon as he called.

"This is what I'm thinking," Riana started, going on to outline the very generous offer she had put together over the weekend. She handed Roberts a single sheet of paper and went on. "For the amount that I'm offering, I want all of the furnishings—such as they are—computers, office equipment and supplies. There'll be no guarantees about staffing. I'm going to need time to interview everyone before I make any decisions about hiring and firing. And I need you to get a copy of the lease. Who owns the building?"

"Drewbegg Realty. Easy to work with. Never had any problems."

"So the current agreement stays the same, right? No rent increases coming up? Nothing I should be concerned about?"

"Right. Our rates are locked in for the next five years. No problem, there," Roberts agreed. "This is great space. Couldn't afford this at today's rates, so you're lucky we've got a long-term lease."

"The suite needs some serious updating, though," Riana could not keep from adding.

Roberts shrugged. "Maybe, but a relocation would be very costly."

"I know. And as long as I can keep this address, I won't have to print new promotional materials. However, installing new phones and computer terminals will be costly enough. The only way this is going to be financially feasible for me is if I stay right here."

"This location was a selling point when I started the franchise," Rodney told her, a lilt of pride in his voice.

"So true. My attorney in San Antonio is drawing up the papers right now. So, if all goes well, we ought to be able to settle this by the end of next week."

"Sounds good," Rodney replied, shaking Riana's hand. "I'll do all I can to make it happen."

Riana spent the rest of the morning reviewing contracts and talking on the phone with Tanisha in the San Antonio office. She went over details related to ongoing clients and made sure everything was moving along smoothly there. With no major problems to report, she relaxed. Tanisha had even taken it upon herself to purchase a baby gift for Donald, the always-helpful security guard at the building, whose wife was due to deliver any day.

"Tanisha, you're really coming through," Riana commented, relieved to have the office in such capable hands. "Things here are a bit fluid," she added, unsure of how else to describe what was going on. "So much needs to be done here and I still haven't made much progress on the Preaux case. Andre had to go out of town on business, delaying my reports, so I may have to stay here longer than I planned, and you may have to hold down the fort a while longer."

"No problem," Tanisha replied. "Everything's under control."

After finishing her conversation with Tanisha, Riana finally got logged on to the Internet. She went to the Uni-Code Criminal Background Check Web site, the service she always used. Even though she didn't have all of the information required for an in-depth search on Andre, she decided to go as far as she could with what she had: Andre's date of birth and place of birth—Baton Rouge, Louisiana. A first pass on the Louisiana site, which provided information on criminal arrests and convictions for the past ten years, showed nothing. Just as she'd thought. A check on the Texas site came back clean, too. Even though her search had been cursory and done without some vital information, she felt secure that Andre had nothing to worry about.

Next, she checked with the hotel to see if there had been any messages. Nothing, the desk clerk told her.

He hasn't called. He isn't going to interrupt his trip to Jamaica to call, she realized, mad as hell that he would take off for the islands and leave her hanging like this. *He's dead wrong if he thinks I'm okay with this kind of unprofessional behavior. He has a cell phone and there're telephones in every airport and hotel in the world. There's no excuse for this mysterious disappearing act.* Incensed by Andre's thoughtlessness, she punched in the number to his office and waited for his voice mail to come on.

"Andre. Riana here. I hate to interrupt your holiday, but I do have business to take care of, and I had expected to hear from you this morning. It's two thirty-five. I'm on a very tight deadline, so if you're no longer interested in working with the Allen Group, please give me a call. I can't drag this interview process out all week." She paused to catch her breath and think of one final word to throw at him when the voice mail suddenly cut off and a live person came on the line.

"A. Preaux and Associates. This is Lester. How can I help you?"

Startled by the man's voice, she sucked in a sharp breath.

"Oh, hello. I thought no one was in the office," Riana said, hoping Lester hadn't heard her tirade.

"Just got here. Glad I caught your call. How can I help you?"

"This is Riana Cole, of Executive Suites."

"Oh, sure. I spoke with you a few days ago. About that job with the Allen Group. Andre told me all about it. I sure hope…"

"I had hoped to hear from Mr. Preaux today," Riana cut him off. "Just wanted to touch base and see if tomorrow might be a convenient time for me to drop by his office."

"Oh, right. He did leave me a note letting me know he'd be out of town today. Don't know where he went, but he said to expect him to be in tomorrow. Do you want to leave a message?"

That's just great. Andre can leave notes for his part-time assistant, but can't pick up the phone and call the person who could influence his future. "Yes." Riana snapped the word, clamping her teeth together as if breaking ice. "Tell him he has until five o'clock tomorrow to get back to me, or I'll have to let George Allen know that he's not interested in the position."

Chapter 14

On Tuesday, Andre's flight from Miami to Houston landed five minutes early and it couldn't have been soon enough for him. Luckily, he had grabbed a seat in first class, so he was able to deplane as soon as the flight attendant opened the door.

Hurrying down the Jetway, he pulled his cell phone from his pocket and called Charles Frazer, only to get his voice mail.

"This is Andre Preaux, and I'm back from Jamaica. I'd like to talk to you right away. I found my sister-in-law and she can use your help. I've got news about Jamal, too. I'd like to come by your office first thing tomorrow. Call me if that won't work for you."

After clicking off, he punched in the speed dial to his office, hoping Lester had smoothed things over with Riana, who he knew must have called, furious with him. He couldn't help it. She didn't even know he had a brother named Jamal, and Frazer had sworn him to secrecy about his mission, so he couldn't have told her the truth if he'd wanted to. Besides, he didn't want to lie to Riana, making up some fantasy story that would only sound fake and make things worse. The best thing to do was keep his personal business to himself. He was back home, and that was all that mattered.

The trip floated in his mind like a fast-moving montage: airplanes, buses, crowded city streets and green-gray mountains. Exhausting, but definitely worth it. He'd even had a chance to see Lonny, and the sight of his nephew sitting at a scarred card table in the cramped hot room above the café made him even more anxious to help Kay and her son get out of Jamaica.

But they have to get out alive, he thought, fully convinced that dangerous men who had worked with Jamal were definitely keeping an eye on her. *No one should have to live like that,* he told himself. *I just hope she's willing to talk to Frazer and that he can keep her safe.*

As Lester filled him in on what had been happening the past few days, Andre took long strides through the terminal, anxious to get in his car and head home. He was not surprised to learn that Riana had called again, clearly upset this time, and that she had expected to hear from him before five o'clock. Andre glanced quickly at his watch. Five thirty-three. He'd already missed her deadline. Quickly, he called Riana's hotel. No answer. Her cell phone went to voice mail, so he left a message for her to call him at home, no matter how late. He called his office again.

"Lester. I just deplaned. This is the middle of rush hour. Traffic into town is gonna be a bitch. Would you keep calling Miss Cole, and if you get her, tell her I'll contact her at her hotel later tonight. I'm not gonna get home for at least another hour."

Ninety minutes later, Andre stepped out of the elevator in his building and into his open-space loft, aware that Lester had already left for the day. Too tired to think about unpacking, he tossed his bag on the floor near the elevator and headed toward the kitchen, where he pulled a cold beer from the refrigerator, popped the top and took a long gulp, savoring the taste of the icy beverage as it slid down his throat and revived him.

Flying always left him feeling like a parched piece of leather, and there was nothing like a cold beer and a warm shower to help him recover. The silence in the apartment was soothing after the hustle and bustle of the trip, followed by a tense drive home among a tangle of cars, road-hogging trucks and exhaust-fume-spitting buses. All he wanted was an hour of peace and quiet to think things through before he met Riana.

Andre turned off his cell phone, disengaged his office phone, and tuned the TV in his bedroom to ESPN, but muted the sound. Unbuttoning his shirt, he went into the bathroom, ran the shower, and then stripped off the rest of his clothes and stepped in. When the warm water hit him, he sagged in relief and lifted his face to the pounding stream, glad to be home, glad he'd found Kay, but wishing he had a clue about what he was going to tell Riana.

Riana was furious. *He's got a lot of nerve, leaving a message for me to call him back!* She was tempted to make good on her threat to call George Allen and remove Andre from her short list of candidates, but instead she decided to try a different tack. She looked at the clock on the bedside table. Six fifty-five. Not too late for their overdue meeting, she calculated, grabbing her purse, her car keys and the papers Andre *was* going to fill out for her that night.

Andre heard the entry buzzer ringing as soon as he emerged from the shower, so he hurried over to the sometimey intercom, which functioned when it wanted to, and pressed the response button, holding it down as he spoke. "Yes, who's there?"

A jumbled answer floated up through the grate, not surprising Andre. The building-wide system had been top-of-the-line when initially installed years ago, with fancy art-deco grilles covering each unit and knobs shaped like faceted diamonds. It was old and unreliable, but Andre had no plans to replace it, as it was part of the original charm of the building. For now, it served him as best it could.

Rubbing a towel over his head, he asked again, "Lester? That you?"

Once more, a garbled mess came back at him. Curious, Andre went over to the window that faced the parking lot and looked down. "Riana," he murmured, recognizing her champagne Lexus immediately. Quickly, he pressed a button to light the lobby and spring the front-door lock. Then, bypassing underwear, he stepped into a pair of jeans and pulled a V-neck shirt over his head. Barefoot, he started for the elevator. Since Riana was obviously dead set on conducting a meeting with him tonight, he planned to greet her warmly, welcome her to his office and escort her upstairs. Just as he did with all of his clients.

As soon as the door latch clicked, lights came on inside the building. Riana pushed against the heavy wooden door fitted with wide iron straps and stepped cautiously inside, unsure of what she would find, startled by the scene that greeted her.

The jewel tones in the geometric-patterned marble floor shone vibrantly beneath a wash of muted light coming from row after row of alabaster pendants suspended from a vaulted ceiling. Tall fluted columns, topped with severely arched caps, rose at intervals throughout the space, creating a sense of intimacy within a huge open foyer. Along the walls, shell-shaped sconces made of hammered copper stood guard over what resembled an art-deco-lover's treasure vault that had been abandoned and forgotten.

Deep, built-in bookshelves and cabinets, made of ebony and trimmed with tarnished brass, stood empty and dust-filled

against walls that were stained and peeling layers of wallboard.
A musty odor rose from the piles of broken plaster and debris
that filled the shadowy corners and many of the narrow first-
floor windows, which she suspected had once been set with
beautiful works of stained glass, were boarded over with
buckling squares of plywood. But still, the timeless beauty of
the aging structure remained very much in evidence, answering Riana's question about why Andre had purchased the place.

Though elegant in a tragic way, the place was eerily silent,
sending a chill over Riana's arms in spite of the musty warm air
inside. She felt as if she had just stepped into an old film noir
movie where tough-talking detectives and smart-mouthed blondes
wearing too much jewelry waited in the shadows to greet her.

The sudden rattle of an approaching elevator startled Riana,
bringing her thoughts back to her mission. She swung her gaze
toward an alcove where a set of double metal doors, surrounded
by an intricate border of mosaic tiles, shimmered in the dim
yellow light. When the doors slid open and Andre emerged,
Riana exhaled with a whoosh, truly glad to see him.

"What a surprise," Andre said, stepping partially outside the
elevator door to lean against the frame and block the door from
closing.

Riana approached, her heels clack-clacking on the jewel-
colored marble, echoing throughout the vacant lobby. Eyes
narrowed. A fist at her hip. She was ready to take him on. "I
called. Twice. Didn't Lester give you my message?"

"Yes, he did," Andre acknowledged in a voice that was surprisingly calm. "I planned to call you again tonight, but you're
here now, so welcome to Prairie Towers. I'm sorry it's taken
me so long to contact you. Forgive me?"

She opened her mouth to fling a snappy remark his way, but
decided against initiating an all-out argument. She had come
to get him to fill out the papers; a nasty exchange of heated

words might ruin everything. What else could she say except, "Yes, I guess I have to." After a short hesitation, she glanced around the lobby and then told Andre, "Your building is so unusual. Awesome, really, even in this state. Have you renovated much of it yet?"

"Only one floor. The top floor, where I live and work, and I still have a lot to do to my office. Water, electricity and gas are fully functioning, though, and I'm making progress. My plan is to convert each floor into loft apartments that will include office space for small business owners, entrepreneurs and creative types, like artists or writers. No musicians, though. Can't turn the place into a rehearsal hall."

With a chuckle, Riana inclined her head in agreement. "Expanding on the work-at-home trend that's so popular right now?"

"Exactly. A lot of start-ups and entrepreneurs are running their businesses out of a spare bedroom or a garage because they can't afford a mortgage *and* high-rent office space. At Prairie Towers, they can get a good amount of square footage to divide as they wish into living and working spaces, with only one mortgage to pay."

"Efficient use of space," Riana admitted, knowing he was dead on target with his approach.

"Let's go up. I'd like to show you my loft and my office."

"Yes, I'd like that," Riana agreed, stepping inside the elevator, her earlier annoyance quickly fading.

Andre pushed the "up" button, and then planted himself in Riana's line of vision as the creaking elevator rose. "So, you like my renovation plan?" he ventured.

"Yes, and I have to admit, I was surprised when I walked in. From the outside, I never would have guessed that this building had so many unique and beautiful features," she told him, trying to figure out if he was pleased or upset with her for showing up on his doorstep unannounced. He was barefoot. In jeans and a T-shirt, the kind of clothes he had worn when they dated. Must have just gotten home. And he seemed way too calm, as if he had a secret that he didn't plan to share.

"Don't find many old buildings with such authentic period details still intact," he commented as the elevator creaked along.

"It's lovely. Loads of atmosphere. Once it's fully restored, you won't have any trouble renting space," Riana said, eager to make small talk until they got down to business.

"That's why I bought it," Andre replied, giving her a satisfied expression. "It'll take a chunk of money and the touch of some very skilled workmen to bring it back to its former glory, but in the long run, the investment will pay off. Property values in this area are going to shoot sky-high when downtown developers realize there are few plots left to build new office space and remain inside the Loop."

Smart move, Riana thought, silently praising Andre. *He's really become a serious businessman.* "You ought to be able to pick and choose your tenants, once this building is renovated."

The elevator stopped. The doors slid open, but Andre didn't move. He placed one hand on the door to hold it open and turned to Riana. "Yeah. Renovating is key. That's the tough part, you know? Deciding what's worth saving and what I should toss. It can be chancy, because once you tear something apart, it's not so easy to put it back together and make it as good as it was when it was new." He waited a beat while his words hit home. "Don't you agree?"

An involuntary shiver made Riana shift from one foot to the other. She averted her eyes and took a deep breath, knowing what he was trying to say. "Yes. You're right. Fixing things that have been broken can be difficult. But not impossible." She walked past him, quickly exiting the elevator, not about to get into a verbal sparring match about their past. She had to focus on fulfilling the contract she had with George Allen.

"So, this is where I live and work," Andre started in a lighter voice as he moved into the open loft and swung an arm to one side. "My home over there, my office on the other side of that movable wall."

"Interesting," Riana commented, casting a quick glance into Andre's open living space where a black leather futon and two matching chairs anchored a sculpted Oriental rug in hues of bold orange and brown. A low wall of bookshelves crammed with books divided the living room from a small kitchen, where two barstools fronted a waist-high counter created from a thick slab of marble balanced on concrete columns. To the left, behind a folding screen, she could see the edge of his bed and a partially open door that led into the bathroom.

"You like loft living?" she had to ask, knowing it was not for her. She liked defined rooms with walls and windows, and the sense of security they provided. Even at work, in order to concentrate, she had to have a wall at her back or she felt nervous, even a bit vulnerable.

"I love it," Andre replied as he led her away from the elevator and into his office. "A lack of walls keeps things easy, uncomplicated, and it makes for an efficient use of space. If I get tired of the arrangement, I can change things around whenever I want and not have to tear out walls or move doors."

"Wouldn't work for me, but I guess I can see why it appeals to an architect," Riana commented, entering his office, which contained two desks, a computer station and a drafting table. He perched on the corner of his desk, while she sat down on the stool at his drafting board and crossed her legs, immediately regretting her choice of seats. Sitting so low, it made Andre loom over her, like a strong dark bird observing its prey before it pounced, and his presence suddenly intimidated her.

Their Friday night meeting at the Dive Lounge, and even their encounter in the Aquarium parking lot had not left her feeling this nervous. Then, she had felt secure because they had been in a public place where she knew he could only go so far, but now that they were alone—in his private space—memories of the times they'd shared in his old studio apartment seeped in to radiate a warm glow, intensifying her insecurity. How could she forget the bubbly Jacuzzi tub? The seductive jazz music that played on the CD player propped against the wall. Scented candles creating shadows of their naked bodies on the ceiling. The scent of jasmine wafting through the room. The way he'd turned her bones to marshmallow mush with just a touch of his hand.

"So, what do you want, Riana?" Andre began, prying her from her unexpected reverie.

"Right." She cleared her throat and opened her briefcase, ashamed of her temporary lapse of attention. She removed the papers she needed Andre to complete and handed them to him, eager to do what she'd come for and then escape this tempting situation as quickly as possible. "I need the following, in order to complete this stage of the recruitment process—your date and place of birth, your driver's license number, all of your former addresses, your mother's maiden name and your Social Security number and the answers to a few standard security-related questions. I did run a quick check on the Internet, and as far as I can tell, you're clean. No surprises, I hope?" She laughed nervously and then flashed a what-did-you-expect kind of look. "You've never struck me as the type to harbor deep dark secrets anyway, so I'm sure this is routine."

Andre simply chuckled his response with an offhand shrug.

"Once my work is complete, I can give George Allen the go-ahead, and he'll invite you to San Antonio for a personal interview. If you impress him as the kind of person he wants as part of his design team, and I'm sure you will, then the project is yours. Very simple. Nothing complicated here."

"You're really pushing this through," Andre observed as he took the papers from Riana and looked them over. "I'll have to do some digging to find my former addresses. When I first came to Houston, I moved around a lot. One crappy apartment after another, but I do remember that studio apartment I had over on Jenkins Street. Don't you? I know you remember that big Jacuzzi tub..."

"Please, Andre. Don't go there." An ache tore into Riana's heart to hear him talk about the past.

"Why?" he gently probed.

"It makes me uncomfortable, that's why. It was so long ago. Bringing up all that stuff won't change what's happened between us. Let it go, please."

"But I don't want to. And I don't want to let you go again, either," he replied with an ease that made Riana tense.

Her mind was congested with doubts, fears and most of all, temptation. Why did he have to make this reunion so damned difficult when it could have been so simple? She shook off his words, returning to her mission. "Just fill out the papers, okay?"

"I'll fill them out later," he replied, a flicker of a break in his voice. He set them aside and leveled a disturbing stare at her.

Riana moved forward on her stool, avoiding his gaze and planting both feet on the floor. Looking up, she zeroed in on him, knowing she had to recapture control of the situation. She filled her lungs, drawing air in through her nose as she lifted her chest and prepared to get back to business. "When?" she stated, flinging the word at him like a dart.

However, Andre didn't flinch, in fact he simply blinked at her, clearly dodging the question.

"Not good enough, Andre," Riana countered, her voice and her temper now rising. "Tonight. You have to give me this information tonight. I have a telephone conference scheduled with Allen tomorrow morning and I need to have this part of the process finished before we talk."

"How long will it take you to complete your part?" Andre asked, as if toying with her impatience.

"I don't know. Most of tonight. If I get started right away. I'm going to do a lot of the background check online by using the Web sites of various agencies, but then, I may have to make some follow-up phone calls tomorrow to clarify any gaps or discrepancies. You'd be surprised by how many people have the same first and last names, or a messed-up Social Security number, or no recollection of a former address. If I have any questions, though, I'll call you first, just to be sure everything is correct."

Though he nodded his understanding, he told her, "Sorry, but your paperwork will have to wait. Can't do it right now. I'm really tired, Riana. You see, I just got back from—"

"Jamaica," Riana finished his sentence with a hint of satisfaction. *Very little gets past me,* she thought, enjoying his startled reaction. "Did you have a nice time in the islands?"

Chapter 15

Riana watched as Andre's lips curved down in surprise, pushing his eyebrows high on his broad forehead. He slid off the corner of his desk, circled it, sat down in his high-backed leather chair, and began moving from side to side. Seated, his eyes were now level with hers, leveling their playing field, too. He wanted to play games with her, well, she was prepared to join in.

"How did you know where I went?" he asked suspiciously.

"Oh, I learned about it by accident, really. I'm not having you followed, if that's what you're implying. You remember my cousin Felicia?"

Andre inclined his head.

"Well, Felicia was working the night shift at the airport on Saturday. She saw you boarding a flight to Miami. She checked your itinerary and saw that you were going on to Kingston, Jamaica. Was she wrong?"

"Hmm." Andre laced his fingers together and studied them. "No, she was correct. I went to Jamaica, all right."

"A quickie getaway vacation?"

"No, I had some business to take care of. That's why I couldn't call."

"Oh, really? Please. Give me a break! Just because you were traveling didn't mean you could blow me off. You have a cell phone. There are pay phones everywhere. Face it, Andre, it was rude of you to take off like that. Why are you dragging your feet all of a sudden? If you don't want to pursue this position with the Allen Group, just tell me now so I won't waste any more of my time, or yours. Why can't you be honest with me?"

The wail of a police siren outside filled the empty space that followed, a screeching sound that seemed to do what Riana couldn't. She wanted to scream her frustration at Andre, let him know how annoyed she was with what seemed like his deliberate attempts to interfere with the job she was being paid to do. She had gone after the candidate that George Allen wanted despite her reservations, but for some reason Andre was determined to mess things up. If he kept this up, she'd have no problem dropping him as a candidate and starting over.

"You're right," Andre finally conceded. "I should be honest with you. I do want the position with the Allen Group, but I don't want to rush the recruitment process, either. I have several important matters I need to take care of before I can do anything about Allen's offer."

"Okaaay…" Riana drew out her response in a mellow voice, wanting to get a better feel for the situation. She would let him explain. Try to be more accommodating. Slow down a bit and listen. If humoring Andre would help her fulfill this contract, so be it. She snapped her briefcase shut and stood. "What kind of issues do you need to take care of? Work-related projects? Some new design you're doing for a client?"

"I can't say much about it right now."

"In Jamaica?" Riana ventured.

Andre nodded.

"Really? And how much time do you think you'll need to finish it?"

"I don't know. Maybe a few weeks."

"A few weeks? I don't think so. Surely you don't expect me to hold off on my recruitment of you until you're ready?" Now, Riana's words resounded with a sharper edge.

Slowly, Andre moved his head up and down, studying her through his lashes. "I hope so. I hope you'd do that—for me."

"And why should I?" she had to ask.

"Because you know me. I'm not a stranger whose résumé you located on a Web site. I'm the man you once sat beside in class, the man you used to study with. You helped me pass a very difficult course, Riana, and without your help I never would have become the man George Allen wants to work for him. You listened to me when I told you about my plans of becoming an engineer, and when I told you how much I wanted to have a successful career. You were the only person I dared to tell my dreams to, and now you're in a position to make them come true. Kinda ironic isn't it?"

His words drifted to Riana like a gentle plea, yet they ricocheted inside her like tiny bits of glass. He sounded so honest, so bitingly sincere, and his words told her that he wasn't playing games, that he wasn't plotting to string her along and then drop out of the running simply to satisfy some need for revenge. He was asking for her understanding—as she had once asked of him. How could she turn away?

"The timing isn't right? Is that what you're saying?" Riana continued, hoping she had read him right.

Andre stood and came around his desk, standing so close to her that she could smell the fresh scent of soap that still clung to his skin, feel the heat of his body.

"Yeah, that's it. The timing is off," Andre replied in a voice that was husky and rough around the edges. "Just like it was for us four years ago, remember?" He shifted closer, extended a hand and brushed a finger over Riana's cheek. "When you left Houston and returned to San Antonio, I was broken up for a long time, Riana. I hated you, I loved you, I wanted to call, I didn't want to hear your voice. But through all the confusion, I knew one thing—I missed the hell out of you and I loved you. I must have gone through every possible stage of pain and misery until I found a way to put you out of my mind and go on."

"How'd you do that?" she whispered, a rawness in her words that underscored the thread of curious apprehension that was beginning to unwind.

"I told myself that I was honoring your wishes by giving up on our relationship," Andre confessed. "I convinced myself that I was making *you* happy, even though I was making myself miserable. I did what you wanted me to do because you asked me to. Now, I'm asking you to do the same. Give me a few weeks, Riana, and I promise I'll do everything possible to make sure the Allen Group contract is yours. It's business, isn't it? You want the contract and I want the job, so we ought to work together. Can you do that? For me?"

Unable to resist his touch, his plea, the correctness of what he'd said, Riana reached up and took Andre's hand in hers, stroking his fingers with hers. He had a point. When she had needed him to honor her request, in spite of what she knew it would cost them both, he had done so. For her. The least she could do was try. "I'll do what I can to buy some time on this, but you've gotta understand that Allen calls the shots. He's the one with the deadline."

"I understand, but will you try to slow it down? Can you?"

"I'll do my best."

After giving her a crooked, almost bashful smile, Andre leaned in, kissed Riana gently on the cheek, and whispered, "Thanks," in her ear.

Swinging back her head, Riana tried to ignore the fluttering sensation that his kiss initiated between her thighs, the pulse of warmth that lingered there, the weakness that filtered from her lips to the soles of her feet. *This can't be happening,* she told herself, craving more than just his peck of a kiss on her cheek. This was the only man she had ever really loved, the only man whose body she longed to feel joined with hers. And he was asking for her help, letting her know in his own way that he had forgiven her for hurting him in her impulsive rush to get on with her life.

In an instant, she knew that she would give him, not only the time he'd asked for, but her heart and soul once more.

The muffled sound that Riana heard coming from her mouth seemed to vibrate in the stillness that descended over them, intensifying the emotionally charged moment. Placing one hand at the nape of his neck, she urged his mouth to cover hers, and when it did, she accepted him hungrily, devouring the long penetrating thrusts of his tongue as she melded her body to his.

The bump of his sudden erection against her leg sent shock waves of longing through Riana, edging her closer and closer to that point where she knew there would be no turning back. The thought of losing herself in loving Andre once again filled her mind so completely that she did not resist when his fingers inched their way beneath her blouse, to the hooks of her thin lace bra, which he easily released to free her breasts. She strained against him when his palm swept over one hard nipple, then the other, making her cry aloud and break off the kiss. She buried her head in his shoulder and filled her nostrils with his scent, holding on to him as she felt his passion vibrating inside. It had been four long years since they had come together willingly, and the reunion was tenderly, yet cautiously unfolding.

When he swept her blouse off her shoulders and let it fall to the floor, she dissolved, discarding all uncertainty and fear. The temptation to love him was too great, he was much too close to her, too easy to embrace.

"Andre," she moaned, almost in a growl, knowing what she wanted, knowing what she'd have to do to make it happen, too. "Love me. Now."

With a tug, she helped him pull his shirt over his head, and then folded herself into the contours of his chest, letting the floodgates of her need for him open without restraint as her fingers moved to the zipper of his jeans.

"You know we belong together," he said in hushed tones, saying exactly the words that were spinning in her head. "We clicked from the beginning, and now you're here again. The past doesn't matter. What matters is that we've found our way back to each other and I swear, I don't plan to ever let you go."

Knowing he was right, Riana clung to Andre, accepting the rain of kisses he showered over her face, her neck, her bare, hot breasts as he stepped out of his jeans and stood naked before her. She slid her hands over his back and down to his buttocks, hard and smooth as sculpted stone. Blood rushed to her head when he picked her up, carried her to his bed, and placed her down with an easy shift of their bodies that sent Riana hurtling back in time.

Slowly, he began to undress her. She melted under his touch. His moves were the same, though even better than she remembered, and the familiar ritual splintered her restraint. Her long-held denial of her true feelings for Andre gave way to a sense of rightness that forced Riana to relax and let herself be loved. Pulling Andre close, she shamelessly gave in to the heat they had created, eager to play in the fire she had prayed she'd feel once more.

As Andre touched and tasted each curve, angle and crevice of her body, Riana explored his. When the heel of his hand massaged her spine, her index finger traced the outline of his ear. When his knee slipped between her thighs and gently moved them apart, her legs swept up to wrap around his waist, and she anchored her body to his.

With a thrust that brought exquisite moans of resignation and delight from them both, Andre settled over Riana in one pleasure-filled movement.

He was hers once more, and she did not feel his weight, only the lift of her heart as they rocked to a rhythm that neither had forgotten, a rhythm that carried them higher and higher into their own special world.

Chapter 16

A sense of satisfied contentment buzzed inside Riana as she tilted her nose toward the bedroom ceiling and inhaled the delicious aroma of Andre's blueberry pancakes. He had insisted she stay in bed while he showered and made them breakfast, and now the smell coming from his kitchen was almost as heavenly as the night they had spent together.

With a stretch of her legs, she filled up the other side of the bed, still slightly warm from Andre's presence. Pulling the gray-and-white striped sheet up over her shoulders, she crushed a handful of the cloth in a fist and pressed it to her cheek, savoring the familiar woodsy-lime scent of Andre's skin, content to be back in his arms, back in his bed, back in his life.

Smothering a giggle, she let her thoughts drift back over their impulsive, but oh-so-right reunion last night. After their initial encounter, which had left them both breathless with joy and unable to deny their attraction, they remained in each other's arms and talked long into the night, with occasional breaks to sip a glass of wine or change the music on the CD player. They made love again, and talked forever, eager to catch up on the four years they'd been apart. Not surprisingly, they both confessed to suffering through a series of unfulfilling, shallow relationships that had gone nowhere, with neither finding the perfect person to settle down with, making Riana realize how much of a chance she had taken, giving up the best man she'd ever known, and how lucky she was to have found him again. Now, all she wanted to do was make love to Andre, hold him close, and prove to him that she was never going to slip away again.

"Blueberry pancakes with whipped butter cream," Andre announced as he entered the bedroom holding a tray with two mugs of coffee and one big plate piled high with his fluffy, syrupy creations.

Riana hurried to sit up and shoved her pillow behind her back against the tall curved headboard of Andre's sleigh bed.

Andre placed the tray on Riana's lap, handed her a fork, and then settled in beside her. "Dig in while they're hot," he ordered, cutting off a piece for himself which he shoved into his mouth. "Hmm. Haven't lost my touch," he mumbled between chews. "If I say so myself."

After tasting a sugary bite, Riana agreed. "No, you haven't lost your touch. In fact, I think you've improved. Been practicing on someone?" As soon as the question slipped out, she regretted it. Glancing at Andre out of the corner of her eye, she grimaced, but held her tongue.

Andre pointed his fork at Riana and jabbed the air as he spoke. "For your information, I have *not* made these pancakes for any other woman. Not one time since we broke up. Not even for myself, now that I think about it. They reminded me too much of you, I guess, so I lost my appetite for them."

"I'm sorry. I didn't mean…" Riana stumbled over her words, wondering if subconsciously she had really meant to ask the question, hoping to find out if he might have been faithful to her in just this little way. Blueberry pancakes after a great night of sex had been their special ritual. She swallowed a sip of hot coffee. Andre's voice had been hard, and now his eyes shone with hurt. She had really struck a nerve. "I was joking. Okay? Forgive me?" she prodded, giving him her most contrite expression.

Ducking his head, Andre managed a quick nod and then resumed eating, closing that topic of conversation.

"Tell me about Jamaica," Riana began, wanting to change the subject. "Is it a big project you're working on? A hotel, a tourist resort?"

"Nothing like that," Andre mumbled in an offhand manner. He gulped a mouthful of coffee from the mug and then set it on his bedside table. "It's a business transaction I need to complete. The details are kinda up in the air. Don't know how it'll go."

"So you might have to go back to Jamaica?" Riana asked.

"Possibly," Andre replied nonchalantly.

"Maybe I could go with you next time? I've never been. I'd love to see it." When Andre didn't respond, she rushed on. "Oh, I wouldn't get in the way, if that's what you're worried about. I can entertain myself when you're tied up in meetings, and then we could do some fun things together when you're free. I know how hectic it is when you have business to take care of, but it might be nice to relax for a while, too."

"We'll see," he told her in a less-than-enthusiastic manner, picking up his napkin. He swiped it over his lips and then swung his feet to the floor. "In fact, I gotta get going right now. An early meeting with a client downtown."

Riana mocked a frown at the clock on his dresser. "It's only seven-thirty! You have to leave now?"

"Yeah. I'd better get going, but you stay put for as long as you want. Take a shower, relax. Lester won't be in today. He and his partner, Todd, are spending the day apartment-hunting. So, there's no reason for you to run off."

After Andre left, Riana did take a quick shower, located one of his large T-shirts in a top drawer and put it on, and then poured herself another cup of coffee, in no real hurry to go back to her hotel. She reviewed the preliminary contract for Rodney Robert's franchise, ready to close the deal as soon as her accountant approved the figures she e-mailed to him. If all went well, the next day, she'd arrange for the transfer of funds from her money-market account to Houston, to be prepared for when they moved toward closing. A call to Tanisha proved everything in the San Antonio office was under control, so there was no need for concern there. To be honest, Riana was so high on happiness that she could hardly focus on anything other than the bliss of being back with Andre. However, she did have to call George Allen and try to buy some time.

"He's got a lot going for him," she told Allen when she got him on the line. "Good work ethic. Very efficient office space. Forward-thinking. Our initial interview on Friday went well, and I'm working on his background check. Shouldn't have any problems, just need a few more details to complete it. He's a level-headed guy with a solid reputation for turning out top-notch work and doing it on time. I spoke with city councilman, Oliver Winder, one of the judges for the Space City Improvement Award. Only had good things to say. Said he's a talented, capable guy with a bright future in the industry. I think I can safely recommend Andre to lead your design team."

"Sounds good so far. But the criminal background check is necessary," Allen replied. "I can't get him bonded and insured for this kind of a project without proof of a clean record. Government red tape, you know?"

"Oh, sure. He understands that it's just a formality. However, Andre is a lot busier than I'd thought he'd be. Seems he's in the middle of a big project in Jamaica that he wants to finish before he commits to anything new."

"What kind of time are we looking at? I'm on a tight deadline here. I don't know if…"

Allen's hesitancy made Riana tense. "A week. Maybe a little more," she hedged, trying not to lie. "And in the meantime, why don't we go ahead and set up his personal interview with you, so you can meet him, feel him out for yourself. By then, his Jamaica project should be in its final stages."

"Yes, we could do that. Might save some time. How about next Monday? I'm in the office all morning."

"Good. I'll see if that works for Andre and get back to you."

"Fine. Call my secretary and set it up. I'm looking forward to meeting Preaux."

With that bit of business finished, Riana felt as if a huge weight had been lifted. Somehow, she'd buy Andre the time he needed.

An urge to skip work for the rest of the day hit her, and her thoughts turned to playing hooky to hang out at Andre's until he returned. She wandered over to the CD player and put on a vintage Al Jarreau. When the singer's smooth voice swelled into the room, Riana smiled: she and Andre had the same taste in music. They also enjoyed the same kind of food, wine, Jacuzzi baths, and now that his firm was taking off, he better understood what she had been facing when they were together four years ago. They both had businesses to run. It seemed as if their separation had allowed them to grow closer, instead of apart.

It was nice, being in Andre's apartment alone. She liked the fact that he trusted her to be there, as he had in the past, and she could suddenly envision them as a married couple, sharing a home and sharing their love as their high-powered careers zoomed forward.

Riana padded barefoot across Andre's Oriental rug to the overburdened bookshelves crammed with novels, biographies, art and architecture tomes and a good supply of reference books, too. She scanned the shelves, smiling. They had pretty much the same taste in reading material, too.

Finding an oversized World Atlas, she pulled the book out and sat on the floor with the pages opened to a full-size map of Jamaica. "Ocho Rios, Negril, Kingston," she murmured, trying to envision the blue water, the white sandy beaches, the tropical mountains all around, a bit annoyed that Andre had not rushed to say that he would take her back to the island if his project required a return visit. It would be wonderful to spend time at the ocean, where it was beautiful and calm. They could rent a little beach-front place, take late-night swims, sit in the sand in the moonlight, drink rum and make love. With a sigh, Riana closed her eyes, envisioning the blissful time they would have.

While she was thinking about Jamaica, Andre's office phone rang. Riana stood, wondering if she should answer it. Her cell was still turned off. Andre wouldn't be able to get through to her any other way. She went into his office, reached for the phone, and then decided against it. He hadn't given her permission to answer his business line, and she didn't want to overstep any boundaries. However, she did take a peek at the caller ID: 011-876-6567, and immediately recognized that it was an international call. Could 876 be the country code for Jamaica? she wondered, starting to turn away.

However, when she caught sight of the profile paper she had given Andre last night, she paused. It was still sitting in the top of his in basket, and still blank. *He'd better hustle his butt and fill this out so I can close this deal,* she thought, looking around

Andre's office, tempted to do a little snooping. She could probably locate his Social Security number and his driver's license
number somewhere among his files, complete the profile page,
do the more in-depth background check and be done with it.
But she knew she wasn't going to do that. He trusted her, she
trusted him. She wasn't going to mess things up.

Riana returned to perusing the World Atlas, ashamed of her
reaction. *Go slow. Don't press him. He'll come around when
the time is right.*

Andre stepped into Frazer's office just as the agent was
hanging up the phone.

"Good. You're here," Frazer said, swiveling around in his
government-issue chair. "Hoped you'd make it. I have a unit
meeting in fifteen minutes, but I wanted to hear what you found
out. Sorry, I don't have more time. Sit down, please. Tell me
what you know."

Andre sat down in the chair across from Frazer, eyes alert,
ready to spill all that Kay had told him, praying that Frazer
would agree to help her get out of Jamaica and off the no-fly
list so that she and Lonny could come to Houston. Trying to
rush, but not about to leave out any important details, he re-
traced the steps of his trip and filled Frazer in on what he knew.

"You believe Jamal is dead?" Frazer asked when Andre
finished.

"Yeah. I do. The harbor explosion was in the papers. I read
all about it, and if he *was* on that boat, he was blown to bits."
Andre tapped his finger on the arm of his chair, as if empha-
sizing his point.

"She willing to give up some names? Give a statement to
the local police about what she knows?"

Now, Andre rubbed his top lip with his thumb, considering
his response. "Jamal associated with some pretty dangerous

characters. They've convinced Kay that she's not going to have any trouble from them as long as she stays away from the police. She's in a difficult position. She wants to cooperate, but she's afraid. She's living like a fugitive, cramped in two rooms above a grimy café. That's no way to live and no way to raise a child, either. I hate to think of how difficult it must be for her and my nephew, suffering like that."

The freckles on Frazer's face seemed to darken as he studied Andre. "If you can convince her to talk to us, we might find a way to get her out of Jamaica and settled safely here in Houston."

"And once you've got what you need, maybe you can help me erase my juvenile arrest for good?"

"Well, let's be real here," Frazer sat back, rocking in his chair. "First, she spills what she knows to the authorities. We check out her story. If what she has to say helps solve Eddie Brooks's murder, then she's got a good shot at getting our help."

"And my old prison record?"

"I can't make it go away, but I might find a way to bury it so deep in the system that it'd take a professional law enforcement officer to find it."

"That would be a big help." The thought of his record being so difficult to find that no amateur would know how to locate it gave Andre hope. "Now, about Kay," he went on. "Won't she be somewhat vulnerable during the time it will take for you to question her and then follow up on her leads?"

"A chance she'd have to take."

"Sounds risky."

"She lived with a very risky man. He's dead. She ought to want to do this, especially for her kid."

"I'll talk to her," Andre promised.

"Do that, and then let me know what she wants to do."

Leaving the Federal Building, Andre headed to his car, considering his options. If Kay agreed to tell all, he might have to go back to help her through the ordeal. But how could he leave now? Especially with Riana back in his life? No way could she go with him, but how could he tell her no?

Just thinking of Riana sent an unexpected jolt of desire through him. Last night's lovemaking was still raw and fresh, filling his head and swelling his heart. They had come together with even more passion and tenderness than before and he knew they were going to make it this time. She wanted him. He wanted her. Nothing else mattered as far as he was concerned.

Andre returned home to find Riana still there, dressed in one of his oversized T-shirts. It was black with gold letters across the front that read, Spring Fun Run for Food, from one of his many charity fund-raiser runs. She was sitting on the sofa, her long bare legs tucked beneath her hips, talking on her cell phone. The sight of her made him go weak with contentment and flash hot with longing, too. It felt right—having her there in his apartment, settled among his things, looking as if she belonged there and would always be waiting for him when he came home. It was a scene he had imagined so many times over the years, and now it was a reality, exactly as he had hoped it might be one day.

She looked up at him and waved, and then covered the mouthpiece of her phone.

"Felicia," she whispered. "She's having a party and wants us to come."

Giving her a nod of approval, Andre left Riana to finish her conversation and went into his office, saw the message light blinking red on his phone and engaged the voice mail. It was Kay, and she wanted to talk to him right away.

"She'll have to wait," he murmured under his breath, hoping she was not in danger. After erasing the call, he went into the kitchen, removed a soda from the fridge, popped the top and took a long swallow. Bending down, he scanned the shelves, scowling. No more sodas left. Apparently, Lester must have drunk them all while he was gone. Andre made a mental note to buy more.

He shut the refrigerator door and was about to turn around when he suddenly felt Riana's arms slip around him from behind. He smiled and leaned back into her surprise embrace, his hands clasped tightly over hers, savoring the feel of her pressed up against him.

"I didn't expect you back so soon," she murmured into his back.

"I told you I wouldn't be long," he replied, smiling even more broadly as she rubbed her cheek along his spine and slipped her hands lower on his torso. His entire body tingled with a sudden need for her, which he could feel growing in his groin. When he was with Riana he was helpless to deny that he wanted all of her, and was willing to do whatever she asked of him to have it. "And I thought you'd be gone by now," he uttered, struggling to pull his mind from her roaming hands and the insistent bulge growing in his slacks. "Didn't you say you had work to do?"

"I did it from here," she replied, in a self-satisfied tone, rubbing her breasts over his back. "Called my office. Everything is going fine. No major issues that require my attention. I spoke with George Allen, also. He's so hot to get you on board, he didn't make a fuss about waiting for you to finish your Jamaica project before you start."

Now, Andre turned in the circle of their embrace and looked down at Riana, studying the exquisite planes of her face, her perfectly sculpted nose, the way her light brown hair swung over one eye. "He didn't balk?"

"Nope. In fact, he seemed to understand completely. I don't want you to feel as if I'm putting any pressure on you, but I would like for you to meet with him as soon as you can."

Andre nuzzled the soft spot beneath Riana's jaw, and then kissed the lobe of her ear. "We'll see," he said in a deep voice, too distracted by her beauty, the feel of her hands on him, and his own rising lust to talk business. "Just let me think about it, okay."

Tilting back her head, Riana pinned him with a mischievous grin. "Okay. You can think about it. So, what's on your agenda for the rest of the day?"

Without answering, Andre grazed his teeth along her neck, fastened them onto the neckline of her T-shirt and tugged at the fabric until he had eased it off one shoulder. He made a small circle with his tongue on her bronze skin. The taste of her flesh quickened his pulse and ramped his craving up another notch as he slid his hands low, and then cupped them beneath her hips. "You're the only action item on my agenda, if that's okay with you."

"I'm down with being acted on," she teased right back. "How long do you think this meeting is going to last?"

"The rest of my life, I hope," he replied, his voice so thick with longing he could barely utter the words.

Having Riana back in his life fulfilled his every dream, but having her back in his bed right then was top priority. When she arched into the kisses he began placing on her neck, he felt her firm bra-less breasts straining against the thin piece of fabric that separated her from him. It pleased him to realize that she was as anxious to make love as he was, and holding on to her with one arm, he ran a hand beneath her shirt and massaged one breast, then the other with a feathery touch, stroking nipples which had hardened into nuggets of sinful pleasure.

A sharp sob flew from Riana's lips, stopping him short. Concerned, he pulled his hand away and squinted at her. "What's wrong?"

She didn't answer right away and the pause was agonizing. Andre began to feel his erection fade, his joy slip away.

"I love you, Andre. That's all," she finally said. "Nothing's wrong. Just keep doing what you're doing and everything will be fine."

"You don't have to tell me twice," he replied, his mouth devouring hers as his fingers worked their magic.

Chapter 17

The two dozen jewel-toned roses arrived at six, the Tex-Mex caterer pulled in at seven, and by eight, the DJ—Felicia's sixteen-year-old nephew—had his station set up by the bar in the den and was trying out his music. Riana had arrived at Felicia's about noon to help her prepare for the party, which was turning into a major event. Immediately, Riana had been swept into Felicia's pressurized excitement when they decided to add drama to the ambiance by stringing lines of bright gemstones throughout the house, turning it into a treasure trove of glitter.

Felicia, dressed in dark-rinse jeans studded down the sides with fiery-green fake emeralds, a soft cowl-neck blouse in a vibrant shade of sapphire, and sandals encrusted with rhinestones entered the kitchen just as Riana hung the last string of luminous pearls in the doorway leading to the patio.

"Looks like a Turkish sultan's palace in here," she told

Riana, going over to pull back the pearl drape curtain and peek out at the patio where round tables covered with glittering sequined cloths waited for guests under a rented canopy. "You done good, girl."

Grinning, Riana took a bow. "Thank you very much. Glad I could help out. You said you wanted the place to look bejeweled, so I followed your instructions. Now, what else needs to be done?"

Felicia waved her fingers, sending sparks of light from the huge gemstone rings on both of her hands. "Not too much. Let's hit that doorway over there and then you need to get dressed before Malcom arrives. He's coming early and I want you two to talk, get to know each other before everybody else arrives. See if you can get him to open up about our relationship."

"Having issues with Malcom?" Riana teased, sensing an ulterior motive in Felicia's request. "You want me to check him out and then give you my opinion about where he stands?"

"Damn straight. Sometimes I think he's playin' me and sometimes I think he's just too good to be true." Felicia shook her head. "Blows hot, then cool. Drives me crazy. Just wanna make sure I'm not readin' things wrong. We've been dating for a while now, so I'm thinking this is an exclusive relationship, you know? But then he casually drops hints about parties he's gone to without me and people I don't know."

"Doesn't mean he's seeing anybody else," Riana added, trying to sound supportive.

"I know, but it means he might be shoppin' for a brand-new model, true?"

"I guess so...." Riana replied, feeling the concern that radiated from her cousin's face. "Leave it to me. I know just the questions to ask to get the answers you want."

"Good. I'm counting on you, cuz. Now, what about Andre? What time is he coming? He has my address, doesn't he?"

"Yes, Felicia. He hasn't forgotten where you live, and he'll be here about nine," Riana replied, glad she had spilled the news about her and Andre to her cousin, even though she'd had to eat her earlier words of denial. "In fact, he hasn't forgotten anything. It's like we've never been apart."

"Girl, didn't I tell you you weren't through with that brother?" Felicia shot back. "Talkin' that smack about, 'it's just business between us,'" Felicia mocked in a high-pitched voice. "He's takin' care of *business,* all right. And I'm glad you got enough sense to let him."

"Felicia. Please. We do still have real business to take care of. I'm trying to convince him to drive back to San Antonio with me tomorrow."

"So you can spend a lazy Sunday on the River Walk with your honey?"

"That's part of it," Riana coyly replied. "But on Monday, Andre has an interview set up with George Allen." Riana sighed. "The problem is, he doesn't know about it yet, and I sure hope he agrees to go."

Felicia stopped what she was doing and looked over at Riana, a length of beads entwined in her fingers. "Uh-oh. I hear something in your voice that shouldn't be there. Why wouldn't he go to the interview? Andre's got all the credentials. What's missing?"

A hint of a scowl pulled Riana's brows together. Biting her lower lip, she thought for a moment, and then told Felicia, "His criminal background check. I should have completed it last week, and it's still not finished."

"And why haven't you done it?"

"Because Andre is dragging his feet on giving me the information required for the search and he hasn't signed the release I need to access some of the more sensitive records."

For a long moment, the only sound in the room was the

voice of Mary J. Blige's "Be Without You," coming from the DJ's station in the den. Finally, Felicia ventured a question. "What's up with him? What's your boy hiding?"

"I don't think he's hiding anything. I think he's deliberately stalling the process. He has a big job in Jamaica he said he wants to finish, so he asked me for more time."

"Oh? You believe him?"

"Yeah, I do," Riana said, wishing she felt better about Andre's request, but knew better than to press him. She draped the last string of pearls over the entry and got down from her stepstool. "All done," she told Felicia, wanting to end their conversation about Andre, telling herself that he would come through once they got to San Antonio.

"Well, if you believe your honey, that's all that matters. Now, you go and get dressed," Felicia ordered, giving Riana a playful shove toward the hallway. "I'm gonna check on the food."

"I'm gone," Riana replied, hurrying up the stairs and into the same bedroom where she had stayed while taking her class in Houston four years ago.

Shaking off thoughts about Andre's upcoming interview, she hurried to finish dressing. A swipe of blush, a lipstick retouch, another coat of black mascara and her makeup looked good as new. A few bumps with the hot curling iron on the ends of her hair and her do sprang back to life. Gold lamé halter top. Round hoop earrings dripping with crystal teardrops. A struggle to squeeze into a pair of pale-blue jeans with a rhinestone floral pattern trailing across the hips. And Lucite wedges sprinkled with a dusting of silver.

Feeling fine and festive, excited and ready to party, Riana gave herself a close inspection in the mirror and grinned. "Been a long time since I've felt this way. Like a college student on spring break." Pausing to savor the moment, she realized that maybe her sister, her mother and her father were right: she had been working too hard for too long. There was more to life than contracts, meetings and negotiations. She deserved to have some fun.

By ten o'clock Felicia's house was so full of partiers that shoulders rubbed shoulders and there was little room to move without taking someone with you. But the guests didn't mind. In fact, they were like a big happy family sharing laughter, jokes, high fives and backslapping that went on all evening long. The party rocked along with Felicia meeting, greeting and fussing over everyone, only breaking away from her hostess duties to join in the riotous sessions of the Harlem Shuffle that would break out at any moment and make the whole house vibrate.

When a slow tune came up, Riana nestled in Andre's arms as they moved to Lionel Richie's voice, her body absorbing his heat as they swayed from side to side—as they had done with every song that allowed them to slip into each other's arms and get lost in their sizzling reunion. Looking over Andre's shoulder, Riana saw Malcom and Felicia locked in a similar embrace, and the sight made her smile. Malcom's height was a match for Felicia, who Riana knew was five-ten in flats. His rich brown skin, wavy hair and suave good looks reminded her of a young Billy Dee and he was even wearing a white linen suit with a black shirt, a definite fashion statement.

"Malcom's a very nice guy," she said to Andre, who simply murmured a vague response. "I spent some time with him earlier in the evening and he was not bashful about admitting how smitten he is with Felicia."

"Good for them," Andre managed, tightening his hold on Riana.

She molded her body even closer to his. "Felicia has nothing to worry about. The guy's in love. I told her she needs to relax and stop second-guessing every move he makes."

Now, Andre leaned away and peered down at Riana. "You been giving her advice about love?"

Riana lifted her shoulder in a quick shrug. "No, only my opinion. That's what she asked for, so I told her what I thought."

"Hmm," Andre murmured. "And what does a man in love look like?" he asked.

"He looks happy and confused and worried and elated. Kinda like you," Riana tossed back, swaying with Andre as he swept her into a turn and refocused on the music.

"Nothing wrong with that," he blatantly admitted, voice firm with pride.

Fanning herself after the end of a long dance set, Riana escaped outside to the patio while Andre went to the bar for two glasses of wine. She sat down at one of the round tables, sank back on her spine and looked up at the stars. The night was clear, warm and magical. The starry display overhead competed with the shimmering glow of Felicia's decorations, making Riana feel as if she had stepped into fantasy fairyland where she was the princess and Andre, her prince.

All evening, Andre had been attentive, buoyant, spontaneous. He let everyone know that he was totally into her, and each time she caught him looking at her with those intensely seductive eyes, a slow tingle started in her chest and slid into her stomach, tightening it in desire. Even when his hand wasn't at her back or on her arm or clasped with hers, she could feel the heat of his touch radiating toward her, vibrating the air between them.

Earlier, when Andre had walked into the party, Riana had seen the catty stares coming from sisters standing around the room. A flash of heat zipped through her body, welding her in place as she watched his long legs eat up the space between them. He was wearing low-rise jeans that hugged his hips with a silver belt buckle anchored at his waist. His light-beige chambray shirt was open at the neck, displaying a generous amount of smooth, hairless chest in delicious caramel-brown. The only thing she'd enjoyed more than watching the curious women watch him, was the kiss he leaned down to plant on her lips.

"Having a good time?" Andre now asked, handing Riana a glass of white wine.

"Wonderful," she told him, raising her glass to touch rims with his. "Felicia has pulled off another one of her legendary parties, and I think this one will go down as the best yet."

"You and your cousin are pretty close, aren't you?" Andre asked in a deeper voice than he had been using, suddenly sounding serious. He reached over to take her hand in his.

"Yeah," Riana replied, tracing a finger over the inside of his wrist. "Our birthdays are only two days apart, September twelfth and fourteenth, so when we were younger, my mom and my aunt always let us celebrate together. I really believe that's when this party bug first hit Felicia. She always planned our birthday bashes, and they were the most outrageous parties you could imagine. We stayed tight through high school, and even after I left for college to go to UT and she went off to Prairie View, we still got together as often as possible."

"But what about your sister? Are you as close with her?"

"Right. Britt. She's busy being a wife and raising a family, so her social circle doesn't exactly collide with mine. We stay in touch, but we don't hang out, party or shop together. Know what I mean?"

"Sure. Completely. I can tell that you and Felicia have a good time together. That's nice," Andre remarked with a hint of sadness that made Riana wonder if she had said something wrong. Long ago, he had told her that he had no family to speak of, only a few cousins back in Louisiana whom he had not seen in years and did not care to know.

"Yeah. I can't imagine not having her around," Riana added,

and then asked, "Did you ever have a close cousin or a friend… when you were young?"

"I've been on my own since I was a teenager," Andre told her. "Kind of a loner, I guess. My family wasn't exactly the kind that had dinner together every night, if you know what I mean. I never really got to know my dad, even though he lived in the same town. My mom died when I was…away. Never had anyone to rely on but myself. Had a few buddies I used to hang out with when I was doing construction work, and they were cool, but I moved on. Things started changin' fast for me. My studies and then my work took up all of my time and I've never worried much about makin' new friends." His low chuckle sounded strained.

"Hey, even though I have a mother, a father, a sister, a bunch of nieces and nephews and lots of cousins in my family, I still feel pretty much alone sometimes," Riana said, trying to make Andre feel better. "It's hard to meet everyone's expectations, you know? They all think they know what's best for me. I ought to stop working so hard. Stay out of debt, don't expand my business. Be careful. Be cautious. Ugh!" She faked a gag. "I don't pay any attention to them. I like my life the way it is, and I'm going to live it as I please."

"For real." His tone was rough with emotion. With a quick tilt of his glass, he finished his drink and lowered his lashes as he spoke. "Wanna dance some more or are you ready to leave?"

His question lit Riana's eyes. She knew what he meant, knew what she wanted, and sensed that his anticipation was as intense as hers. "Let's go. If you want, we can move our party to another level," she whispered sexily, knowing she was not going to struggle to keep from falling into his arms as soon as they were alone. She'd already lost that battle, and was more than content to surrender.

"Let's roll. I'm with you," Andre told her, standing and offering her his hand.

* * *

Riana's hotel room was at the back of the building, facing a landscaped area where people didn't gather and no parking was allowed. That made for the kind of peace and quiet that she appreciated, and added to the sense of privacy she enjoyed.

As soon as they entered her bedroom, Andre untied the straps of Riana's halter top and let it fall to her waist. Bending, he slid his tongue over her chest, across one breast and then fastened his lips over the other to suckle hard, yet gently.

Shivering in pleasure, Riana fell back onto the bed and pulled him down with her, sweeping them into a delicious whirlwind of tasting and touching and stroking that continued until all clothing had been shed and their bodies were locked together.

In the dimly lit room, Riana accepted Andre with tender urgency, guiding him into her with a shudder of satisfaction. As he moved in and out, stroking her with a gentle, but ever-increasing urgency, the intensity of her love for him swelled, sealing all cracks of doubt. They'd reclaimed their love, physically and emotionally, and she would never again hold back.

His hardness filled her up. She tensed the muscles that she knew would draw him even deeper into her core, no longer concerned with maintaining that cool facade of a "business-only relationship." That lie had been shattered for good, and now all she wanted was to focus on the passionate journey that they had begun.

In paced, deliberate pulses, she rode the wave, moving with him, feeling his flesh, slick with perspiration slide over hers as he explored her body with his hands and his tongue. His kisses left her breathless, barely satisfying her hunger for him, urging her to demand more and more until he brought her to fulfillment. Within seconds, he too, exploded in release. Panting in each other's arms, she listened to his gasps of contentment, drenched in the passion that had swept her to such heights.

Afterward, still locked in an embrace, they lay in bed and talked about their future: her bid for the Houston office of Executive Suites, and his upcoming job—the reason she had come to Houston in the first place.

"When I spoke to George Allen about slowing the process down, he was okay with that, but still pretty adamant about meeting with you."

"I dunno if I should do that right now," Andre started.

"Why not? At least go to meet him… Don't you want to make sure Allen is the kind of man you want to work with?"

"Hmm," Andre murmured. "That's a good point. Maybe I should go. When?"

"Monday?" Riana ventured, holding her breath. Allen was expecting her to deliver. Andre had better not complicate her plan. "It's the only time he'll be available for a while. I think he's going out of town on Tuesday."

"Then I guess it wouldn't hurt for us to meet, even though I haven't really committed to taking this on."

"Exactly what I was thinking. We could drive up tomorrow, spend Sunday hanging out on the River Walk, and then you'd be there for your Monday-morning meeting."

Shifting onto his side, Andre propped himself on one elbow, chin on his fist. Looking down at Riana, he said, "Sounds doable. Do I need to get a hotel room?"

Reaching up, Riana placed a finger over Andre's lips and snuggled closer. "Naw. I've got plenty of room at my house. Besides, I don't want to let you out of my sight. Not for a minute."

"Isn't being together like this some kind of conflict of interest?" Andre teased.

"I dunno. I'm not hiring you, just recommending you," she replied in a breathy voice. "You're my special client, so you get special treatment."

"That so? I'm curious about what that includes," Andre laughed, pulling her to him.

Riana lifted her face to his. "Whatever makes you happy."

"Pretty generous offer," he tossed back, lips curving into a grin.

"And one I'm sure you will not turn down," she murmured, thinking, *Everything will fall into place once we get to San Antonio,* before surrendering to Andre's flurry of kisses.

While Riana slept, Andre worried, hoping he wasn't setting himself up for disaster. *I need the money, as well as the clout that this kind of contract brings. George Allen has to take me on. I'm qualified to do the job. But will he hire a man with a juvenile felony conviction to design a prison for the federal government? Frazer's got to come through for me.*

Andre turned onto his back and stared into the darkness, listening to Riana's even breathing. She was doing her part, now he had to do his. And that meant not disappointing her. *All I have to do is go to San Antonio, enjoy my time with Riana and then impress the hell out of George Allen. No biggie,* he told himself, trying to feel convinced that nothing would go wrong.

Chapter 18

"A. Preaux and Associates. This is Lester speaking. How may I help you?" Lester Tremaine chewed his bottom lip impatiently, anxious to get back to the long list of things that Andre had asked him to take care of while he was in San Antonio. There was so much to do, and if Andre was lucky enough to snag the Allen Group design, Lester knew his workload would double.

"I want to talk to Andre Preaux," a woman said.

Lester detected an island accent, one he'd never heard before. "Mr. Preaux is out of the office. Would you like to leave a message with me?"

"Oh. A message. No."

Thinking she sounded a bit confused and hesitant to go on, Lester offered her another option. "Would you like Mr. Preaux's voice mail? I can transfer you over, if you prefer."

"Yes. That will be fine. Thank you."

With a punch of a button, Lester switched the call to Andre's voice mail and then hung up, curious about the female caller. He had an excellent memory for voices and knew this was a new one. He waited until the red light on the phone had gone off, signaling that she had finished with her message, and then entered the code to retrieve it, something he did every day. He and Andre had a system that worked well for them. Any call that came in over the office line was Lester's responsibility. Andre's home line and cell phone were off-limits.

Pen poised to take down whatever the woman had said, Lester engaged the call.

"Hello, Andre. This is Kay. I've been thinking so much about you since you left. If only I could have come back to Houston with you. It makes me sad that we are so far apart, but I'm so glad you came to visit me in Jamaica. I must see you right away. I can't wait long. Here is a safe number you can use to reach me. I'll be waiting for your call."

"Well!" Lester huffed, rolling his eyes. "So, that's where he went! Andre's got himself a sweet island girl tucked away in Jamaica." Twirling his pen, Lester grinned, a smug twist to his lips. He had suspected for some time that there might be a romance going on in Andre's life. His boss had been so different lately. Smiling all the time. Taking mysterious calls on his cell, which he made sure Lester didn't overhear. At first Lester had suspected that it might be Miss Cole who had turned Andre into such a sweet doe-eyed puppy, but now he knew who it was, and he wondered what Kay looked like. "Probably a gorgeous full-bodied woman with flowers in her hair." He sighed. "Being in love is just so wonderful. Good for Andre! It's about time the guy broke loose and got some. Whew! I don't know why he's been such a loner for so long."

After sitting for almost an hour in the reception area of the Allen Group's offices, Riana had read almost every magazine on the table, and could not stomach another article on office politics or how to get along with an incompetent boss. Setting the glossy publication she'd been reading aside, she simply let her thoughts drift, going back to the day before, to the marvelous time she and Andre had had checking out the city. It had felt good to have him on her turf as they explored the business district, the historical sites, the tourist attractions and even the offices of Executive Suites, Inc.

Andre had been impressed with her office, stunned by the fantastic view of the Alamo city that she enjoyed every day, and had complimented her several times on her choice location. They'd gone shopping in the Mexican market, eaten tacos at an outdoor stand, and eventually wound up back at her house, where they sipped the mean margaritas that Andre whipped up and made love while listening to a romantic serenade from Julio Iglesias.

"Miss Cole. You can go in now. Mr. Allen is ready to see you."

Riana's head jerked up from her reverie when she heard her name being called. Quickly, she rose, smoothed her suit jacket and followed the young lady down a corridor to a set of double doors. Once inside, she made immediate eye contact with Andre, who was seated with George Allen in a small conversation area of the man's spacious, light-filled office. Both men were smiling. *That's a good sign,* she thought, sinking into a plush burgundy chair that nearly swallowed her. Scooting to its edge, she crossed her legs at the ankles and nodded at Allen. "How'd it go?"

He winked at Riana and thumbed his fleshy chin. "We got ourselves a winner here! This young man is perfect for the job. I hated to make you sit out there and wait so long, but we had a lot to go over."

"No problem. I hope my client fits your needs."

"Oh, I don't think you could've done better. We need go no further. Preaux is the one. Let's get the contracts rolling."

Flashing a look of relief at Andre, she lifted both hands in a gesture of agreement. "I'm delighted. I felt he had the credentials you were looking for, as well as the vision for your project."

"Precisely." Now, Allen turned to Andre. "*Any* architect can design a building. But not all of them have the sense of respect for the complexity of the elements that go into the process. You've got that, young man. It's not something that's measurable, but it's what I was looking for. We're going to get along fine."

"I appreciate the opportunity," Andre added, sending Riana a glance of thanks and a hint of a smile.

"Good. Good." Allen stood, prompting Riana and Andre to do the same. "Miss Cole—" he zeroed in on Riana "—you go ahead and get with Pat, my human resources manager, and give her what she needs to finalize everything while I show Andre around." He turned to Andre now. "I know you have a project to wrap up before you can start with my group, but that's okay. I'll wait. You're here now, so I want you to meet the rest of the team. Get a feel for the way we operate. You're going to be spending quite a bit of time here in the very near future."

Before Riana could make a comment, Allen had whisked Andre out the door, chatting animatedly as they entered the corridor. However, once they were out of view, she did a hard air pump with her fist and bit back a smile. The contract was going through! The bonus was hers! Andre had been selected to fill the opening with the Allen Group. What a coup for him! And her! Just as she'd thought—everything was working out exactly as she'd hoped.

After leaving Allen's office, Riana suggested a celebration lunch at Plaza de Rosas and Andre quickly agreed.

"You really worked this out, Riana. I might have lost this opportunity if you hadn't persuaded Allen to wait a while to put this through, you know?" he told her as they sat in the entry, waiting for a table at the popular lunch spot.

"I told you I'd do what I could, didn't I?"

Andre nuzzled her neck before replying. "Yes, and it means a lot."

Their eyes locked and held, and she knew she would have kissed him right then and there, if his cell phone hadn't gone off.

"God," he murmured, glancing at his phone. "Lester. Excuse me. Something must be up."

Andre got up and stood off to the side as he took the call, but Riana could not help overhearing the conversation.

"Yeah. Frazer. I know who that is."

A beat.

"What did he say? Oh, are you sure?" A long pause. "Okay. I'll give him a call right now." Immediately, Andre punched in another number.

"Frazer? Yeah, I got your message. Kay called you?"

Silence.

"I guess so," Andre went on. "Better book my flight. I can fly out from here later today."

Riana frowned to hear that. Andre was going back to Jamaica? Today?

"Right," Andre went on. "I've got my passport with me. No problem. Thanks, I'll call you later."

He returned to Riana just as the waitress arrived to tell them their table was ready. They made their way to a booth in silence. As soon as they were seated, Andre broke the news.

"I've gotta fly to Jamaica tonight."

"So I gathered. Couldn't help but overhear. Something come up with your project there?" Riana asked in as pleasant a voice as she could muster, though she was certainly not happy with the news.

"Yeah, seems so."

She watched him closely, thinking that he seemed rather uneasy, but was trying to come off as relaxed. "Maybe I could tag along," Riana prompted, recalling their talk about going there together one day.

With a lift of his shoulders, he shook his head. "Not this time. I'll be moving around too much."

Disturbed by his quick refusal even to consider her going with him, she asked the question that had been stuck in her mind since overhearing his call. "Who's Kay?" she blurted out, feeling as if she deserved a little more information.

Andre's head swiveled away from the menu he'd been perusing. His eyes popped wide. Riana could imagine tiny wheels spinning in his head as he searched for just the right words, and she didn't like how long it took for him to reply. "Oh, she's…co-ordinating everything," he tossed off, though clearly distracted.

"With Frazer?" she couldn't help from asking.

"Yeah. I'm working with both of them." Lips pressed together, he studied Riana for a few seconds. "I told Frazer to get me a flight out from here, if that's okay. I hate for you to drive back to Houston alone."

"Don't worry about me," Riana told him, holding back from saying what was really on her mind. Why was he being so damn mysterious? What was he doing? Designing a top-secret nuclear power plant in Jamaica? She had thought they were close enough for him to trust her with anything related to his work. Obviously not. "Think I'll stick around here for a few more days anyway. Take care of some work at the office. I have two clients who need…."

"I'm going to miss you like crazy," Andre said, taking her hand, interrupting her effort to keep the conversation going.

"I'll miss you, too. I've gotten too used to having you around," she whispered, speaking the truth while feeling as if she'd been punched in the chest.

Andre squeezed her fingers reassuringly. "We're both going to be very busy for the next few days. Time will zoom by, you'll see."

It better, Riana glumly thought, unhappy with the way her romantic getaway with Andre was ending.

After Riana dropped Andre curbside at San Antonio International Airport later that afternoon, he hurried through the double glass doors and disappeared into the terminal without a backward glance. His heart was taut with worry, yet tense with love. This was not the ending he had envisioned for their time together and he hated leaving Riana so suddenly, and under such murky circumstances, too. No wonder she'd turned cool toward him and sent him off with a short peck on the lips. He wished he could have been more open with her about why he had to leave, but he'd had no choice. He had to proceed with caution.

Frazer had told him that Kay had called, that she was willing to talk to the authorities, but only if Andre agreed to come to Jamaica and be with her, and then escort her and Lonny out of the country once it was all over. She was terrified of being attacked, abducted or tortured by the men whose names she planned to give to the police, so once she told the JCF everything she knew, she wanted to leave immediately.

Andre scanned the rows of departing flights on a nearby monitor, got his bearings and moved on, shifting his carry-on bag from one shoulder to the other, Riana's unhappy expression still etched in his mind. He'd make it up to her when he returned. Maybe take her to Hawaii for a short break before he started work with the Allen Group. Frazer had said he would try to bury Andre's record, and when he returned to Houston, he'd be able to give Riana all the information she needed to finish processing his paperwork, taking a chance that Frazer's word was good. There was nothing else to do.

Andre glanced up when he heard the announcement that his flight had started its final boarding. He had to run, but he made it to his gate just in time, and was the last passenger to take a seat on American Airlines Flight #458 to Miami, with connections to Kingston, Jamaica. He forced himself to relax, glad that this trip would be the last one he planned to take to the island.

Chapter 19

"You gonna eat that shrimp?" Felicia asked, fork poised above Riana's plate, ready to pounce.

"Be my guest," Riana replied, unable to make the effort to take another bite. She pushed her barely touched salad across the table toward her cousin and leaned back in her chair. Captain Papa's was her favorite Houston seafood restaurant, and when Felicia had suggested they meet for lunch, she had immediately decided to come here. But now, she had no appetite. Hadn't had one yesterday, or the day before that, either. In fact, she'd barely thought about food since returning from San Antonio three days ago, existing on diet sodas from the vending machine and whatever fruit remained in her hotel mini-fridge.

All around her, noontime diners chatted animatedly, waiters hurried past balancing trays of steamy seafood, and soft Caribbean music played in the background. However, nothing about the festive atmosphere lifted her spirits. In fact, the hustle and bustle and the lively steel-drum tunes were driving her mad, turning her thoughts to Andre.

"Hey. This is supposed to be a celebration lunch, isn't it?" Felicia said between bites of Riana's grilled shrimp. "This morning you closed the deal on Executive Suites, Inc., and are now an official Houston business owner." She reached for her glass of peach iced tea and lifted it high. "To Riana. Recruitment mogul extraordinaire."

Mustering a weak smile, Riana clinked her glass with Felicia's, but then set it down without taking a sip.

"You mind tellin' me why you can't at least *act* happy about what you've accomplished? When I invited you to lunch, I didn't think I'd have to bring along a box of tissue, but from the look on your face, I guess I should have."

Riana blinked several times, and then let go of the tension she'd been holding in her shoulders. With a droop of her body, she focused on Felicia. "Sorry. I know I should be happy right now, but I'm not feeling it. Too many other things on my mind."

"Like Andre?"

Riana nodded. "It's been four days. Not a word. I can't believe he's doing this to me."

Pulling a frown that drew her eyebrows low and her lips into a pucker, Felicia set down her fork and pushed her face closer to Riana's. "Let's review the situation, girlfriend," she stated with a tad of annoyance. "Did he promise to call every day?"

Riana gave a negative shake of her head. "No. He said he'd be very busy, moving around the island, taking meetings, so if he didn't get back to me right away, not to worry."

"Exactly. And what else did he tell you?"

"That he'd be back as soon as he could."

"Okay. And didn't he also tell you he'd be *working?* You, of all people ought to understand that, Miss Workaholic. Cut him some slack, Riana. In my opinion, no news is good news. He'll be back."

"When?" Riana wanted to know.

"When he's finished doing whatever it is he's doing in Jamaica, I guess."

"Right. I wish I knew what that was."

After promising Felicia that she would improve her attitude and stop worrying so much about Andre's lack of communication, Riana gave her cousin a quick embrace, got into her car, and watched as Felicia drove away. She felt frozen in place, as if Andre's absence had sucked all of the energy from her body, leaving her restless and edgy. Felicia was right: she ought to be celebrating the successful purchase of her second franchise instead of moping around with near-tears in her eyes. What was the matter with her?

I love him. Always have, always will. That's what's the matter with me. And I have to love him enough to trust him. I shouldn't have sent him off with a cold peck on the lips. I was wrong, and I ought to tell him so.

This silent admission—long overdue—provided a surge of confidence that shook her from her lethargy. She didn't have to wait for Andre to contact her; he needed to know how much she missed him, how much she wanted to hear his voice and feel that magic connection between them. It was time for her to do some communicating of her own, even if all she could do was leave a message on his hotel phone. At least he'd know she was thinking of him.

Quickly, she called Andre's office, praying that Lester would answer. He did.

"A. Preaux and Associates. Lester speaking. How can I help you?"

"Lester. Riana Cole here. Have you heard from Andre?"

"Umm, no, I haven't, but I didn't expect to. Do you want to leave a message?"

"Yes, I want to leave it at his hotel. Do you know where he's staying?"

"I…I don't think he's at a hotel, to tell you the truth."

"Oh? Where else would he stay?"

"Probably with Kay."

"Kay? I'm sorry, I don't understand. Isn't she the manager for Andre's design project?"

"Project manager? What are you talking about? As far as I know there's no Jamaican design on Andre's drawing board. If there were, I'd certainly know about it. He told me he had to go to the island to see a friend who needed his help."

"Then who *is* Kay?"

"Kay is Andre's friend, and a very special friend, I'm beginning to think. She's called here a few times. Seems like a real nice person. I'm happy Andre has someone to spend time with down there. He needs to relax more, you know?"

"Yeah, seems like he's been doing a hell of a lot of that lately."

"Well, my other line is ringing. Any message?"

"No, Lester. No message. Thanks, you've been very helpful."

The air inside the car crowded into Riana's chest and made her feel as if she were suffocating. How could he do this to her? Take off to Jamaica to help a *friend,* leaving her to believe he was working? Lester had no reason to lie, unless Andre had kept this particular contract a secret. But why? And why couldn't he have been up front about his friendship with this woman, Kay? If that's all it was. Obviously, Lester had some reason to believe that there was something more going on between them.

I hope Andre hasn't been using me to get a boost for his career, Riana suddenly calculated, her imagination beginning to flare. *If I find out he's been lying to me about a design project in Jamaica, I could call George Allen and tell him that Andre Preaux is not the trustworthy, honest man I thought he was.*

But how could she do that? It would infer that she had been less than thorough in her assessment of a candidate, that she had been taken in by Andre's charm. Even their romantic entanglement might surface and cause problems. After all, Andre was a client, and she had her professional reputation to consider. Besides, halting the contract would mean forfeiting the bonus money she deserved.

When she had taken out her loan to purchase the franchise, she had included additional funds for renovations, and was hoping to use her bonus from the Allen contract for the much-needed electronic upgrades. No way could she let that money slip away. She needed the extra cash now more than ever, and Andre was not going to mess that up.

Riana swallowed hard to force back the tears that clogged her throat. Andre would explain everything when he returned. Until then, she had to pull herself together and not surrender to her misery and sulk the rest of the day. Work called. What better cure was there for the blues? Instead of feeling sorry for herself, she'd get busy and whip her new office into shape.

Riana returned to the Houston office of Executive Suites fired up and ready to take control. Earlier that morning, Roberts had signed his franchise over to her and she had presented him with a hefty check. She was pumped by the familiar surge of excitement that came from taking on a new challenge, even though it would require a great deal of work to bring the place up to her standards. Now, she was ready to start.

After concluding their transaction, Rodney Roberts had cleaned out his desk, picked up the only living plant in the place and tipped his head to his staffers. When he walked out, the staff had immediately begun to murmur among themselves, and before the elevator doors had fully closed on their old boss rumors had started to fly. The new owner was going to close the office, move it to the suburbs, fire everyone and hire all new staff.

Sensing unrest among her new charges, Riana had sequestered herself in Roberts's old office and concentrated on her plan. Now, it was time to unveil it.

At one forty-five she swept through the entrance and told Terri, the receptionist, to put the phone lines on voice mail, hang a closed sign on the front door and call everyone together for her first staff meeting, to be held in the open reception area.

Dragging chairs, the twelve employees crept cautiously from their cubicles to gather in whispering clumps, clearly apprehensive about their fate.

As soon as everyone was settled, Riana came out of her office, prepared to take over the reins of her new enterprise.

"The last thing on my mind is letting any of you go," she started, going on to inform them that everyone who wanted to stay was welcome to do so. "I want to get to know each of you, so I'll be conducting individual interviews over the next few weeks before any staff changes occur. However, in the meantime, I plan to make some major adjustments in the way this office operates, the way it looks, and how we'll measure achievement of our goals and objectives. We're a team now, and I hope we can work together to make Executive Suites, Inc. of Houston the number-one producer in the state."

"You mean you want to knock San Antonio out of that spot?" Conrad, a sallow-faced man with a droopy mustache, threw out. Everyone in the room laughed and poked elbows at each other.

He's got a point, Riana thought. *I am competing with myself.* But she plunged ahead in an enthusiastic tone. "Why not? Nothing would give me more pleasure than to own the top *two* producers in the state. Pitting you guys against the Alamo giants might really heat things up."

"We could have a challenge," Zoe, a slender woman with soulful brown eyes and a sweet smile, piped up. "You know, with prizes or trophies, or something like that." She glanced shyly at her coworkers, her voice trailing off, as if afraid that she might have said the wrong thing.

"I agree with Zoe," Sara boldly interjected, giving her neck a hard jerk, flipping her shoulder-length braids to her back. "At least we'd have a spark of life around here." She turned to Riana, one thin eyebrow arched. "Nothing against Rodney, Miss Cole, but he wasn't much into team-building. Really, he wasn't much into anything. We've kind of always worked solo."

"I understand what you're saying, Sara. And you, too, Zoe. You'll soon find out that I'm a very different kind of owner. I may be the CEO, but I'm also a part of the team. We do this together. And there's no reason why we can't become the best. If you're willing to give it your all, we will."

The unexpected burst of applause that erupted startled Riana, forcing a genuine smile for the first time in days. She had a new business to get up and running, goals to meet, an outdated office to redecorate. Suddenly, her disappointment with Andre seemed of little consequence. Work was her true friend, a constant that would not hurt, disappoint or betray her. She had never let personal issues interfere with her professional goals before, and she wasn't about to start.

"I appreciate your vote of confidence," Riana told her staff, relieved that they all seemed to be on the same page. "So, let's get started. The office is officially closed for the rest of the day."

Whoops of glee spilled out. Smiles brightened faces that had earlier been filled with apprehension and doubt.

"A Friday afternoon off. Whew! Thanks for the long weekend," Jake, the youngest of the staff and the only computer whiz among them, called out.

"Hold up! I'm closing the office, but you're not going home," Riana clarified, lifting a hand in caution. "We have some serious housecleaning to do. I want everyone to return to their cubicles and get busy. Dump old files, remove everything from your walls, dejunk your desktops, and someone please take care of that nasty refrigerator. We're tossing the microwave oven and getting a new one. Tomorrow, painters are coming in to paint this place, new carpet will be laid in a few days. I've already ordered new computers, and yes, we will have DSL. And Terri, an entirely new phone system is on its way. We're coming out of the dark ages, gang. Let's do it! Okay?"

Chapter 20

The road that skirted the western edge of the island was a twisting ribbon of steamy hot asphalt that led Andre directly to the near-hidden turnoff that Agent Morris had described to him on the phone that morning. Swinging his rental car off the main highway, Andre started up the narrow mountain road, leaving the ocean behind, traveling under a canopy of red-blooming vines and dark-green leafy branches. The bright tropical sunlight began to fade, darkening his path so quickly that Andre had to turn on his headlights and slow down to make sure he didn't stray off the road and wind up stuck in the soft sandy shoulder.

He'd been in Jamaica for four days, and at last he was going to meet the special agent that Frazer had sent to interview Kay. It had taken a lot of calling back and forth between Kay, Frazer and Agent Morris—the U. S. Marshal stationed on the island—to set the whole thing up: Morris was bringing Kay up to the cabin and he had instructed Andre to come alone, at four o'clock, not before.

After a long stretch on a steep uphill climb, the thatch roofed cabin that Morris had told him to watch for came into view. He slowed down, feeling nervous for the first time since agreeing to come back to Jamaica.

Being alone on foreign soil, high in the mountains in a very secluded area, and involved in a situation that could turn dangerous at any moment, didn't sit well with Andre. No one knew where he was, or when to expect him back at his hotel. He could simply disappear. Anything could happen and no one would know.

Andre shut off the engine of his rental car and remained behind the wheel, staring at the front door of the cabin. There were no other cars around. Deciding to stay put until he felt better about the situation, Andre slumped down in his seat to wait for other signs of life.

Just as he had settled in, the door to the cabin opened and Kay emerged. Andre bolted upright. Right away, he could see that she'd been crying. He hurried to get out of the car, slammed the door shut and walked across the open area that fronted the tiny house in quick steps.

"Andre! You're here. Thank God!" She cried out, increasing her pace toward him, arms open.

"I thought I was the first to arrive," he told her, glad to see her at last.

"A car arrived to pick me up in Kingston early this morning, brought me here and left me with *him!*" she told Andre, pointing back at the cabin. "His car is parked out back. Oh, Andre, I can't believe this is happening."

She slumped against him, he held her safe, while looking over her shoulder at a hulk of a man, dark-skinned and imposing, who was emerging from the cabin. He stood in the doorway, hands at his waist, eyes on Kay. Andre flinched, fearing the worst.

"Who's that?" he hissed into Kay's ear, not liking the way she was shaking in his arms or the sound of her cries muffled against his shirt, wondering what had happened during the hours she had been alone with the stranger in the cabin. "What's been going on?"

With a near-convulsive jerk, Kay pulled away from Andre, looked up at him and shoved one hand into the pocket of her skirt.

"This! Agent Morris gave me my passport and one for Lonny, too!" She waved the small square documents in Andre's face, her brown eyes glistening with tears of joy. "We can leave. Finally, we can leave this place and all the bad memories it holds." She paused to wipe her eyes. "I told the agent everything, and he's been on his cell phone with the authorities who are rounding up the men who most likely killed the policeman. Agent Morris said the men I have identified have been under suspicion for a long time. Thank you. Thank you, Andre, for saving my life."

Andre connected with Agent Morris's stern glare and nodded at the man, who finally broke into a half smile that allowed Andre to relax.

"Sorry we had to leave you out of the loop on this, Preaux, but this is the way we had to do it," Morris said, walking closer. "I have a few more questions for Mrs. Preaux and then she will have to give the same information to the JCF in Kingston. Hopefully, she'll be free to leave the island after that. She's cooperated fully with me and I'm grateful for her help."

Andre shook the man's hand. At least for Kay, the ordeal was almost over. Next, he'd have to find out what Frazer could do for him.

Andre entered the mountain cabin and sat with Kay during the conclusion of her extensive interview with Agent Morris, during which the U.S. Marshal grilled her with brutal intensity, though he did preface each question with "Please, tell me if you can…"

Once Morris had gotten all he needed from Kay, he drove her back into Kingston, with Andre following close behind, where she was taken to the JCF and interrogated by the local police, who were a lot less polite than the marshal had been. Pushing a tape recorder into Kay's face, they launched their investigation, their questions detailed and often presented in the tough street language used by the thugs they were trying to catch. It didn't take long for Kay's earlier upbeat attitude to dissolve into wary apprehension as she responded to the barrage of inquiries thrown at her. But she answered each question and gave the JCF names and detailed physical descriptions of the men she had seen coming and going during her time with Jamal, without breaking down.

It wasn't until the chief of the local constabulary came into the interrogation room and informed her that her husband's body had been recovered from the ocean that her strong facade collapsed. Kay's face crumpled into a mask of grief when she learned that they were holding Jamal in the morgue, waiting for her to identify him. Tears fell from her eyes and she sobbed quietly into a handkerchief while following an officer into the cold sterile room, clutching Andre's hand.

Andre felt a tear escape his half-closed eyes. He was unable to believe that Jamal was dead. Looking at his brother's charred, waterlogged body was the most difficult thing he'd ever done, even though he felt more relief than sadness. The half brother he had resented as a kid, imitated in youth and feared for as an adult was gone.

Andre struggled with his mixed reaction to Jamal's death, knowing that the self-destructive force that had driven Jamal to such a tragic end was over, and that Kay and Lonny would be spared from having to live on the edges of his frenzied, dangerous world.

Jamal's remains would be cremated, the officer said, and his ashes given to Kay to take to Houston, so she could bury him in a local cemetery.

"I never want to come back to Jamaica," Kay told Andre. "When Lonny gets old enough to ask questions about his father, at least I will be able to take my son to visit his father's grave. That's the least I can do."

Once the authorities released Kay and gave her clearance to leave, Andre took her back to the café to retrieve Lonny from the babysitter, and to move them both into the hotel room adjoining his. She packed quickly, stuffing only her necessities in a few battered suitcases, leaving behind a stack of her oil paintings, which filled every space on her walls.

Andre was impressed with her work: vivid island street scenes, bright birds and tropical flowers, serene compositions of the sea and the sky—all done in a whimsical, free-flowing style that captured the spirit of her homeland. "I want to buy this one from you," Andre told Kay, selecting a miniature oil painting of a steel drum band performing at a calypso party, enclosed in a frame that was studded with a glittering rainbow of multicolored bits of glass.

"Take it as a gift. Please." She shook her head, holding up a palm.

"No, I want to pay you," he insisted, and despite her protests handed her a fifty-dollar bill. The painting resembled a fine piece of jewelry, a fitting gift for Riana, he thought, a peace offering for having abandoned her in San Antonio.

It was dark when Andre finally got Kay and Lonny settled at the hotel and was back in his room, flopped on the bed. He sank into the fluffy comforter, feeling as if he had climbed the steep, vine-covered mountainsides on foot. He lay quiet, absorbing the intensity of the strange day, which had started out in the cabin in the mountains and ended at the morgue, where both Kay and Andre had paid their last respects to Jamal.

Andre massaged the muscles at the nape of his neck, thinking that he ought to call Riana even though it was very late. His mission in Jamaica was complete. At last, he could concentrate on Riana, give her the attention she deserved and focus on their relationship. *Get things back on track. If only I could have told her the truth about why I had to go away, but doing so would have compromised too many people. Now, I can tell her everything.*

Though the emotional strain of the day had nearly turned his body and his mind to mush, he picked up the phone and placed the long-distance call to Riana.

She sounded groggy when she answered, mumbling a soft hello. He hurried to apologize for not calling earlier, for leaving so abruptly, for not being able to return sooner than he'd thought.

"Unfortunately, I still have to sort out an unexpected problem that only I can take care of," he added, not ready to go into details about Kay, Jamal and the FBI. "But I'll be back in Houston late Monday. I'll call as soon as I get in. I'll explain everything then," he promised.

Her response was little more than a murmured, "Sure, I understand." She didn't ask him how he was, didn't tell him that she missed him, and didn't give him a chance to tell her that he loved her before the line went dead.

Flipping onto his back, the phone still in his hand, Andre felt the same icy emptiness that had paralyzed him years ago, when Riana had decided to leave.

Chapter 21

Riana removed a load of laundry from the dryer, dumped it onto the folding table, and grabbed a T-shirt, which she gave a hard shake. With hands that moved without thought, she worked through the pile of warm clothes, one eye on the bright red numbers on the clock above the washing machine, certain Andre's plane had landed.

"He's got a hell of a lot of explaining to do," she said to herself, slamming a folded pair of capris into her laundry basket. When they'd parted in San Antonio, she'd been miffed that he could desert her without much of an explanation after such an intimate weekend together, but she'd understood that he had work to do. However, why hadn't he felt he could trust her with the truth, whatever it was? *How can I love someone who will not be honest with me?* she wondered, her mind beginning to fill with doubt.

* * *

The second-floor apartment in the quiet complex near Hermann Park was exactly the kind of place Andre had hoped Frazer would find for Kay. Before leaving Jamaica, he had placed a call to the agent and filled him in on Kay's plans. Frazer had agreed to find a furnished, rent-by-the-month apartment in a neighborhood where she would be safe, and said that the agency would place her in a modified witness-protection status until the investigation in Jamaica was closed.

Frazer had come through on short notice, taking a huge worry off Andre, who wanted Kay and Lonny to be close by since there was no way they could live with him in Prairie Towers. He wanted to do all that he could to support Kay and his nephew as they started over in Houston: help her get a green card, a job, a car and everything required to transition into her new life. Who knew? Kay and Riana might hit it off and become friends, too, creating the kind of family he'd never really had.

With Jamal dead, Andre knew it would be up to him to inform his father that his youngest son was gone. All Andre had was a fifteen-year-old address for Rex Preaux in Baton Rouge. He had a phone number that was just as old. Knowing Rex, he had probably moved a hundred times since Andre last saw him, but he'd send a letter anyway, just in case it got forwarded.

Andre regretted he'd never been able to build an adult relationship with Jamal, and their estrangement still left an ache in his heart. He had never stopped hoping that Jamal would tire of his thuggish ways, decide to change and reach out to embrace his only brother. But it had never happened. Jamal was dead, ashes in an urn, and it would be up to Andre to step up and be a father figure for Lonny, who most likely would have drifted into his father's shady world if Jamal had lived to raise him. Lonny barely knew what was going on, though he had been told that his father was in Heaven with the angels and would not be coming back. He was a bright kid who deserved a shot at a better life than the one his father had squandered.

"This is beautiful," Kay remarked as she moved from one sunny room to another, Lonny's hand in hers. "So spacious. And clean." She gingerly opened a louvered door and peeked in. "This closet is bigger than the room Lonny and I shared in Jamaica. I don't know what to say." She turned around and faced Andre. "You've done too much for me, Andre. How can I ever thank you?"

"You don't have to do anything but stay here and be happy," Andre told her. "You're family. That's all that matters." He gave her a quick hug, and then stepped back. He reached into his hip pocket, removed his wallet and took out several bills, which he offered to Kay. "I've got to run. Some business that can't wait. You and Lonny get settled. There's a supermarket at the end of the block. Go and get what you need for tonight. Tomorrow, I'll go to the bank and…"

"I have some money," Kay quickly interjected, refusing Andre's offer. "I managed to save some of what I earned at the café and from sales of my paintings, too, because the Americans always paid in American dollars. Guess I've been hoping that I'd be able to pay my own way if a time like this ever came. Right now, I'm okay."

"All right, but if you need money, or any help, please ask, Kay. I don't want you to think of this as charity. You're family. Houston can be expensive, and I don't want you or Lonny to worry about anything."

Shaking her head, she told Andre, "I'm not worried. I'm a pretty resourceful woman, and as soon as I get settled, I plan to start painting again, and then, you can just point me to the nearest flea market, and I'll be fine."

"A real entrepreneur, huh?"

"It's called survival, Andre. And I'm sure you know what that's about."

"I do," he replied, giving her another fast hug. "I'll check with you tomorrow. You've got Frazer's number and my cell-phone number, so call if you have any problems. I'm not that far away."

It was a short drive from Kay's apartment to Prairie Towers, where Andre planned to drop his bag, make a quick call and then head over to see Riana. As soon as he entered his loft, he was hit by an overwhelming sense of relief to be back home and finished with his role as amateur secret agent Preaux.

Surprisingly, Lester was still in the office, busy doing the mail that had stacked up while Andre had been away. Andre had deliberately kept Lester in the dark about Kay, Jamal and Riana, too, but now that everything seemed to be falling into place he knew he had some explaining to do.

"Hey, Lester. How's it going?" Andre asked as he slid onto the stool at his drafting table and propped one elbow on the corner.

"Well, hello to you," Lester quipped, jerking his head back. "I was just finishing the mail and I worked up that report you need for the shopping-center design."

"Thanks. I'll need that for my meeting with Richard Vail. Next Wednesday, isn't it?"

Lester flipped a page on the calendar on his desk. "Right. Ten o'clock." Then he gave Andre a big wink and a smirk of a smile, and said, "So! The traveler returns! I thought you'd be in earlier. Didn't your plane arrive at two?"

"Yeah, but I had some business to take care of first," Andre replied, wondering where he'd start with all that he needed to tell Lester.

"I see. So how was it? I want to hear all." Lester grinned, closed the folder he'd been working on and hunched forward, ready to hear the details of Andre's trip.

Andre exhaled and massaged his neck, rotating it to free up the tension of the day, and then launched into the reason for his trip, giving Lester a full blow-by-blow account of the events of the last three weeks, and as he talked, Lester's eyes grew wider, his gasps of surprise more frequent.

"Get outta here!" Lester interrupted. "You and Miss Cole? The recruiter? Oh, my God. You're telling me Kay is your sister-in-law? Not your…girlfriend?"

"Right. My brother's wife. Why would you think she was my girlfriend?"

"She sounded like she was so close to you when she called. Really close. I just assumed…well, I guess I got it all wrong. Ohmagod," Lester repeated, biting down on his bottom lip. "It never occurred to me that you and Miss Cole…"

"Riana. You can call her Riana, now."

"Well, I kinda told Riana that I thought you had a special friend in Jamaica. You know. That Kay was someone special."

"Lester! You did what?" He spat the words, sending Lester a scalding glare.

Scrutinizing Andre with apprehension, Lester began to mumble. "I may have led her to believe that you and Kay were more than friends. How was I supposed to know Kay was a relative? You never mentioned you had family in Jamaica."

"You weren't supposed to know. And why in the world were you discussing my personal life with Riana anyway?" Now, Andre was truly angry, his temper rising steadily.

"Oh, I don't know. You'd been so happy lately, so different. I've always wished you had someone special and I was sure you'd found a girlfriend. I surely never suspected it was Riana Cole! I'm sorry, Andre. Really sorry. If you want me to, I'll call her and explain everything. Tell her I was way out of line even to mention your personal affairs. I'll call right now. She's still at the ESA Greenway, isn't she?" Lester rambled, already reaching for the phone.

"Yes, she is, but no, don't call her," Andre stopped him. Slowly, he forced himself to calm down, determined not to overreact. He scratched his chin, thinking. "I'll take care of it. She'll understand."

Cautiously, Lester drew back his hand and eyed Andre with suspicion. "Am I fired?" he asked in a timid voice. "I'll understand if you want to let me go."

Andre gave up a soft laugh. "No. You're not fired. I can't manage this office without you and I guess I have to admit that I'm just a little flattered that you noticed the change in me."

"Of course. You're in love," Lester stated with authority. "Anyone can see that."

Andre stood, nodded, and beamed an open smile at his assistant. "Yeah, I'm in love, all right." He stretched out his back and tilted his head to one side. "And you know what? I'm very happy about it."

After Lester left, Andre noticed the red light blinking on his personal voice mail, and punched in the code to retrieve his messages. A reminder from his dentist about a Wednesday afternoon appointment. Riana checking to see if he'd made it back. George Allen's human resources manager requesting that he fax over his personal profile so she could finalize his contract.

"George will be out of town for a while," Pat said, "so, the start of the Tierra Trace project has been pushed back until early November. However, he wants me to move forward, and I'd like to get you fully on board while he's away, so everything will be in place when he returns."

Clicking off his voice mail, Andre sat at his desk, thinking about the last message. That damn personal profile. He'd been haunted by it for weeks. He reached into his in-box, removed the paper and began to fill it out. Nothing left to do but provide the requested information, put it all down on paper, take his chances and get this over with.

It didn't take long for him to answer all the questions—he had mentally reviewed them enough times to have them memorized. He signed his name at the bottom of the page, swearing the information he had provided was truthful, and then slipped it into his fax machine and sent it on its way. Once the buzzer sounded to confirm the delivery of the document, Andre let out a low stream of breath. "It's out of my hands now," he told himself, eager to go see Riana.

The door to Riana's suite had barely shut before Andre was embracing her, kissing her, tempering her doubts. Braced against him, she sagged into his chest, torn between a need to believe that they shared a very special bond and her disappointment with him for not telling her the truth. His tongue flicked over hers, sending tiny shock waves of pleasure through Riana, chipping away at her irritation, which had been steadily building since her conversation with Lester. She drank in Andre's presence, thrilled to have him back, wishing they weren't going to have the conversation she had rehearsed in her mind, perhaps spoiling everything.

Pulling back, a flush of worry came over her before any words had been spoken. Suppose what he said, or didn't say, brought their runaway reunion to an abrupt halt? She didn't want to think about that.

Riana raised her eyes to his, searching for a sign that would tell her all was well, convince her that Lester had been way off track. *He must have been mistaken,* a voice in her head kept telling her, while her heart floundered in uncertainty.

"Tell me about Jamaica," she started, easing away from Andre, her words thick with caution. "Did you accomplish what you set out to do? Or did you get distracted?" Letting go of his hand, Riana walked over to the seating area by the window, where two club chairs faced a small round table. She sat down. Andre slipped in across from her, a puzzled expression building on his face.

"Distracted? By what?" he asked.

"Or by whom, perhaps?" Riana added, giving away nothing. *Let him dig his way through this without my help,* she decided. "You know, it must be nice to be able to take off on a Caribbean holiday twice in one month. You must really love Jamaica."

"I don't care for the place at all, really." Leaning back, he looked down at her with a squint. "Anyway, I told you, I went to Jamaica to take care of some business."

"Oh, yeah. Business. I forgot. Guess you can call any kind of a relationship business, as long as a transaction takes place."

Andre moaned, swiped a hand across his jaw and shook his head, clearly annoyed. "Okay. Stop the double talk. Spit it out, Riana. There's something you're holding back, so let's hear it, all right? I have a lot to tell you, but before I say anything, I want to hear what's on your mind."

The dam of emotions she'd been holding in check for days burst as soon as she opened her mouth. "How dare you lie about doing a project in Jamaica so you could go spend time with some woman friend, supposedly in a bind? Lester told me that you have no design project underway in the Caribbean. You have a special friend named Kay, who's been calling you quite often. What's up with that, Andre?"

"Lester shouldn't have told you all of that."

"Well, he did."

"Oh, shit. Lester doesn't know what he's talking about. Kay called my office a few times about something very important, and he got the wrong impression."

"Kay. So, that *is* her name. If she's only a friend, why couldn't you tell me about her? Why be so secretive, sneaking around like that? Lester knew about your friendship with her and I didn't? Why not?"

"Riana, I'm not seeing another woman, not sneaking around, and have no interest in anyone other than you. Kay is my sister-in-law."

"Your sister-in-law? Please. I thought you were an only child. Had no immediate family, only a bunch of second and third cousins back in Louisiana that you don't care about."

"Kay was married to my half brother, Jamal, who's been living in Jamaica."

"A half brother in the Caribbean? How convenient. You never mentioned him, either. What else don't I know about you, huh?" Riana threw her questions at Andre, her voice rising, anger taking over. "You've had plenty of time to tell me about these long-lost family members. Why have you been so damn mysterious?"

"I *had* to be," Andre replied, in a voice raw with torment. "And if you've finished yelling at me, I'll tell you exactly what was going on. The whole truth, I promise, okay?"

Huffing her response, Riana folded her arms on her chest and pushed her hips far back into her seat, tilting her body toward him. "I want details. Everything." She clamped her mouth shut, prepared to listen while Andre explained himself.

Starting at the beginning, Andre told Riana about growing up with Jamal in Baton Rouge, how he fell into a shady world of drugs and gangs as a youth. He told her about meeting Agent Frazer in Hermann Park, about the murder of Eddie Brooks, why the FBI believed Jamal was connected to the killing. Kay's status as the wife, and then the widow of Jamal, put her in a dangerous position, resulting in a listing on a suspicious-person, no-fly list which prevented her from traveling to the United States. Andre said he had agreed to cooperate with the FBI in order to persuade Kay to give them the names of people connected to Jamal's drug posse. He talked about Kay's fear for her life and the future of her son, and why he had had no choice but to help her through the ordeal to get her and his nephew, Lonny, out of Jamaica.

"They arrived in Houston with me. I'm her only contact in the United States. I had to come through for her, and my nephew, too. They are all the family I have now."

"So you made up the Jamaica project to buy time with George Allen so you could help Kay?" Riana clarified.

"Right," Andre replied. "And for your information, I faxed my personal profile sheet directly to Allen's human resources manager today. Everything is in order. As for the Jamaica project, I hated to deceive you, but I couldn't tell anyone about Kay. I might have put her and her son in danger, and besides, Frazer didn't want too many people involved, told me to keep my mouth shut."

The mystery has been solved, Riana realized, hating herself for ever doubting Andre. A slight shudder rippled through her body—a mixture of relief, guilt and a sudden desire to hold Andre close. She looked at him in a new way, sensing the strength of commitment that it must have taken for him to get involved in his brother's dangerous world. He had done this to salvage what was left of his family: Kay and Lonny were all that remained, but Riana knew that she wanted to be a part of it, too.

Rising from her seat across from Andre, she went to stand behind him, leaned down and wrapped both arms about his neck and placed her chin on his shoulder. "My brave, courageous undercover agent," she murmured in his ear. "Forgive me? Please? You know I love you very much."

He turned his head to the side, their lips met and held, Riana deepened the kiss until she could hold her breath no longer.

Andre rose from his chair and turned to Riana. "I know you

do, and I love you, too. It's difficult to think about anything but being with you. I missed you like hell, I ached from thinking about you, and I knew you weren't happy. But, it's all behind us now. No more separations. Ever. That's what I want."

"Together forever?" Riana whispered, quizzing him with an arched eyebrow.

"Yes, forever. If you want it, too." He ran his hands along her arms, and then clasped them at her back. "We can be happy anywhere. Houston, San Antonio. Wherever. It doesn't matter where we live. We can make it work, can't we?"

Riana nodded, unable to speak, overcome by the tone of commitment that Andre was using. She had never heard him sound quite so serious. "Are you…"

"Asking you to marry me?" he finished her question.

Again, Riana could only nod.

"Yes. I want you to marry me. Soon."

"How soon?" Her voice was jagged with emotion.

"Very. There's no reason to hold off, is there?"

Now, she found her voice as the veracity of what he was proposing sank in. "Well, think about it, Andre. You have the Allen Group job coming up, I'm launching a new franchise, then there's Prairie Towers, which you're in the middle of renovating…"

His fierce kiss interrupted her rambling excuses. Putting a finger to her lips, Andre told her, "And we can face all of those things together. Nothing we can't handle. Our careers are no longer going to dictate how we handle our relationship."

The look on Andre's face melted Riana's heart and she knew he spoke the truth: it was time to focus on their future together and she was more than ready to take what they had found to a higher level.

Andre loves me, he wants to marry me, and this time I'm not going to run away. Riana snuggled closer to Andre, yielding to his touch, letting him guide her away from the sitting area and over to the bed. All she wanted to do was make up for the time they'd spent apart, show him how sorry she was for doubting him. The flutter of anticipation that swelled up inside Riana created a rush that made her light-headed with joy. She felt her legs give way when he pulled her down on top of him, and then floated into his embrace as he settled beneath her. With a few quick tugs they shed their clothes, impatient to get lost in each other.

Sitting astride Andre, Riana pressed her thighs into his waist, flattened her palms against his smooth brown chest and then rubbed his skin with her knuckles, delighting in his murmurs of anguished pleasure. She leaned low, brushing her bronze breasts over him, teasing him with one warm sweep of flesh, then another, while whispering silly lust-filled words in his ear, inflaming herself as much as him. With her lips at his ear, she felt the heat of his skin warm her cheek, saw the beads of perspiration gathering on his forehead, smelled his woodsy, masculine scent—so familiar and so heavenly. Impulsively, she took his earlobe in her mouth and tasted gently, initiating a groan from him that ended in a gasp.

Fully aroused, she felt Andre shift and then cup her hips with both of his hands to press himself more firmly into place. She resisted her own urge to cry out when his rock-hard erection slid between her legs and entered her pulsing core. The electrifying sensation of their joining rocked her back for a moment. Her mind spun in senseless circles, and she had nothing to hold on to except the magic of the moment, so she contracted the muscles that increased her pleasure and urged him deeper, arching her back to meet him. In a pulsing ballet of heat-seared thrusts and twists, their bodies united in a slippery mass of arms, legs, hands and lips spiraling higher and higher toward ultimate fulfillment.

Just when Riana knew she had lost all control to the flood

tide of emotions that were rushing through her, Andre moved onto his side and they reversed positions.

Locking her fingers, Riana placed both hands around Andre's shoulders and sank down beneath him, her lips seeking the cords in his neck, the slope of his shoulder, the bulging muscles that defined his upper arms. Shamelessly, she ran her tongue over every inch of skin she could reach while Andre kept one hand at the back of her head, his fingers entwined in her hair. Of their own volition, her lips found his, and she suckled his tongue with a powerful pull that fused them even closer.

She wanted to devour him, disappear into him, and never forget how he felt in her arms. He was all she'd ever want or need, and the thought of loving him for the rest of her life made her shiver in anticipation.

Their recent separation had intensified Andre's need to feel Riana's body next to his, her flesh, warm and soft and sweet-smelling inviting him to paradise. As difficult as it was, he held back from satisfying the red-hot need for relief burning in his veins to savor the way she was responding to him: wild and shamelessly. So fiercely passionate was she that he felt as if she were tied to him by an invisible cord that was keeping them in sync and preventing them from losing their rhythm.

Drawing his lips lower and lower along Riana's exquisite body, he placed a line of kisses from her throat to her belly button, to the triangle of dark curly hair between her legs until his tongue found the tiny slick spot to settle in and pleasure her. Her response was rapid and intense, a low moan that rose in a crescendo of gasps until she stiffened in release and held his lips in place, riding the wave of their love. Gently, she urged his head up into her arms and held him to her breasts as she opened herself to him, giving Andre everything he'd ever dreamed of and more. His climax came quickly, in a string of long shudders that left him weak, yet deliriously fulfilled and content. He slumped against her and held her tight, his lips pressed into her neck.

At last, nothing stood between his love for Riana and the future he envisioned for them—nothing except the fact that he still hadn't told her he had once been arrested on drug charges and had a felony conviction on his record.

Chapter 22

He looks so much like Andre. No wonder everyone thinks he's his son. Riana slipped her sunglasses to the top of her head, removed a tube of sunscreen from her bag, and began slathering a generous amount of the creamy lotion over her arms as she watched Andre toss a bright-white softball to Lonny for the umpteenth time. A smile came to her lips when the little boy finally caught it and then raised a triumphant glove-covered hand in the air. Andre's adult-sized mitt dwarfed the five-year-old's face and made him look even smaller than he was.

"Way to go!" she called over from her spot on the blanket that Andre had spread out for her under a huge oak tree in the middle of Hermann Park.

"He's got the hang of it, I think," Andre yelled back to her before bending down to sight his path, preparing to deliver another hard pitch to his nephew.

The three of them had come to the park to visit the zoo and

the Houston Museum of Natural Science. Afterward, they had ridden the miniature train, rented a paddle boat to explore the lake, and then enjoyed chicken wings that Andre picked up at Frenchy's on the way to the park. Now, they were simply kicking back, enjoying the unusually moderate weather.

August was not typically the ideal time to go on a picnic in Houston, but a rare cool front had swept in overnight to temper the blistering weather. Today, Hermann Park, a lovely, green oasis in the heart of the city was abuzz with people enjoying a much-deserved summer Sunday of picnics, walks or just sitting around to watch the world go by.

It had been Andre's idea for them to take Lonny for the day and give Kay some time alone to go shopping, work on her painting, read a book or simply be alone. It had been nearly two weeks since Kay and Lonny arrived in Houston, and during that time, Kay had been working nonstop to get herself and her son settled in their new apartment and adjusted to life in the sprawling city where public transportation was limited and everyone needed a car. Getting a Texas driver's license was top priority on her list of things to do, and Andre was giving her driving lessons every evening he could spare. Sometimes, Riana tagged along, encouraging Kay, who had never had to drive in the small village where she grew up and was terrified of the Houston traffic, especially the fast-moving freeways.

Riana befriended Kay immediately, finding her to be a slightly shy, sweet person who was devoted to her son. Kay never talked about the family she'd been forced to leave behind in Jamaica or the sad ending of her marriage to Jamal, whose ashes were now buried in a local cemetery. She spoke about her new life in positive words, determined to start over and make the transition from Jamaica to Houston a success for herself and Lonny, who was adjusting surprisingly well. Riana promised Kay that she would do all that she could to help.

Soon after their initial meeting the two women were chatting away like old friends, and Riana was enjoying her role as guide as she showed Kay around the city, pointing out the best places to buy clothes, groceries, household necessities and even oil-painting supplies.

When Andre presented Kay's painting to her, Riana had been impressed by his sister-in-law's talent and believed that Kay's work was good enough to sell in local galleries. As soon as she created enough new pieces to show, Andre planned to introduce Kay to his contacts in the local art scene.

Last Thursday evening, Andre had thrown a small dinner party at his loft, where he and Riana announced their engagement to his family and friends, even though she did not have the ring that they had picked out together, having left it with the jeweler to be sized. Riana wanted to wait and call her family later and break the news herself.

Kay, ecstatic to learn that soon she would have Riana for a sister-in-law, had volunteered to cook Jamaican food for the party. She prepared jerk chicken, peas and rice, mango salsa and coconut shrimp—her favorite island dishes, which everyone devoured. Felicia and Malcom, still together and getting more serious each day, had come. Lester arrived with his partner, Todd, who wowed everyone with his palm readings, a skill he'd recently acquired and one that he enjoyed practicing whenever he got the chance. After scrutinizing the lines in Riana's hand, Todd told her that unexpected news that could be considered both good and bad would soon come her way. Not sure if she should be worried or pleased, Riana had laughingly put his prediction out of her mind.

The gathering had turned into a fun-filled night of reggae music, laughter and great camaraderie, infused with a sense of family. It had been clear to Riana that Andre was overjoyed to have the people he cared about with him at last, and the evening had made Riana realize how truly alone he had been and how much she looked forward to becoming an important member of his family.

"All finished?" she now asked as Andre headed toward her, a hand resting on Lonny's tiny shoulder. An image of him walking with a child of theirs flashed into her mind and sent a jolt of love through her. She had never experienced maternal urges before and the sensation caught her off guard, but it didn't bother her at all. Suddenly, she felt ready to take that big step toward marriage and motherhood, to move into a new phase of her life. She looked from Andre to Lonny and back. This was what life was all about. Family. There really was nothing else.

"Yeah, this guy is a fast learner. Getting too good for me." Andre ran a hand over Lonny's small round head and grinned down at his nephew, his smile full of love.

Riana scooted over on the blanket to make room for the two to sit down, one on either side of her. Placing an arm around Andre, she held on to Lonny's hand. "Well, there's only one thing left to do," she said, glancing from one to the other.

"What's that?" Lonny piped up.

"Go for ice cream, of course."

"Right!" Lonny said, jumping to his feet. He shifted from one foot to the other, anxious to get going. "Can I have chocolate? Two scoops?" He was already starting across the grass toward the ice cream stand on the other side of the park.

"Double chocolate, if you want," Andre called out to him, keeping his small frame in view as the boy raced ahead. Rising, Andre extended a hand to help Riana up from the blanket. He kissed her lightly on the lips. "And you? What do you want?"

"I have everything I want right here," she murmured softly, returning his kiss. "But a double scoop of strawberry butter pecan really does sound good."

* * *

After taking Lonny home, Andre declined Kay's invitation to stay for dinner and made a fast exit, surprising Riana, who felt he might have hurt Kay's feelings.

"I didn't mind staying, Andre. What if she went to a lot of trouble? And you know how much she wants to please you. We should have accepted, don't you think?"

"Oh, don't worry about Kay. I'm learning all about Jamaican hospitality. Every time I show up, she offers me food and she's a great cook, so it's hard to turn her down, but she doesn't expect me to accept. It's the Jamaican way. Don't worry, she's quite content to be left alone with her son, her paintings and her new apartment. I'm just relieved that they're both adjusting so well."

Riana remained silent, listening to the Santana CD that Andre had put on as he swung his Pathfinder onto the freeway. She hoped he was right. She didn't want to offend Kay, who would soon be her sister-in-law, too, and she really did love her cooking. They had snacked on junk food all day in the park and at the moment a plate of Kay's home cooking sounded pretty good. Riana was even toying with the idea of asking Kay to give her a few cooking lessons, which it appeared she would desperately need once she and Andre got married.

"So, what do you want to do for dinner?" she asked, food on her mind.

"It's a surprise," Andre responded in a mysteriously smug manner. "I'm dropping you back at your hotel to change, and I'll pick you up at six. Okay?"

Riana cut her eyes over at him. "Change? Into…." She had no idea where this was leading.

"Nice, but not too nice," he told her, lifting one hand. "You know what I mean, don't you?"

Just like a man, Riana thought as she told him. "Sure, I know exactly what you mean."

After a shower and a long stare into her closet, which was rapidly filling with clothes she had bought on shopping trips with Felicia, Riana chose a pair of loose-fitting black slacks, a white ruffled blouse with a low-cut neckline and strappy black sandals trimmed in silver. Oversized pearl earrings and a black straw bag and she was ready when Andre returned.

A comfortable silence filled the car as they drove along, intensifying Riana's belief that she and Andre were destined to be together, that they had no need to talk all the time. Apparently, he wanted to keep his destination a secret, so she wasn't about to probe. Let him have his fun.

It had been a wonderful day in the park with Lonny, and she was happy to have been invited to share Andre's outing with his nephew, but now she liked the fact that Andre had decided to wind the evening down with a special outing just for them. Lately, he seemed to know exactly what made her happy.

When he turned off Westheimer Boulevard—one of the busiest thoroughfares in Houston, lined with restaurants, strip shopping centers, boutiques, gas stations and fast-food joints—and turned onto a quiet street, Riana began to get curious. Winding his way down a shady section of the street, he came to a gated dead end, beyond which Riana could see an extremely large home surrounded by a smooth green lawn.

She craned forward, wondering whose house it was, examining it closely while Andre punched in an entry code. The gate swung open and they drove through, heading down a long driveway toward the house. When she got closer, Riana saw a small sign on a brass post that read, Largo's—Fine Dining And Private Parties.

"This is a restaurant?" she finally spoke, intrigued by the country-club look of the place.

"One of the best in town. Reservations only. When you make your reservation they give you the code to get in. Not a bad idea, huh? Great food. Beautifully landscaped grounds. You'll see. It's a pretty special place."

The closer they came, the more Riana understood what Andre meant. Large peacocks strutted across grass so smooth and green it looked artificial, their feathers fanned in kaleidoscopes of color. A blue lake in the distance was dotted with swans, both black and white, and a white lattice gazebo stood watch from the shore. Roses bloomed in carefully tended beds along brick-paved walkways and cascaded over doors.

Andre swung to a stop at the entry, handed his car over to the valet attendant and held Riana by the elbow as they made their way inside and to the table he had reserved. The dining room was surrounded by windows, providing a spectacular view of the landscaped property from every seat in the room. After settling in at their table, Andre took Riana's hand.

"Like it?" he asked.

Lips parted, she shook her head in amazement. "This is the most beautiful restaurant I've ever been in. Why haven't I heard of it before now?"

"Guess I was holding back from bringing you here until I was sure…" His voice fell low, as if purposely mysterious.

"That we'd be together," she completed his sentence, her voice just above a whisper.

"I came here for a business luncheon a few years ago," Andre explained. "And I knew right away that this was a place I would only bring someone special. For a very special reason. Guess I was right to wait." He gazed at her as he spoke, the heat between them building.

"I'm glad you brought *me*," Riana told him, feeling herself sink into that bottomless pit of pleasure that consumed her whenever he looked at her that way.

He leaned over and kissed her lightly on the lips, fueling the warm glow that was building inside. "Who else would I bring?" he responded huskily, increasing his grip on her fingers.

Holding on to Andre's hand, Riana gazed out at the lake, feeling as if she had traveled to a faraway place, though she knew she was still in the heart of the city. Beyond this surprising oasis of serene beauty, the rest of the world rushed by. Floating on a cushion of happiness, she turned back to Andre, and let out a small gasp when she saw what he was holding: a round gray-velvet box, opened to reveal the impressive emerald ring that they had picked out. "Let's get married here," he suggested, eyes shining with anticipation as he slipped the ring from the box.

"Andre! It's even more beautiful than I remembered. It's so unusual, and I love it!" Lips pressed together to keep from crying, she watched as he placed it on her finger, and extending her hand, she studied the gem for a long moment, knowing it was the symbol of their future. Gingerly, she touched the clear green stone, her heart pounding in delight. "I hoped you'd say that this was going to be our special place for our special day. Perfect. Absolutely, perfect," she murmured, and then she kissed him hard, sealing the deal.

Chapter 23

The remainder of the week flew by in a flurry of staff meetings, training sessions on the new phone system, dealings with renovation contractors, and briefings with installers who were turning her office into a wireless, computer-networked suite. The upgrades were costly, putting a huge dent in Riana's bank account, but they were absolutely necessary if she wanted the franchise to succeed.

And in the midst of all this upheaval at work, Riana had to fit in phone calls with Felicia to discuss wedding plans, shopping trips to search for the perfect outfit, and consultations with Andre about the reception dinner, which was going to be a four-course sit-down affair with three kinds of wine and a champagne toast.

It was a great relief when Riana finally decided on a white silk suit trimmed in small seed pearls at the collar for herself, and selected soft rose-colored dresses with flowing skirts for

Felicia and Britt. With the clothing and the menu issues settled, she turned the remainder of the details over to Felicia, who was thrilled to be in charge of her most important party yet.

Riana closed the folder of invoices she had been reviewing and clipped a stack of checks she had signed to the outside, ready for Iris to finish processing them. Money was coming in, but it was flowing out just as fast: not unusual during this transitional phase. Riana wasn't worried, the improvements she had made were investments in the franchise that were already paying off. Morale was high among her staff and they had already exceeded their monthly recruitment goals.

When Iris arrived with the weekly reports and the day's mail, which Terri had opened and placed in a folder, Riana smiled. "You look very nice today," she told her office manager, pleased to see that Iris was wearing an attractive forest-green linen suit and a mint-colored blouse. When Riana first arrived, Iris had been dressing in casual polyester pants, big shirts and sandals, paying little attention to her appearance, but now she showed up every day looking like a woman who cared about the image she was projecting: subtle makeup, tailored suits, low-heeled pumps and manicured nails. The transformation was impressive.

"Thanks. You always look so pulled together," Iris began, "I realized that I had let myself go when Rodney was here. Back then, coming to work was a bore, and a chore, too. But you know what? This place is so different now. I love getting ready for work, and it's hard to believe that I used to dread coming here. The atmosphere is charged with energy now, everyone agrees, Riana, you've changed all of us for the better. However," she paused and cut her eyes to the folder she had brought in. "I think you ought to read the letter on top first." Iris clasped her fingers together after she placed the red folder on Riana's desk.

Curious, Riana retrieved the letter, saw that it was from Drewbegg Realty and quickly scanned it.

"What?" she snapped, blinking several times as she reread the notice. "This is ridiculous. They can't do this."

"I know," Iris agreed, vigorously shaking her head back and forth, looking as if she were about to cry.

"Surely Rodney *must* have known," Riana went on. "According to this letter all of the tenants in this building were given a heads-up last year. I have a five-year lease on this space. This is terrible. This cannot be happening!" She pulled Iris in with piercing eyes, as if trying to read her thoughts. "Did *you* know about this? Did Rodney?"

"Hey, Rodney didn't know what was going on most of the time, and didn't much care, either. Even if he had known, he never would have told any of us," Iris complained, moving to sit down across from her boss. "Can you believe the building's been sold? I'll bet they're going to tear it down and put up a new parking garage for that giant office building next door." She shook her head and pushed back her bangs, using two fingers to pat her hair in place. "And just when you whipped this place into shape. We only have sixty days to vacate. What are we gonna do, Riana?"

Riana didn't answer, she was frantically digging into the bottom drawer of the lateral file behind her, looking for her lease. She yanked out the blue folder, flipped through the pages and found what she was looking for, shaking her head as she read.

"What does it say?" Iris asked.

"Umm, let's see. It's buried in here, all right. In event of sale of property compensation to lessees in the amount of twenty-five percent of space improvements, ten percent on the remainder of the lease. Crap. This sucks. If I had known the building was going to be sold, I never would have invested in all these improvements. I'm gonna lose a ton of money," she told Iris, devastated by this turn of events. All of her electronic installations and suite renovations for nothing. Relocating the franchise would be expensive, time-consuming and a distraction she did not need in the midst of all she had going on. "Iris, keep this quiet, okay? Tell Terri not to say anything, either. I've got to make some calls, figure out my next step, and I can't deal with a panicky staff right now."

"Sure, no problem," Iris told Riana, standing, smoothing the wrinkles in her linen skirt. "I won't say a word. You'll work this out, I have faith in you, and you can trust me, Riana. Just let me know what you need me to do."

"Thanks," Riana said without looking up, her eyes still riveted to the paper, her mind whirling with possibilities. She could sue Rodney for negotiating a deceptive sale, but that would cost even more in attorney fees than she would get if she settled according to the terms of the lease. She could pull funds from the San Antonio account to use for the relocation, but that would be like robbing Peter to pay Paul, accomplishing nothing. In fact, it would create unnecessary cash flow problems between the two franchises. Now, more than ever she could use that infusion of cash from the bonus money George Allen had offered.

As soon as Iris walked out, Riana punched in the number to the Allen Group, and was on the line with Pat, in human resources, immediately.

"Oh, Miss Cole," Pat started right in. "We must be operating on the same wavelength today. I was just about to call you."

"With good news I hope?" Riana prompted in a cheerful tone, thankful that this particular contract was complete. It had not been an easy one to bring to conclusion, but it had turned out to be her most lucrative yet, and reuniting with Andre was an even better bonus than the cash Allen had promised. Riana smiled at the thought, knowing how lucky she was.

"I know Mr. Allen is still out of town but I wanted to check on the status of Andre Preaux's contract. I'm sure he's fully on board by now, so I was wondering if you could give me a time frame to settle with my company."

"That's why I wanted to talk to you. I spoke with Mr. Allen this morning and I told him where we stand on Mr. Preaux. He's very concerned."

"Concerned? Really? About what?"

"The fact that Andre Preaux has a felony conviction on his record. With this being a federal project, and a prison, too. I'm afraid Mr. Allen can't hire him."

"A felony? Surely you're kidding." A sharp pain stabbed Riana in the chest and turned her stomach upside down. "Nothing came up on him when I did a first pass on the background check," she managed, her throat so tight she could barely speak. "I used Uni-Code Criminal Background Check, the same Web site that I use all the time."

"Oh, that's too bad. This information really complicates things, you know?" Pat went on, sounding very concerned. "His conviction goes back a ways, maybe that's why it didn't show up in your search. Nineteen-eighty-six. He was seventeen at the time. Found guilty of possession and distribution of illegal drugs."

"Drugs! Oh, my God. What drugs?" Riana had to know. The floor beneath her feet seemed to fall away, leaving her feeling disconnected from her surroundings.

"Marijuana and cocaine. He was supposed to serve his time as a juvenile, meaning his record would have been expunged, but for some reason the system put him in an adult federal prison, so his record was never erased."

"What? I'm shocked!" It was all Riana could say. Her body chilled, as much from the thought that Andre had a prison record as the fact that he had never told her. "Surely you're mistaken." She went limp, overcome by a light-headedness that was swift and intense.

"I wish I were. This is such a surprise," Pat continued. "I confirmed all of this with a call to Louisiana. The authorities verified everything. I'm so sorry to bring you such disturbing news."

Finding her mental balance, Riana immediately focused on how this news would affect Executive Suites and her professional reputation, and it did not take long for anger to replace her sense of shock. "I am outraged, Pat. You understand, don't you, that if I had known about this I never would have recommended Andre Preaux for the position with your firm. This is highly unusual. Nothing like this has ever slipped past me before."

"Oh, of course I understand. You have your reputation to protect, too. Unfortunately, Mr. Preaux must have thought that his record had been purged. He has put all of us in a very difficult position."

"That's exactly right." Riana gripped the edge of her desk to steady herself, feeling as if she might pass out. How could Andre not tell her about this? How could he let her proceed with his candidacy and withhold this potentially disastrous information?

Damn him, Riana mentally cursed. *Damn him for being so sneaky, for hiding his messy past. First, it was Kay and Jamal and Jamaica. Now, this.* She bit back her tears and concentrated on what Pat was saying.

"…so we're back to square one, Miss Cole. Too bad we'll have to start all over. Mr. Allen is very upset with the delay this is going to cause."

"I know, I know," Riana rushed to agree, her mind racing ahead as she plotted how to fix this—losing the Allen Group contract was not an option. "I'll get right on it. I have several other candidates in mind. I'll contact them today and get back to you immediately."

"That won't be necessary, Miss Cole. Mr. Allen has decided

to use Total Staffing Limited for his executive searches from now on. We've used them many times in the past with great success. Mr. Allen said to tell you that he appreciates your effort and wishes you the best. I do, too," Pat finished, and then she said goodbye.

"Thanks," Riana whispered, her heart sinking, her stomach churning, her eyes filled with tears. Todd's palm reading sprang into her mind. At the engagement party, he had looked into her hand and told her that unexpected news that could be considered both good and bad would soon come her way. Where was the good news in this?

Chapter 24

Lester was at lunch, so Andre answered the phone himself, and was surprised to hear George Allen's voice coming over the line from California. A flash point of anticipation hit Andre, and he snapped to attention, eager to hear what the builder had to say, praying that Allen was calling to confirm his start date. If so, the call could not have come at a better time.

Andre had spent the morning putting the final touches on his design for a suburban strip shopping center that had been on his drawing board for months, and he was set to meet with the builder at any moment. Though glad to have been awarded the bid, his heart had not been in the cookie-cutter project, which was a routine job that would pay the bills and keep him working. Tierra Trace was what Andre wanted, as well as the opportunity to work for the prestigious Allen Group. He held his breath as he listened to Allen's greeting, biting back a smile.

"Yes, Andre, I'm in my car, on my way to the office. Just got back from a quick trip to the West Coast. Can you talk?"

"Yes, I've been waiting for your call. Hope you had a nice trip."

"Oh, yes. Lovely place, San Diego. Too bad I didn't have a chance to do much other than sit in meetings. I am swamped, but I had to stop and make this call to you now." A beat. "I just received a disturbing call from Pat, my human resources manager."

"Oh, I'm sorry. You sound upset." What else could he say? Andre steeled himself for the words he knew he did not want to hear, had prayed would not be tossed at him, severing the thread of hope he had been holding on to for weeks.

"I am upset, Preaux," Allen stated in a much more forceful tone than he had been using earlier. "I hate to do this over the phone, but I had to call to tell you that I can't bring you on board, after all. A damn shame, and I truly am sorry, but I suspect you know my reasons?"

Andre squirmed uncomfortably in his chair and expelled a gasp of air, the last bit of hope draining away. So, here it was. His record had caught up with him. He was busted. And he had no one to blame but himself. "Yes, I think I know what you're referring to, Mr. Allen, and I hate that it's come to this."

"Me, too," Allen agreed. "If this weren't a federal project with so many regulations I'd still use you, but I just can't."

"Sure, I understand. I wish I could have…"

"Andre, I was extremely surprised to learn that you had a felony conviction on your record," Allen stated, interrupting Andre's attempt to rationalize his behavior. "Want to tell me what happened?"

Feeling as if his entire world was spinning out of focus, Andre let the pain of his letdown wash through him, resigned to accepting his fate. He had royally screwed things up, and he couldn't fault Allen for dropping him, or Pat for doing her job. He was the one who had rolled the dice and lost, and there was nothing left to hide. All he could do was be honest, apologetic and hopeful that once Allen learned about the circumstances surrounding his youthful arrest, he might not think so badly of him.

"Yes," Andre finally replied, "I'd like you to know everything. And even though I won't get the chance to work with you, I want you to know how honored I am that you wanted me to be a part of your team." Then Andre launched into the unsettling details of his past, eager to get everything out in the open.

"Our youthful mistakes often reach far into the future," Allen said when Andre had finished. "Too bad we can't simply wipe them away for good, but that rarely happens. However, I respect you for all you've accomplished professionally, Preaux, and for risking so much to help your sister-in-law leave Jamaica. That took guts, and you should be proud of what you've done, especially for your nephew. Maybe I can use you on another project one day," Allen said. "I'll keep you in mind if something else comes up. That's a promise."

"I appreciate that," Andre replied, while thinking, *Thank God I haven't totally blown my chance to work with you.*

"A sad part in all of this is that I'm equally sorry that Riana Cole's company wasn't able to deliver," Allen was saying. "She's a bright young lady with all the qualities to be successful. I know she will do well, even without my support, though I had hoped to use her firm exclusively for my searches. I had put a great deal of trust in Executive Suites and now I won't get the man whom I still think is perfect for the job and her firm won't get the attractive bonus I was planning to pay."

"A bonus? Really? For recruiting me?" Andre bent forward, leaning over to stare at the floor as he listened to what Allen had to say.

"That's right. After Riana brought you to my attention, I was worried that you might be a hard one to recruit, so I offered to double Executive Suite's fee if she could get you on board in record time. Never done that before, but I wanted to let her know how serious I was about getting you, and about using her firm, too. She did her job, all right. Too bad it isn't going to work out."

Riana was getting a huge bonus to recruit me? Andre thought, irritated that she hadn't revealed that to him. Resentment flared, but immediately faded. Why should she tell him anything about her business affairs? he asked himself, trying to remain rational. Going after a bonus was a perfectly legitimate business maneuver, and there was nothing wrong in strategizing to get the best deal, so why should he care?

Andre was surprised that he felt offended by what Allen had just revealed, but when he recalled how persistent Riana had been about coming to Houston to meet with him, how hard she had pushed for him to complete his background profile, and how quickly she'd arranged his interview with George Allen, even before his paperwork was completed, he felt betrayed. Once again. He should have known she would go to any lengths to further her career, including using him.

She probably made love with me to get this contract completed within Allen's time frame, he mentally grumbled, hating himself for even thinking such a thing. Was he only another business negotiation as far as Riana was concerned? Did she really love him? Was she capable of separating her work from her personal life?

Riana picked up the phone, slammed it down and then picked it up again. Holding the receiver at her mouth, she froze, unable to punch in Andre's number. She massaged her temples, her neck, worried. She had to talk to him! Confront him about the mess he had created. George Allen was not happy. There would be no deal. No bonus for Executive Suites. No future contracts with the Allen

Group. The realization of what she now faced made her slightly nauseous. Blowing a contract like this was not to be taken lightly. The executive search industry had standards. Word would get around that Executive Suites had not done due diligence on an important job and that she had bungled a lucrative contract. Her professional reputation was at stake and she had to do something about it. *But what?* she silently asked, too confused to think straight, feeling overwhelmed by this sudden cascade of troubles.

For the third time, Riana jammed the receiver back into its cradle, unable to make the call. *Andre has a criminal record. How did this happen? Why didn't I discover this earlier?* She pressed a hand to her chin, trying to steady herself, feeling as if she were breaking into jagged pieces. She had put a lot of effort into this assignment, had invested personally in a relationship with a man she had thought she had known. And it was turning out like this?

God, what a mistake I've made, she admitted, knowing her parents and her sister would delight in telling her that they had been right to worry about the fast pace of her involvement with Andre. They had been correct in asking her to slow down, to stop and think about how much she really knew about the man she planned to marry.

Riana touched the vibrant green emerald on her left hand, a sob inching its way to the surface. When she had been involved with Andre four years ago, she hadn't bothered to drill him about his past, convinced that their affair had no future, that she didn't need a detailed history on a man she would never see again. All she had known about him when they parted was that he had been born and raised in Baton Rouge.

Now, things were different. They were about to start a life together, and still, it was clear, she knew very little other than the fact that he had a half brother who was dead, a mother who had died long ago and a father he had neither seen nor heard from in fifteen years. The only time he had discussed his past in depth with her was when he had told her about Jamal and Kay, and Riana had thought that was the end of it. Apparently, there was a lot more.

The sob she had felt building in her chest broke through and burst from her lips. She held back her tears with a fist to her mouth, not wanting her staff to hear how upset she was. Pressing hard on her lips to regain control, she forced herself to calm down.

Andre had deceived her, embarrassed her, and she was mad as hell at him for ruining a business deal that could have been a fabulous opportunity for them both.

She was in shock, but the saddest aspect of the whole mess was that she knew she still loved Andre. She had looked forward to building a life with him. She would never love any other man. But how could they go on?

Swiveling in her chair, she snatched a tissue from the box on the file cabinet behind her desk, wiped her eyes and grabbed her purse. A phone call wouldn't do the job. She had to see Andre in person.

When the entry buzzer sounded, Andre pushed the release button without using the intercom, glad that his client had arrived a bit early. He hoped he'd be able to conceal his distracted state from Richard Vail and make it through this final meeting so he could close the books on this project and move on.

Move on to what? he thought morosely as he began to straighten up his desk. Not to the Tierra Trace design. And probably not to a wedding at Largo's, either. Riana was going to be furious when she learned about Allen's decision, as well as the reasoning behind it. She would never forgive him for hiding his past, for putting her in such an awkward professional situation, and he dreaded the confrontation they would surely have over this disastrous twist.

While waiting for Vail to arrive, Andre spread the shopping-center blueprints out on his desk and unrolled the neighborhood map that they would need to consult during their discussions of utility-placement and traffic-flow issues. All he wanted to do was finish this meeting and go to see Riana, whom he hoped, would agree to talk to him.

He pushed back from his desk when the elevator doors opened, and got up. Taking a deep breath, he rounded the wall that screened his office from the entry and stopped. It was Riana. And from the look on her face, he knew that she had already received the bad news.

"Oh, hello," he greeted, in as level a voice as he could manage. "I was expecting a client. Richard Vail. But I'm glad to see you, instead."

"Are you really?" she taunted, one hand at her hip, her feet planted far enough apart to make sure he got her message: she was angry. Disappointed. Embarrassed. And ready for a fight.

"Yes, I am glad to see you," Andre insisted. "And I can tell from the expression on your face that you've spoken to George Allen."

"No, I spoke to Pat, his human resources manager. She delivered the bad news. And I have to say that she was very professional about it, even though she could have been quite nasty."

Andre scratched the side of his neck, unsure of where to start, uneasy about the fact that he had a business meeting in a few minutes and his client was on his way. "I'm sorry," he began, easing forward. "I had hoped it wouldn't turn out like this, but I had to take the chance."

Now, Riana stepped closer, both fists at her waist, eyes deliberately widened in wonder. She jerked her neck, showing her amazement at what he had just said. "You had *hoped?* Hoped for what, Andre? That your criminal record would simply up and disappear? That you could con me and con your way into the Allen Group when you knew a clean report from a background check was essential?"

"I never tried to con anyone," Andre defended. "I had been assured that I would have no record once I served my sentence. Even Charles Frazer, my contact with the FBI, agreed that my record should have been expunged. Said he would try to help me clear it up, if I helped him get to Kay. I did my part. I thought Frazer might've been able to help me out. Guess it didn't work."

"Apparently not. And what if George Allen had hired you and later found out about your record? Don't you realize how awful that would have been? The fact that you did time for, oh, let me remember what Pat told me. Possession of marijuana and cocaine with intent to deliver! It won't *ever* vanish, Andre. Please. You've got to be crazy to think all that mess wouldn't catch up with you one day."

"Okay, I understand why you're upset, but you don't know the circumstances. There's a lot more to it than you think," Andre said. "I was only seventeen. Jamal and I were just street kids. Our parents didn't care what we did. I wasn't lucky like you. I didn't come from a family that wanted the best for me or even cared enough to guide me on the right path. I was left alone to raise myself pretty much and I didn't always do the right thing. Sure, I paid a high price for the mistakes I made, but I did the time, grew up and made something of myself. I shouldn't be persecuted forever."

"I don't want to hear it," Riana threw back. "Sing your sob song to some other gullible girl. I could care less about the history of your dysfunctional family. I'm a businesswoman. I have a job to do, and I can do without all that touchy-feely stuff. You must not understand how much damage you've done. I lost a very lucrative contract because of your shady maneuverings and my professional reputation has taken a big hit."

"And your bank account, too, I understand," Andre thre
back, unable to keep from hurling his share of hurtful word
"Allen told me all about your signing bonus. So, now I unde
stand why you were in such a hurry to get me to San Antoni
for the interview. Why you pressed me for the profile infor
mation. You wanted to earn that extra bundle of cash. I'm dis
appointed to think that you might have been making love t
me to get a big payoff for your company. But as you said
you're a businesswoman and it's all business with you." H
snorted a laugh, his disdain just below the surface. "I've alway
known that. Just too bad you weren't honest with me from th
beginning."

"Honest with you! How dare you say that? What abou
Kay? Jamal? The phony job in Jamaica! This is exactly wha
I knew would happen. You don't understand me, at all. You ac
cuse me of being too involved in my work, when I should hav
been even *more* involved. I let my feelings for you cloud my
judgment and I'll never mix personal affairs with busines:
again. Just leave me alone, Andre. Agreeing to recruit you fo
my client was a colossal mistake."

Just as Andre opened his mouth to defend himself, the entry
buzzer rang. "Damn. Richard Vail. I've got to meet with him."
Andre hurried to press the entry-release button and then turned
back to Riana. "Wait for me, okay? We have to settle this today
and I don't want you to leave."

"Oh, yes, I can leave. And I plan to, right now." Riana
stepped toward the elevator, but Andre blocked her path.

"No, no. Please, come in here." He held her by the arm and
tugged her out of the entry. Without waiting for the protest he
knew was coming, he walked her into his living quarters and
stopped in front of his black leather futon. "Sit down, please.
Wait for me here. I won't be that long." He motioned for her
to sit, giving her a look that he hoped would help plead his case.

"We've got to talk, Riana, but not now. I have to meet with Richard and finish up this job."

With a roll of her eyes, Riana pulled her engagement ring from her finger and slammed it down on top of the coffee table. "Sorry. I don't want to talk anymore. Not now or ever again. I've gotta go. I have an office to move, and I need to start looking for new space right away. I have too much to do to stand here and argue with you!"

"You're moving? Why?" This was news he hadn't expected, and he could tell that she was worried, looked as if she were about to crack under the pressure of everything that was coming down.

"In addition to the bad news I received about you today, I was also informed that Drewbegg Realty has sold the building of my Houston office. I have sixty days to vacate, and very little funding to do it! So, you go take your meeting, okay? 'Cause I have to go. Bye!"

Too shaken to beg her to stay, Andre picked up the ring, put it in his pocket, and watched her walk away. When the elevator doors opened, Richard Vail stepped out and Riana stepped in. Andre managed to lock eyes with her for a split second before the doors slid closed, his heart breaking to see the tears streaming down her cheeks.

Chapter 25

Inside the elevator, Riana's shoulders drooped with disappointment. She was so distraught she could barely breathe. Andre's accusations had really hurt. Sure, she could have been honest with him about her initial motivation to recruit him. Yes, it had started out as a business deal, which, unfortunately, she had let turn personal. But what did he expect? That she would refuse a cash incentive to complete an important assignment? That was not her style.

Maybe she *had* rushed the process in order to close the contract and earn the bonus, but that wasn't why she had made love to Andre. She had gone to him willingly, lovingly, eager to give herself completely to him, and as hard as it was to admit, she did not regret what she had done.

She loved Andre. His youthful mistakes didn't matter to her; the past was not important, and everyone had skeletons in their closets, didn't they? He had served his sentence and paid for his mistake—changed his life and moved on to become quite a success. She wanted to feel proud of him, not angry with him, but there were too many other issues involved in this situation for her to ignore the damage he had done.

The wedding is off, she thought with a shudder, wondering how she was going to explain what had happened. The invitations had gone out yesterday, to friends, family and professional colleagues. Her white suit was hanging in her closet, and the substantial deposits that she had paid to the florist and to Largo's were nonrefundable.

Her entire body ached with defeat, and as much as she longed to go back to Andre and try to find a way to make things right, she knew it would be impossible. His bungled attempt to deceive her had struck her as hard as if he'd slapped her in the face, hurting her pride, her company, her livelihood, and he'd made her feel like a fool. No, she couldn't face him now, and perhaps never again—her pain was too raw and his deceit far too fresh for any attempt at a reconciliation.

The elevator clanged to a stop in the lobby and Riana made a speedy exit from the building. Outside, the muggy August heat hit her squarely in the face, drying up her tears within seconds. Shoulders back, head held high—in case Andre was watching from above—she crossed the cracked asphalt in a power stride, got to her car, and once inside, started it up and put the air conditioner on high. Then, she fell apart, shaking as she slumped against the steering wheel and sobbed into her palms.

Why did this have to happen to her? Just when she was beginning to believe that she really could balance a romantic relationship with the pressures of her fast-paced career? New tears erupted. She should have known she was asking for too much.

"I've got to focus," she told herself, sitting up, patting at her eyes with a soggy wad of tissue. "I can't worry about what I've lost, I have to think about what I need to do to hold it all together. I have staff in two locations to think about, clients who depend on my company to come through for them, bills to pay, new office space to negotiate and a wedding to cancel, too. I don't have time for an emotional breakdown over a man."

A man, she thought, fighting to regain control, struggling to convince herself that she had done the right thing by breaking off their engagement. *I'll get over him. Just like I did once before.* But the spasmodic trembling that gripped her body continued to increase, because she knew Andre was more than simply *a man.* He was her lover, her best friend, the person with whom she had hoped to live a long, fulfilling life.

Looking into the rearview mirror, Riana grimaced. Her eyes were puffy, her mascara had run, and her face was dotted with dark-red blotches that looked like streaks of mud. She could not go back to the office looking as if she'd been in a catfight, and she didn't want to explain this disaster to any of her staff members, either.

She called her office and informed Iris that she wouldn't be coming back in today, but she would be checking her Black-Berry for messages. With that settled, she thought about where to go, fighting a slump of despair.

Returning to her hotel room to rant at the walls, pace the floor and second-guess her involvement with Andre was not an option. What she needed was a long talk with someone who wouldn't mind being dumped on, who wouldn't judge her and who might help her sort the whole mess out. And someone who knew Andre, too.

Maneuvering through her phone log, she pulled up Felicia's number and pressed Send, hoping her cousin might be able to get off work early so they could meet for happy hour at the Clutch, the newest spot for after-work get-togethers where they could commiserate over Riana's meltdown. She listened to the recorded message on Felicia's voice mail, a frown replacing her tears. Just her luck. Felicia was in a conference off-site and not expected back at the airport today.

Clicking off, she thought about Kay, the only other person who might know Andre well enough to give her some insight about him, and help her understand how he could have done this to her. Kay must know things about her brother-in-law that would help Riana put the situation into perspective and move on. After all, he had gone to great lengths to assist Kay when she had needed him, and she was the only member of Andre's family whom Riana knew. And most importantly, Riana liked Kay very much.

They had spent a lot of time together lately, and even during the short time Riana had known her, she had seen that Kay was a sensible, forward-thinking and nonjudgmental person. But did she know Kay well enough to discuss this turn of events? Riana mused, putting her car into Drive. *Only one way to find out,* she decided, starting off in the direction of Kay's new apartment.

Riana sipped her glass of ice-cold Caribbean punch as she listened to Kay praise Andre. She had been talking nonstop for fifteen minutes in her lilting island accent, clearly pleased that Riana had come to see her.

"I'm so glad you trust me enough to tell me what has happened," Kay said, reaching over to touch the back of Riana's hand. "Andre is a good man. Look what he did for Lonny and me, and what he tried to do for Jamal. The first time I met Andre, I fell in love with him."

"You what?" Riana reacted, startled from her own misery.

Kay chuckled and waved her hand, the thin silver bracelets on her ruddy brown wrist making a jingling sound. "Oh, not like that! I say I fell in love with Andre because he represented the kind of man I wanted Jamal to become. I used to nag Jamal, 'Let's go back to America,' I'd say. 'You get an education like your brother. Become someone important.' But six months into my marriage, I knew my husband wasn't going to do that. He wanted the street life, loved the danger. Always disappearing for days at a time. No explanations when he came back. The crazy men who hung around him... I knew something was going on, but I hid my head in the sand too long, not wanting to know too much. He treated me good for a while, but as Lonny got older, I knew the boy would soon realize what kind of 'work' his father was into, and maybe get drawn into it, too. I couldn't accept that, so I begged Jamal to get away from the gangs and let us be a real family. He refused. I knew I had to leave him, then. It was a hard decision, but Jamal forced me to go."

"Did you go to live with your parents?" Riana asked, intrigued by Kay's story, and glad that she had come to see her. Listening to Kay, Riana began to better understand the hardships that Andre had faced as a young man, and better appreciated what he had accomplished against such great odds. Working for the Allen Group would have been such a coup for him. No wonder he tried to sidestep his flawed record to go after such a prized position.

"Go to live with my parents? Oh, no," Kay reacted in surprise. "They are poor, have very little, and are barely making it themselves. I couldn't burden them with my problems, and a child to worry about, too. That's when I began to paint. I lived in two small rooms above a café and worked in the kitchen during the day, made my paintings late at night while Lonny slept. I rented a stall at the open-air market and sold my paintings to tourists who paid me good money for them. That way, I was able to survive and save enough money to make sure I'd always have a way to support myself if suddenly no one came to buy my art."

"I don't think you'll ever have to worry about that," Riana said, rising from the chair at Kay's kitchen table to walk over to a half-finished painting that was propped against the wall. It depicted a man and a woman sitting in a small boat surrounded by blue water. "This is lovely, Kay. So realistic and so vivid. They look like lovers, just drifting through life."

"Good for you! Exactly what I wanted you to see," Kay said in an excited voice. "Sometimes we need to simply float along and stop trying to control our world."

"I can't imagine how you do it," Riana commented with envy. "You're truly gifted. I can't draw a straight line."

"That may be so, but you have other gifts," Kay admonished with the assurance of a person who knew what she was talking about. "You're a successful businesswoman, Riana. You own two companies that help other people find work. Very important work. And it must be extremely difficult. You must have patience. Insight. A true desire to get to the heart of who a person is. Otherwise, you could not do what you do. And I'm sure you have gifts you haven't even used yet."

A puzzled expression flashed over Riana's features. She turned and walked back to the table, bent down and gave Kay a quick, hard hug. "I needed to hear that, you know? I don't think anyone has ever interpreted what I do in that way. And it's true. With each client I take on, my goal is to find his or her heart, to match their talents, their gifts, with the position they were meant to have. Sometimes, the process can try my patience, but when a perfect match occurs between a client and the right company, the outcome is worth the struggle. It's very satisfying to make people happy with what they do for a living."

"You see. And you did your best for Andre," Kay interjected.

"But I failed. We both failed each other," Riana murmured, feeling as if she were drifting away from the solid foundation she had worked so hard to build. She and Andre were not like the couple in Kay's painting at all. They were floating off in two different directions, in their own separate boats, and the reality of what was happening formed a cold knot inside Riana.

"Failed?" Kay repeated, clucking her tongue. "I don't think so. You may not have gotten Andre into the position you wanted for him, but you found love in the process."

Riana stilled, listening carefully.

"If Mr. Allen had not contacted you, how else would you and Andre ever have found each other again?" Kay went on. "Wasn't *that* the perfect match? Didn't finding love make you happier than any business deal? I think Andre got exactly what he bargained for when Mr. Allen dropped him. So, Riana, don't you ever think you failed. Maybe Andre wasn't meant to have that job, anyway."

Stepping back from Kay, Riana considered the woman's words, which made a lot of sense and helped put the problem into perspective. "I…I never looked at it that way. But still, it didn't work out for us…"

"Do you love him?" Kay asked sharply, eyes crinkling at the corners.

A pause while Riana took everything in. "Yes," she murmured, unable to deny the truth.

"Then you must put all that anger and disappointment away. Start over. You don't know how lucky you are, Riana. If only Jamal had been able to leave his past the way Andre did, he might still be alive. We would still be a family, him and me. And Lonny would have a father. There's an old Jamaican saying that my mother used to tell my father whenever he was cranky. She'd say, 'My husband, sometimes you just have to swallow the whole pig and deal with the indigestion later.'" Kay laughed under her breath and shook her head. "So maybe you and Andre just have to swallow this situation whole, and deal with the unpleasantness that comes with it. There are worse things to have to do."

"Kay, you're far too wise for your years."

With a flutter of her fingers, Kay grinned. "Jamaican women are born old, I think. Or at least our mothers make us so with their stories and sayings and advice all day long."

The humor in Kay's tone made Riana smile, easing some of the pain that still gripped her. "Enough with the pity-party, huh?" She forced a smile that animated her features, beginning to feel alive again.

"Exactly," Kay agreed. "Andre made a big mistake, hiding his past from you. And you lost a big business deal. That's all." She snapped her fingers, as if telling Riana to let it all go.

"Yes," Riana began, "but then I threw away the man I love. Kinda stupid, huh?"

Kay raised both shoulders in a noncommittal shrug. "Your priorities got crossed up. It happens all the time," she said. "Forgive him, Riana. Move on together. Business matters can wait, but love can't. Men can be slow to see the truth and it takes a woman to light the way."

"Another one of your mother's sayings?" Riana asked with a grin, a surge of energy shooting through her veins.

"No," Kay laughed. "I made that one up myself."

"Makes sense to me," Riana told her, already planning her next move.

Chapter 26

The club was dimly lit, with undersized round tables placed along the walls and an extended bar that took up most of the space in the center of the Clutch. A corner in the rear of the club had been turned into a dance floor where three couples stood locked in each other's arms, grinding in oblivion to Luther Vandross's crooning vocals.

Andre sat alone at his table, engrossed in arranging toothpicks—each of which had once held olives in his three martinis—into a variety of patterns, while nuggets of conversation popped up around him. Drinking alone in a bar was not Andre's style, but he had been too distraught to do anything else. He needed to be around people, hear music and laughter, convince himself that life was going on outside his isolated loft atop Prairie Towers.

He shifted the toothpicks one way, then another, as if doodling on paper with a pen while his mind drifted in and out of the problems he knew he had created. The despair that gripped him was startlingly physical, and he felt as if he had been beaten. His head pounded, his stomach churned, and his eyes burned from all the tears he had shed in private before storming out of his loft and into the Clutch, to sit alone and dwell on his misery.

He took another sip of his martini and glanced around, not surprised to see Lester coming his way.

"Thought I'd find you here," Lester remarked, pulling out a chair. He scrutinized Andre with a quizzical eye and shook his head. "Man, you look like shit. What's going on? That message you left on my voice mail got me worried. What do you mean, it's off?"

With a slow shake of his head, Andre blinked in a signal of defeat. "That's right. The wedding's off."

With a cringe, Lester bent forward. "Hell no. It can't be. I just bought a new tuxedo and I don't plan to give up my role as best man so easily." He was clearly joking, as if trying to nudge a smile from Andre. It didn't work.

Andre gently placed Riana's engagement ring on the table and slid it back and forth with one finger. "She gave it to me this afternoon and walked out. And you know what? I don't blame her. I would've done the same thing."

"Oh no, you wouldn't have," Lester threw back. "I don't know what went wrong, but I know enough to see that you're too much in love with Riana to let her go voluntarily. Now, dish, Andre. Tell me what's going on."

A waitress dressed in a short black skirt and skimpy tight tank top arrived to take drink orders.

"Coffee. I've had enough of this," Andre told her, handing her his empty martini glass.

"Jack Daniel's straight for me," Lester said, and then added, "Better make it a double. I think I'm gonna need it."

Andre told Lester everything, focusing on his disappointment with himself: for trusting Frazer to make things right, for not telling Riana about his conviction and for bungling an important career move.

"I failed to rescue Jamal from the drug world that took his life, I failed in my bid for the design job and I failed Riana, too," Andre finished, splaying both hands on the table.

"Don't be so hard on yourself, man," Lester said after hearing what had happened. "You're a great architect! I only hope I'm half as good as you when I get the chance to do my thing. You'll get other jobs, and with firms just as important as the Allen Group. Don't even worry about that. But you'll never find another woman like Riana. If you love her, man, you'd better not wait too long to make things right."

Andre didn't reply; he couldn't. Talking about what had happened was taking too much out of him. He simply let out a long, low breath and accepted the cup of coffee that the waitress handed to him. He took several sips, and then set it aside.

"She doesn't want to talk to me," he finally replied. "I've been calling, leaving messages all afternoon. We're through, and I know Riana well enough to know that I'm not getting a second chance."

"Don't give up so easily," Lester admonished, knocking back half of his drink. "You haven't failed, because you haven't tried."

With a sarcastic snort, Andre thumbed his chin. The sense of failure that filled him was smothering, pushing his mind back to the stretch he had done in prison, when he'd had plenty of time to ponder his shortcomings. It had taken two long years in prison to drive the point home. He couldn't change who his father was, couldn't bring his mother back to life or erase his rebellious past. All he could do was live a better life once he was released, creating the future he wanted. It had been a struggle, and he had accomplished what he set out to do—almost. Marrying the woman he loved still eluded him, and maybe it would forever.

The impact of his situation crashed down, tightening Andre's chest, stinging his eyes with unshed tears. With a snap, he broke one of the toothpicks in half and crushed the soft wood between his fingers.

"I think Riana will come around. She just needs time to cool off. Surely, she won't leave you for good," Lester offered, intruding on Andre's musings.

"She did once before," Andre confessed.

"And you did nothing about it?" Lester pressed, flinching in concern.

Slowly, Andre nodded, thinking, *But this time I can't stand by and let it happen again.*

"Then you know what you've gotta do," Lester prompted, brows moving high on his forehead. "You don't need to be sitting here, crying the blues all night."

"You're right," Andre finally said. With a chug, he finished his coffee and put a twenty-dollar bill on the table. Losing Riana a second time was not something he planned to accept. She *was* going to talk to him—tonight. "I've gotta go," he told Lester, standing. "Sorry to skip out on you like this, but I have to find her. Fix the problem."

"Go. Please," Lester urged. "Don't worry about me. Todd's on his way over, so I won't be alone very long."

Andre was startled by the way Lester's face lit up when he mentioned his partner, Todd, and a flash of envy shot through him. Lester was in love. He was happy. He was secure in his relationship, had someone to care about, and someone who cared about him, while Andre was miserable and alone.

Not for long, he vowed as he left the club and climbed into his Pathfinder. Immediately, he called Riana's hotel suite. No answer. Her cell phone rolled over to voice mail, and even Felicia didn't answer when he tried her number.

Where is she? he worried, desperate to see her, ready to do anything she asked of him if she would give him a second chance. He pulled the emerald ring from his pocket and looked at it in the streetlight coming through the windshield. She had been so happy when they picked out the ring—the symbol of their future. How could everything they had found together have dissolved so quickly?

Because I took a risk that didn't pay off, he reminded himself, as he slid down behind the wheel, holding the ring in front of his face. Staring at the luminous jewel, he made up his mind. *Our wedding will go on as planned. I'll renovate an entire floor of Prairie Towers and give it to her for new office space. I can go after another design project with a firm just as prestigious as the Allen Group, and without hiding my past, either. I've got to press forward, believe in our love and pray that we'll find a way to move past this.*

He started the engine, drove to Riana's hotel and knocked on her door. No answer. Frustrated, he sat down on a bench in the hallway, prepared to wait for her, no matter how long it would take. Sitting there, cloaked in misery, he passed the time by mentally searching for the words he would need to say to Riana if he wanted her to forgive him. All he knew was that he had to try, and keep on trying until she was his once more.

Fifteen minutes into his wait, a hotel maid came along, pushing her cart of towels and cleaning supplies as she made her way toward him. When she stopped at Riana's door, slipped in the key card and opened it, Andre stood up, curious about what she was doing.

"Uh, excuse me. Are you going to clean that room now?"

The woman whirled around and looked Andre up and down, as if he had no business asking such a question. "Why? Are you waiting to get in? Don't worry, it'll be ready in fifteen minutes. Come back then, okay?"

"No, you don't understand. I'm not checking in. I'm waiting for the woman who stays in that suite."

The housecleaner lowered her lashes to half-mast, as if sizing him up before she spoke. "This suite? It's empty. The front desk asked me to come and clean it right away for a late arrival. That's not you?"

"No. I told you I'm not checking in," Andre repeated, coming up behind the woman to look over her shoulder. He peered into the suite, and could see right away that she was right. All traces of Riana were gone and the rooms had that dim, messy look that confirmed they were no longer occupied. "Do you know when she checked out?" he asked.

"No, I have no idea," the woman said as she pushed her cart into the room and pulled a set of sheets off the top tray. She gave the sheets a hard shake and got about her work.

A surge of panic struck Andre as he hurried back to his car and got in. *San Antonio,* he decided, and turning his car toward Interstate 10, he headed west, more determined than ever to make things right with Riana.

The two-and-a-half-hour drive whizzed by so fast that Andre surprised himself when he realized how quickly he had arrived at Puerto Valdez Avenue. He swung to a halt at the curb in front of Riana's house; a neat little structure that he thought resembled a cottage in one of Kay's paintings, *The Refuge* was the title.

Very appropriate, Andre thought as he watched the house, his heart full of regret, yearning for forgiveness. He'd hurt Riana deeply, blindsided her with a complicated matter that he should have handled better. Lights burned in the windows at the back of the house and her champagne Lexus was parked in the driveway. He shut off his engine, took a deep breath and pulled out his cell phone. *She's home, and she's going to talk to me. We'll settle this even if it takes all night.*

* * *

"Leave me alone," Riana muttered as she scowled at the name on her caller ID. It was Andre. Again. And she wasn't going to answer. First of all, it was eleven o'clock at night and she was far too tired to get into it with him. Secondly, she had promised herself that when he called, as she knew he would, she wouldn't do anything hasty, like forgive him too quickly, or rush back to Houston to be with him. She needed time away from him to sort out her feelings and get over his betrayal. If only he knew how she really felt, he would back away, give her some space to cool off, allow them both to rethink the way they had handled their relationship.

When the phone stopped ringing, Riana turned the ringer to mute, went into her bedroom and slipped into her nightgown, desperate for a good night's sleep. She was exhausted after what seemed to have been the longest, most difficult day in her life.

As soon as she'd arrived back in San Antonio, she had gone straight to the Allen Group and met with George Allen to offer him a personal apology for the way the Preaux case had turned out. Even though she had lost their contract, she wanted to end their business relationship on a professional note.

Never burn bridges, or let anyone burn them for you, Riana had reminded herself, recalling the advice of her former boss, Madeline Betts, words that she had never forgotten.

"It wasn't entirely your fault," Allen had said, looking at Riana with those steely gray eyes that could just as easily turn gentle. "Preaux placed you in a difficult position, and I do understand what happened. However, he needn't worry. I've already got a job coming up next year that I have in mind for him."

"That's very generous," Riana had replied, feeling the tension she had carried all day beginning to ease.

"I respect you for coming here and I accept your apology,

Riana," Allen had told her. "Most certainly, I'll use your firm again, and often enough for us to get to know each other much better."

His goodbye handshake had been firm, and their meeting had ended on a positive note, sending Riana back to her office overlooking the Alamo with a spring in her step and a heavy weight lifted from her mind. Back in her familiar suite, she had buried herself in work, anything to keep her mind off Andre.

Now, sitting on the side of the bed, stretching her legs, she felt weary to the bone, but satisfied with her newly devised plan. Tomorrow was going to be another hectic day. She planned to meet with her banker first thing in the morning to arrange for an increase in her line of credit to cover the move of her Houston office. Then she needed to hold a staff meeting to discuss several new contracts, and congratulate her staff on their excellent weekly reports. Next, she wanted to go online and locate a Houston Realtor who could help her search for a new office suite, and find a moving company to execute the relocation. She had to stay busy, lose herself in work to forget about her troubles with Andre, for a little while at least. If she dwelled too long on what they were going through, she'd break down in tears again, and she had cried enough.

Slipping between the sheets, she turned out the light, plumped up her pillow and sank down. *At least he's still calling,* she thought, imagining him sitting alone in his loft apartment in Houston, as miserable as she was. *Let him stew a while longer,* she told herself, feeling better about the next day.

When Andre saw Riana's bedroom light go out, he panicked. She wasn't answering her phone. She was going to sleep. It was definitely time to take action. Jaw tensed, fueled with the courage of a man determined not to back down, he got out of his car, went up to her door and pressed the bell. He could hear it chiming inside.

"What in the world?" Riana muttered when she heard her doorbell ringing so late. Cautiously, she slipped out of bed and made it down the hallway using only the light from the street-lamp outside to guide her way. At her door, she paused and listened for a moment, thinking that perhaps she had imagined hearing her bell. But then, it chimed again. Three times, forcing her back a step.

"Who is it?' she cautiously called through the door. Home invasions were not uncommon throughout the city, but she had never had any problems in her neighborhood. She didn't want to take any chances.

"Andre."

His voice sent a chill of surprise, bound with a touch of relief through her, and she let the word resound in her mind for a few seconds before she calmly responded, while struggling to keep her delight from showing. "Andre? I thought you were in Houston. What are you doing here? I told you I didn't want to talk to you."

"May I come in?"

She bit her lower lip and smiled, determined not to make this easy. In a coy manner she told him, "That depends."

"Depends? On what?" He slammed his query against the closed door, obviously very frustrated.

"On why you came." The lilting sweetness in her response made Riana suppress a giggle.

"Why? Dammit, Riana, I came because I miss you, I love you and I am begging you to forgive me for all the problems I created. I'm sorry. Truly sorry."

"You should be," she told him, placing her face closer to the door, almost able to feel him through the barrier. He sounded so desperate and so miserable. *Just like I felt when I learned about your past,* she thought, aching to feel his arms around her while wanting to make him suffer a tad longer. Out of habit, she started to flick on the porch light, but stopped. Kay's words of advice popped into her mind. *It takes a woman to light the way,* Kay had said, and now Riana planned to do just that.

"I think it would be best if you come back tomorrow," she finally told him, suppressing a chuckle. "I'm going back to bed."

"No way," he shot back immediately. "We're talking this out tonight."

"It's too late, Andre. I have a big day ahead of me tomorrow. So much to do. I need sleep and I'm very tired," she sagged against the door, fingers on the dead-bolt lock, her body already tingling with a need for him.

"Hell, I'm tired, too. I had a miserable day, also, you know? I drove nonstop from Houston to see you, and I'm not going away until you let me in and talk to me."

"Oh, I dunno," Riana teased, quietly turning the dead-bolt lock. "What'll you do if I don't let you in?"

"Start yelling. Wake up your neighbors. Cause a big scene."

Riana sprang the lock, pulled back the door and faced Andre. "I wouldn't do that if I were you. My neighbors might think I was being assaulted or something."

In an instant, Andre was inside the house, standing in the shadowed entry. He slammed the door closed behind him, reached for Riana and crushed his mouth to hers, propelling her back against the wall. She didn't resist his probing tongue, or the pads of his fingers as they roamed her skin, or the strong hold he had on her body. As her defenses began to wilt she could feel herself spiraling into that pleasure zone of bliss that always swept her away when he touched her.

With her lips still locked with his, she guided him down the dark hallway, lighting the way into her bedroom and over to her tangled sheets, where they sank down together amid murmurs of relief and joy.

Chapter 27

Labor Day

From the overpass on the freeway, Riana could see that a crowd had gathered in the street in front of Prairie Towers, an odd sight in the usually quiet neighborhood. She pushed her face closer to the darkened window of the white limousine, anxious to see what was going on.

"It looks like something's happening next door to your building," she told Andre, pointing to the knot of people standing around, watching heavy construction equipment roll into the vacant lot.

Andre leaned over her, his lips deliberately brushing hers as he passed. "Another kiss for my bride," he said with a wink as he scrutinized the scene. "Looks like a new building is about to rise on lower Main," Andre murmured, nodding. "That's a very good sign, you know? Things are shaping up in the area faster than I'd hoped."

"Fantastic," Riana agreed, entwining her fingers with her husband's as they both sank back into the soft leather seats of the limousine that was taking them to the airport to start their honeymoon in Hawaii, which they had decided not to postpone.

"And when we return, I'm going to start renovating the new Executive Suites space at Prairie Towers," Andre told her, slipping an arm around Riana. "And on the first floor, I'm putting in an art gallery for Kay."

"Are you sure it won't cramp your style, having your wife working in the same office building with you?" Riana teased. "You might get bored, having me around all the time."

"Not at all." Andre nuzzled the soft hollow of her cheek. "Just means I won't have to go very far to see you. Day…or night. No stressful traffic. No commute time. Think of how quickly you'll get home from work."

Riana let out a soft laugh. "That's true. But when I do get home, there'll be no talking about work, I promise."

"That's right," Andre agreed. "Once we enter our private space, all I'll want to do is make love to you." He leaned forward, pushed the button to close the privacy screen, and then turned to Riana. "As we could right now, Mrs. Preaux," he taunted, a mischievous gleam in his eye.

Riana moved her gaze from his twinkling eyes, to his full sensuous lips, to the strong jut of his jaw, and then she touched his cheek. An involuntary shiver of anticipation swept through her as she sank back in her seat and looked at Andre, her husband.

"Everything was perfect today wasn't it?" she murmured, relieved that the big day had come at last.

"Couldn't have turned out better," he agreed, placing a line of kisses along her neck. "Thank God the weather held."

"I told you it wouldn't dare rain on our wedding day," she

lazily commented, and then added, "I can't believe how quickly my sister and Kay became friends. And you! You can be quite the charmer! My mother was hanging on to you as if *she* were the bride."

Andre laughed off Riana's comment, nibbling at her ear. "But she wasn't the bride, today. You were," he said, outlining the curve of her cheek with a feathery touch. "And a most beautiful bride, too." Their lips locked solidly and held. "We have forty minutes to kill until we get to the airport," he started, his fingers poised at the top button of her cream-colored satin blouse.

"I know, so stop talking and kiss me again, and again, and again," Riana urged, sinking down on the seat, enveloped in Andre's embrace, knowing that their love, their work and their lives would be forever entwined.

* * * * *

DON'T MISS
THIS SEXY NEW SERIES
FROM KIMANI ROMANCE!

THE BRADDOCKS

SECRET SON

*Power, passion and politics
are all in the family.*

HER LOVER'S LEGACY by Adrianne Byrd
August 2008

SEX AND THE SINGLE BRADDOCK
by Robyn Amos
September 2008

SECOND CHANCE, BABY by A.C. Arthur
October 2008

THE OBJECT OF HIS PROTECTION
by Brenda Jackson
November 2008

The second title in a passionate new miniseries...

THE BRADDOCKS

SECRET SON

*Power, passion and politics
are all in the family.*

Sex and the Single Braddock

ROBYN AMOS

Determined to uncover the mystery of her powerful father's
death, Shondra Braddock goes to work for Stewart Industries
CEO Connor Stewart. But her undercover mission soon
gets sidetracked when their sizzling attraction explodes
into a secret, jet-setting affair!

Available the first week of September wherever books are sold.

KIMANI™
ROMANCE

She was on a rescue mission;
he was bent on seduction!

SECRET AGENT
S E D U C T I O N

TOP SECRET
ROMANCE ON THE RUN

Favorite Author
Maureen Smith

Secret Service agent Lia Charles needs all her
professional objectivity to rescue charismatic
revolutionary Armand Magliore, because extracting him
from the treacherous jungle is the easy part—guarding
her heart against the irresistible rebel is the *real* challenge.

Available the first week of September wherever books are sold.

KIMANI™
ROMANCE

www.kimanipress.com   KPMS0820908

Where there's smoke, there's fire!

MAKE IT
HOT

Gwyneth Bolton

Brooding injured firefighter Joel Hightower's only hope
to save his career is sassy physical therapist Samantha
Dash. But as the sizzling attraction between them
intensifies, Samantha must decide whether a future with
surly Joel is worth the threat to her career.

The Hightowers
Four brothers on a mission
to protect, serve and love.

Available the first week of September wherever books are sold.

KIMANI™
ROMANCE

www.kimanipress.com

For All We Know

NATIONAL BESTSELLING AUTHOR
SANDRA KITT

Michaela Landry's quiet summer of
house-sitting takes a dramatic turn when
she finds a runaway teen and brings him
to the nearest hospital. There she meets
Cooper Smith Townsend, a local pastor
whose calm demeanor and dedication are
as attractive as his rugged good looks.
Now their biggest challenge will be to trust
that a passion neither planned for is strong
enough to overcome any obstacle.

Coming the first week of September 2008,
wherever books are sold.

ARABESQUE®

www.kimanipress.com   KPSKI040908

NATIONAL BESTSELLING AUTHOR

ROCHELLE ALERS

invites you to meet the Whitfields of New York....

Tessa, Faith and Simone Whitfield know all about coordinating
other people's weddings, and not so much about arranging
their own love lives. But in the space of one unforgettable year,
all three will meet intriguing men who just might bring them their
very own happily ever after....

Long Time Coming

June 2008

The Sweetest Temptation

July 2008

Taken by Storm

August 2008

ARABESQUE®

www.kimanipress.com

KPALERSTRIL08